TREMBLING

Jason and Azazel, Book Two
V. J. CHAMBERS

Punk Rawk Books

TREMBLING
© 2009 by V. J. Chambers
www.vjchambers.com

Punk Rawk Books

ISBN: 978-0-9841206-2-8
Printed in the United States of America

10 9 8 7 6 5 4 3 2 1

TREMBLING

Jason and Azazel, Book Two
V. J. CHAMBERS

PART ONE

"O! Beware, my lord, of jealousy,
It is the green-eyed monster which doth mock
The meat it feeds on."

-William Shakespeare, *Othello*

CHAPTER ONE

michaela666 (01:34:22): Is it done?

aird92 (01:35:01): yep. success. it's all good.

michaela666 (1:35:24): And it went well? No snags? No interference from Jason?

aird92 (01:36:12): dude's damned clueless, r u kidding? went perfect.

michaela666 (01:36:54): You're sure? They shouldn't be underestimated, you know. The two of them together are quite powerful.

aird92 (01:37:17): i know this, ok? stop worrying. everything's fine.

My brain felt like it had exploded while I was sleeping and the pieces of brain matter were straining against my temples, trying to get out. My head hurt.

I squeezed my eyes shut against the bright Florida sun that was streaming through the window. Damn it, but my head hurt. Really, really bad.

Tentatively, I opened one eye. The room was blazingly bright. I closed my eye again. Maybe it was better to keep my eyes closed.

Wait.

I opened my eyes again.

Where was I?

Jason's room? Jason's bed? Why was I in Jason's bed?

How had I gotten here?

Damn it. I didn't remember going to sleep. I must have been really drunk when I went to sleep. Blackout drunk. I didn't think I'd ever been blackout drunk before. What *did* I remember from the night before?

A loud voice sliced into my temple. "I don't how many times I've told you that you two are not supposed to sleep in the same bed!"

That was why I had woken up. Hallam was yelling at Jason. Ugh. I pulled a pillow over my head, but I could still hear them.

"Jesus, Hallam, I carried her to her own bed, but she crawled in here with me," Jason was saying. "I couldn't get her to go back. Nothing happened. She was way too drunk."

I was? I didn't remember any of that at all.

Jason was my boyfriend. He and I lived with Hallam, who was our legal guardian. Hallam was pretty cool most of the time. He didn't have any problem with my going out and getting wasted or coming home at four in the morning. But he was insistent that Jason and I did not sleep in the same bed. He said he didn't want us to conceive our firstborn on his watch. But that was silly, because when Jason and I actually did get to have sex (which was rarely), we were careful. Really, Hallam was just a prude, and that was all there was to it.

"I don't want to hear excuses, Jason," Hallam said. "You two know the rules. You both agreed to them."

It was amazing how, in just a few short months, Hallam

8

had begun to sound remarkably like a parent. He was only twenty-two, just five years older than Jason and me. But he sounded fifty.

"You're blatantly disobeying," Hallam went on.

"What was I supposed to do?" Jason demanded. "She could barely stand, she was so wasted."

Really? That wasn't good. Okay, okay. What had I done last night?

Um, I'd gone to a party on the beach with Jude and some of the other guys from work. I worked at a movie theater here in Bradenton, Florida. I remembered that I'd been drinking a lot of shots. I'd been talking to some guys around a bonfire. For a long time. And then . . . I'd lost Jude. I couldn't find him anywhere. And I was so drunk. . . So . . . I called Jason, because I couldn't find Jude, and I was freaked out. Being alone like that. And drunk. And then . . .

And then, *nothing*.

God.

That was terrifying.

"She's been drunk a lot lately, hasn't she?" asked Hallam.

"She's seventeen," Jason said. "It's what young people do!"

Jason was seventeen too, but when he said that, it sounded like he was so much older than me. In some ways, maybe Jason was. He'd been through a lot in his young life. Jason had spent his childhood on the run from men with guns, who were trying to kill him. He'd held his mentor Anton in his arms while Anton bled to death. Jason had shot

9

five men in the head point blank to save me from getting killed. It made sense that Jason would seem older than me.

But.

"You're seventeen too," Hallam pointed out. "You're not getting fall-down drunk."

Why was Jason so much more responsible than I was? After all, while it was true that Jason had been through a lot, the last six months of my life had been no picnic either. I'd found out that my entire town was controlled by a Satanist coven who wanted me to kill Jason. Then I'd seen my parents and my aunt all shot dead in front of me. Yeah. Things weren't easy for me either. Most days, I felt older than seventeen.

"Well, someone's got to stay sober," Jason muttered.

Great. He didn't sound happy. But I guess I couldn't blame him. It didn't sound like I'd been much fun last night. I really shouldn't have gotten so drunk.

"Just keep her out of your bed," said Hallam. "I don't care how drunk she is."

I heard the door to Jason's bedroom slam as Hallam stormed out.

Sheepishly, I pulled the pillow off my head and looked at Jason. "Hey," I said.

"Good morning," said Jason, but he didn't sound at all happy about it.

Jason was probably one of the most beautiful human beings I'd ever seen. He had dusky skin, perfect and unmarred, huge dark eyes, and a shock of dark hair that tended to fall into his eyes. Looking at him, no matter where I was or what I was doing, nearly always took my breath away, made me tremble inside.

"I'm sorry?" I said. I hoped he wasn't going to be too mad.

Jason sighed. He sat down on the edge of the bed, next to me. "What are you sorry about?"

"Sorry I got so drunk," I said.

Jason shook his head. "It's not your fault," he said. He reached for me. Stroked my cheek with the back of his hand. "It's Jude's fault."

"Jude?" I asked. For some reason, Jason did not like Jude very much.

"He got you all messed up and then he just abandoned you," said Jason.

It was true that Jude had disappeared last night. But I wanted Jason to like Jude. Jude was probably my best friend. "We were at a party," I said. "I'm sure he just got . . . distracted."

"Don't defend him," said Jason.

"He's my friend." I had to defend him. If I didn't, Jason would never start liking him. Ever.

Jason rolled his eyes. "I don't know why you spend so much time with that jerk, anyway."

"He's fun!" I said.

"Right," said Jason. He looked down at his hands. "Unlike me, right?"

"Jason!" I rolled over in bed, frustrated. My head

11

pounded angrily at the sudden movement. "There is no reason to compare the two of you. You're Jason. He's Jude. You're both fun, just in different ways."

"I just feel like I never see you anymore. You're always hanging out with him. You're never hanging out with me."

"You sound jealous."

Jason shrugged.

"Jesus, he's gay!" I exclaimed. "He's like a girl."

"Except he's not a girl," said Jason.

"Oh my God," I muttered. I sat up in bed, carefully this time, so as not to upset my throbbing head. I crawled over to Jason. Hugged him from behind. "Don't be jealous of Jude," I murmured, kissing Jason's neck. "You shouldn't be jealous of anyone, ever. No one could ever be to me what you are. You're . . . Jason."

Jason turned his head and his lips met mine. "I know that," he whispered in a husky voice. It always made me swoon. It was the voice meant only for *me*. He didn't talk to anyone else in that voice.

I caressed his face. Ran my finger over the line of his jaw. He winced.

I leaned forward. "Are you hurt?"

"It's nothing," Jason said, standing up.

I flopped back on the bed. "What did you do?" I demanded. "Did you get in another fight?"

"I . . ." Jason trailed off.

"Jason!"

"I'm sorry," he said. "But you should have heard this

12

guy. He had it coming. That bastard."

"What happened?" I asked.

"I couldn't find you when I got to the party," said Jason. "But I found that jerk, Jude, and he said he put you in a tent. And you were fine." Jason glowered into space.

"A tent?" I had no memory of being in a tent.

"Yeah," said Jason. "That dickwad just dumped you there and ran off."

"At least he put me in a tent," I said. Wow. How drunk had I been? A thought suddenly occurred to me. "Oh God. You didn't beat up Jude, did you?"

Jason shook his head. "No."

"Good," I said. Because if my boyfriend had beaten up my best friend, it probably would have meant I didn't have a best friend anymore. And the thought of Jason punching skinny, prissy Jude was almost too much to handle. He would have *destroyed* Jude.

"Jude never could have gotten a punch on me," said Jason.

Of course not. I snorted.

"So I found the tent, and this guy was standing outside. I looked inside. You were in there, passed out. And you were only wearing your bikini."

"What?!" I demanded. I had gone to that party *clothed*, dammit. "Where were my clothes?"

"In the tent," said Jason.

So how did they get off? I didn't ask that question out loud. Concerned, I wiggled my pelvis. It felt . . . fine. "What happened?" I repeated.

Jason didn't look at me. "The guy outside the tent said that he wouldn't say anything if I . . ." Jason trailed off. He whipped his head around and looked straight in my eyes. "He said to save him seconds."

I covered my mouth with my hand. "Oh my God."

"Yeah," said Jason. "And Jude just left you there. With people like that around."

"So you beat up the guy outside the tent?"

"I did. I wasn't going to, because it wasn't like he did anything. I just told him to shut up, because you were my girlfriend. And he said, 'Your girlfriend looks like a drunken slut.' That's when I beat him up."

"Oh," I said. I was quiet. "How bad?" I finally asked.

Jason shrugged. "I don't know."

"Did they have to call an ambulance again?" I asked.

"I don't know. I took you and left."

I didn't say anything.

"He was bleeding a lot, I guess," said Jason. "Maybe I broke his nose. I don't know."

"Oh God, you shouldn't have done that."

"Can you blame me? He was clearly a total bastard."

"I just don't think it's a good idea for you to do things that might attract attention to us," I said.

Jason sat back down on the bed. "Azazel, we're safe," he said.

"I know," I said. "But I don't trust the Sons. And I just feel like every time you do something like that, it sends out a

14

beacon to them screaming, 'Here we are!'"

"They probably know where we are, anyway," said Jason. "They're a huge, powerful organization. I'm sure they haven't just forgotten about me."

"Maybe they did," I said. "Maybe they did." I wished I could believe that. I wished I wasn't worried nearly every second of every day that the Sons of the Rising Sun were going to burst into our house, guns blazing, kill me, and take Jason. We were blackmailing them with information we had, and so far it seemed to be working. But every day, I worried that it wouldn't work anymore. They'd find some way around our deal. They'd come for us.

Jason lay down next me on the bed. He gathered me in his arms. I buried my head in his chest.

"We're safe," he whispered into my hair. "I swear we're safe. I swear I'll keep you safe."

And I wanted to believe him. I did.

"All I want to do is keep you safe," he said. "You know that, right?"

I lifted my head to look at him. He was so heartbreakingly beautiful. "I know."

"That's why I hit that guy," said Jason. "When it comes to you, Azazel, I just . . . I can't think straight. If anyone ever hurt you, I'd go absolutely insane. You're so important to me."

I kissed him. "I love you," I said.

"I love you," he said.

We kissed again, Jason's hands stroking my back. I

moaned softly.

And Hallam stormed into the bedroom. "Out!" he thundered. "Azazel, get out of this bed!"

I got out of the bed, folding my arms over my chest and glaring at Hallam. "We were just kissing," I said.

"Sure," said Hallam. "It's all just kissing until someone gets pregnant."

I rolled my eyes. But I went to my own room anyway. I needed to find some ibuprofen.

* * *

It was nearly eleven-thirty, and I had to be at work at noon. I worked at the Regal Cinemas on Cortez, a ten-minute drive from our apartment if the traffic wasn't bad. Which it always was. Jude said that in the summer, there was no traffic in Bradenton at all. Once all the "snowbirds" left, no one was left in Florida except the people who lived there full time. Snowbirds were rich, old people who came to Florida during the winter to escape the snow up north. Since Jason, Hallam, and I had only lived in Bradenton since November, I had never witnessed a summer in Bradenton.

Bradenton was a very, very big town compared to Bramford, West Virginia, where I grew up. However, according to most people, it was a relatively small place. It was located about forty-five minutes south of Tampa and twenty minutes north of Sarasota, on the west coast of Florida. The rent there was a little cheaper than what you'd pay in Sarasota, which was why we'd decided to live in Bradenton. At the time, I wasn't in touch with my grandmother, who was insanely rich and lived in New Jersey, so we didn't think we'd have enough money to live in Sarasota.

When we first moved to Florida, we didn't really have much money. Hallam had a little bit of cash which he'd squirreled away. Jason and I had a fraudulent credit card. We were barely able to get enough money to move into a three-bedroom apartment. We got jobs as quickly as we could. Hallam insisted that both Jason and I finish high school, so we had to get jobs that wouldn't interfere with our studies. I started working at the movie theater, and Jason got a job waiting tables. Hallam, who was highly educated and British, somehow managed to swindle himself into a job as a professor at New College, the honors college of Sarasota. Both Hallam and I still had our original jobs. Jason, however, had been fired four times. He kept getting in fights. Currently, he had a job working at another restaurant, but he was in the kitchen, so he didn't have to deal with the public.

We had a very hard time at first, because we didn't have a car, so we had to rely on buses and on favors from co-workers. Sometimes it worked out, sometimes it didn't. Finally, Jason suggested that I should get in touch with my grandmother. She was my only living relative, besides my three adopted brothers.

I didn't want to contact Grandma Hoyt at first. I was worried that the Sons could use her to get to me, or that she might be in danger. After all, it was the Sons who had shot my parents. They didn't seem to have qualms about killing whoever got in their way. Jason and Hallam were sure that the Sons were out of the picture, so eventually I did.

Grandma Hoyt bought me a car, and started sending me a pretty decent allowance every month. It helped make our situation more comfortable, but I still worked, because I liked having the extra cash. Besides, with Jason working as well, if I stayed home, I'd be alone most of the time. I really didn't like being alone anymore. I got really freaked out when I was by myself in our apartment. I didn't know if I was really worried about the Sons busting in and shooting me or not. But I did know that I got very, very frightened, and I couldn't handle it.

So I worked. That afternoon, I was so hung over and miserable that I really wished that I didn't. But I dragged myself into the shower, got dressed, ate something, and went to work. The night before, I'd left directly from work and gone to the party, and I'd accidentally left my uniform in the staff workroom. When I arrived, Jude was waiting for me, holding my uniform.

"Girl!" he exclaimed. "I cannot believe you are standing!"

"Oh my God, Jude! How drunk did I get last night?"

Jude shook his head in awe. "You were wasted," he said. He handed me my uniform. "Better get changed. We've got to start slinging popcorn in two minutes."

"Ugh," I muttered, taking the uniform from him.

Jude was tall and very skinny. He was a quarter Cherokee, so he had dusky skin and dark eyes. (Like Jason, in fact, who was also a quarter Native American, but Muscogee.) Jude liked to wear heavy eyeliner, but at work, it was against the dress code, so Jude only wore a little bit. He also had three holes in each of his ears, plus a nose piercing. He had to take out all his piercings for work too. The theater couldn't do much about his hair, however, which he dyed various unnatural shades. Currently, his hair was electric blue. Last week, however, it had been bright orange. I'd seen it green, purple, and fire-engine red. Jude also made it a point to paint his nails. At the moment, they were purple and sparkly.

"Come into the bathroom with me while I change," I said. "I want to know everything about what happened last night."

"While you change?" Jude said.

"Yeah," I said. I took him by the arm and pulled him into the staff bathroom with me.

The staff bathroom didn't have stalls. It just had one toilet and a sink. It was for either men or women. Once inside, I locked the door, and pulled my shirt over my head.

"So where did you go?" I asked, folding my shirt and searching for my uniform polo.

Jude wasn't looking at me. He was staring at the floor, like he was embarrassed.

"I'm sorry," I said. "Does it make you uncomfortable that I'm taking off my clothes? I just thought . . ."

Jude looked at me, grinning. "No, girl, you're fine," he said.

"Okay," I said.

Jude took a deep breath. "I wouldn't have left you if I thought you were so drunk," he said.

"I didn't mean to get that drunk," I said.

"You weren't when I left," he said.

"Left?"

"I didn't leave the party," Jude said. "I just started chasing this yummy boy with long blonde hair."

I unbuttoned my jeans and wriggled out of them. "And?"

"Oh, he turned out to be straight."

"Sorry."

Jude shrugged. "Whatev." He glanced at me and then looked away. I *was* making him uncomfortable. I needed to try to remember that being gay did not make Jude a girl. Maybe I was being rude. "So, what do you remember?"

"Not much. I remember looking for you, not being able to find you, and calling Jason."

"Oh yeah," said Jude, "your boyfriend's intense, isn't he?"

Intense? That was one way to put it. "How do you mean?"

"He hospitalized that guy. I've never seen anyone fight like that. He was like a machine."

Damn it. Why was Jason always getting in fights? "He had to go to hospital, huh?"

"Yeah. Broken ribs."

Ribs? "Dammit," I said, shaking my head. I thrust my leg into my uniform khakis. Jason had to stop this.

"You remember the fight?" Jude asked.

"No. Jason told me about it."

Jude nodded. "You don't remember anything, then?"

I shook my head. "Not really."

"Is that weird?" he asked. "I've never blacked out before."

"Neither have I," I said. I remembered drinking, but I really didn't think I'd had *that* much to drink. The whole thing was weird. I buttoned my khakis thoughtfully. "Jason said something about that guy outside the tent. Like he said something about me."

Jude raised his eyebrows. "What did he say?"

I was probably being paranoid. "Jude, you don't think I was like roofied or something, do you?"

Now that I was fully dressed, Jude was looking right at me. "Why would you think that?"

"Jason said that when he found me I was only wearing my bikini. And the guy told him to save him seconds."

Jude made a horrified face. "Eew."

"Yeah."

"Well, are you okay? I mean, do you think . . .?"

"Oh, no. I'm fine. I mean, I don't think *that* happened. But maybe someone was trying?"

Jude crossed to me and hugged me tightly. "Omigod," he said. "I am so sorry. I will never leave you alone at a party again."

Work would have been torturous without Jude. He kept me laughing, whispering jokes about what the customers

21

were wearing or saying when no one was looking. I really liked Jude. He was one of my favorite things about living in Florida. I'd always wanted to live someplace like this. Someplace warm. Near a beach. And being able to be close to Jason was a definite plus. Jason was my soul mate. Nothing could be too bad whenever he was around. But in all honesty, my life was far from perfect anymore.

Six months ago, my biggest problem had been that I thought I was the oldest virgin on earth. I wasn't a virgin anymore, but sometimes, I almost wished I could go back to my life before. Then, my parents were alive, and I loved them. I lived in a busy, crowded home full of teenage foster boys, but I didn't realize how great it was to feel loved like that. I didn't realize how great it was to trust people implicitly. Now, I didn't trust anyone. I had nightmares a lot. I dreamed about my parents getting shot. I'd see it over and over again, in slow motion. The surprised look on their faces. The blood. The way their bodies had crumpled. In the worst dreams, the ones that always made me sit up straight in bed, screaming, I'd see Jason's face when he was shooting the members of the Sons who'd killed my parents. He looked determined and dangerous. Frenzied. Angry.

After that nightmare, Jason would rush into my room, and he'd be so sweet and comforting that I'd wonder how I could ever feel frightened of him. He was perfect. He was wonderful. He was mine. He wasn't scary.

But other times, when the dream didn't go that far, I wouldn't wake up without screaming, just seeing the image of my dead parents engraved on the back of my eyelids. And I'd think about other things. I'd think about Michaela Weem, Jason's crazy mother, who had screamed at me that together Jason and I would destroy things. She had told me that Jason was destined for violence on a grand scale. She had wanted me to kill Jason. Michaela Weem had believed that Jason was too dangerous to live. And she'd been able to convince a lot of people that she was right. I tried to tell myself she wasn't. I loved Jason more than life. I would die for him. I would kill for him. He was all that I had.

But Michaela had been right about one thing. Once. She'd told us that together Jason and I would "drive men mad." And we had. When we kissed, a whole group of the Sons had stopped shooting and completely lost their minds. If she'd been right about that, maybe she was right about . . . But no. No. Jason was not going to enslave the world. I didn't think that. I *refused* to think that.

Between freaking out about the Sons trying to kill me, reliving the trauma of my murdered parents, and worrying that my boyfriend was actually the anti-christ (instead of the messiah, which was what the Sons thought), my life was not exactly a cakewalk. I longed for the days when I worried about my history exam or whether girls at school were gossiping about me. All of that just seemed ridiculous and childish now. Sometimes, I felt very old. Jude was right. Jason was intense. Ever since he'd appeared in my life, everything had been intense.

That was why I liked Jude so much. He made me feel

23

normal, like a regular teenage girl again. One who thought about parties and boys and make-up. I used to think that kind of stuff was shallow, but now I wished like hell it was all I thought about. I missed it. I felt like my innocence had been stolen or something.

Thanks to Jude, the six hours of my shift went by pretty quickly. Afterwards, we sat outside of the theater, drinking huge sodas (one of the perks of working at movie theater). I was waiting for Jason to pick me up. We only had one car, and I hadn't wanted to monopolize it. Jude was just hanging out with me.

"You wanna go to that party at Rachel Kline's next weekend?" he asked.

"God," I said. "I'm not sure if I ever want to drink again."

Jude laughed. "I've heard that before."

"Hey!" I said. "I don't drink that much."

"You can hold your own, girl," said Jude, with a touch of admiration.

I rolled my eyes. "I just like to have fun. Is that so wrong?"

"You are fun," said Jude. "That's why I like you so much."

I'd always been such a goody-goody back in West Virginia. Now that I was free, I was able to make my own decisions. Hallam thought I was a teenage alcoholic, but then, Hallam didn't have a very high opinion of me. I was over-sexed. I drank too much. I didn't study enough. He was like the father I never wanted. Sometimes, I thought about packing up and moving to New Jersey to live with my grandmother. She had custody of my younger brother, Chance. But I didn't really think that Jason would be welcome, and there was no way I'd go anywhere without Jason. So I put up with Hallam, because I had to.

"Well, Jude," I said, "you're kind of fun, yourself."

"Kind of?" he said. "I am a blast, and you love it."

I laughed. Jude *was* a blast.

"So, party, then?" he asked.

"Maybe," I said. "I'll ask Jason if he wants to come. He might have to work, though."

Jude raised his eyebrows.

"Jason can come, right?"

"Keep him on a leash. He can't beat anybody else up."

I sighed. "I can't believe he did that."

"He was protecting you," said Jude. "It's sweet and all, and I understand, but didn't he get in a fight at school last week?"

"Yeah," I said, inwardly groaning. Jason had anger issues. "Speaking of Jason, where the hell is he?" He was at least ten minutes late.

"Call him," said Jude.

"I'll give him another minute or two," I said. "You don't have to wait if you don't want."

"Are you kidding? Of course I'm going to wait with you. I wouldn't let you sit outside the theater by yourself."

"Thanks," I said. But I remembered that earlier that day Jason had called Jude a jerk, and I wondered if it was a good idea for Jude to be there when Jason pulled up.

I scolded myself. It wasn't like Jason just started punching people for no reason. He had to be provoked. The guy he'd beat up last week at school for instance, had been threatening some poor freshman girl and being really vulgar. To Jason's credit, he hadn't started the fight. He'd asked the guy to cut it out. The guy had started swinging. It was just really stupid to try to fight Jason. Jason was too good at beating people up.

"Maybe I will call him," I said to Jude. I got my phone out of my purse and selected Jason's name out of my recently dialed log. Holding the phone up to my ear, I waited while it rang.

Jason picked up. "Azazel," he said.

"Hey," I said. "Are you coming to pick me up?"

"Crap," he said. "What time is it?"

I told him.

"I'm sorry," he said. "We've got a little situation here."

My heart started to race. A situation? It was the Sons, wasn't it? What had happened? "What?" I said, serious now.

"It's Lilith," he said.

CHAPTER TWO

To: Edgar Weem <eweem@risingsun.org>
From: Renegade Son <settingsun007@yahoo.com>
Subject: Monthly update
Edgar,
Not much has changed. Jason is still behaving violently. He's been badly beating several other boys in the area, both at school and work. He's still completely and utterly devoted to Azazel.
I look for other tell-tale signs, but he seems like a normal kid otherwise. Nothing else to report.
Hallam

The last time I saw my best friend Lilith, she was wearing a silk black robe and explaining to me that everyone in my entire town (including her) was a Satanist. She was telling me that my parents, my principal, and my teachers all thought that I was the Vessel of Azazel and that I was supposed to kill Jason for the greater good. The time that I'd seen her before that, I'd found out that she'd been sleeping with my then-boyfriend Toby for years. I wasn't really on speaking terms with Lilith anymore.

But there she was, sitting in the living room of our apartment in Florida, looking pretty much the same as she had months ago. Her hair was still red. Her boobs were still gigantic. And she didn't look the least bit sorry.

Standing in the doorway with Jason, I glowered at her. I'd wanted him to fill me in on the way home, but I hadn't really given him the chance to talk, because I'd spent the entire ride ranting about how I couldn't believe that Lilith had the nerve to show up at my house. If Lilith was expecting some kind of tear-filled, happy reunion with me, she had another thing coming.

"What are you doing here?" I demanded.

"Hi Zaza," she said, smiling tentatively.

The sound of my old nickname made me cringe. My parents used to call me that. "It's Azazel," I said.

"Sorry," she said.

I crossed my arms over my chest. "Well?" I said. "Why are you here?"

"Azazel," said Jason from behind me, "maybe – "

I turned on him, silencing him with a look. He backed away, making a hands-off gesture. "I'll let you two catch up," he said, and tried to duck into the kitchen, away from us.

"No way," I said. "You're not going anywhere." I clutched his arm and yanked him over to me, so that we were standing shoulder to shoulder. A united front. Against Lilith.

"You're mad," said Lilith.

"Duh," I said.

Lilith nodded. "Of course you're mad," she said. "Why wouldn't you be?"

"You screwed my boyfriend behind my back and tried to

get me to kill Jason," I said. "So, yeah, I'm pretty much mad. Pretty much hoped never to see you again. Pretty much want you to get the hell out."

Lilith's face fell. Then she nodded. "Okay," she said, standing up from the couch and slinging her duffel bag over her shoulder. "I understand."

"Wait," said Jason.

What? I looked at Jason, shocked. Why was he saying that? He was supposed to be on my side.

"She ran away from home," said Jason.

"So?" I said.

"So, she's got nowhere else to go," he said.

"I don't care," I said.

"She needs help," he said.

"She doesn't deserve my help," I said.

"Why not?" he asked.

"You know why not," I said. "Because of what I just said."

"The stuff about Toby?" he asked.

"Yeah," I said.

Jason nodded. "You still care about Toby?" he asked, not looking at me.

"No," I said. It was a moot point. Toby was dead, anyhow. The Sons had killed him the same time they'd killed my parents.

"Good," said Jason, turning to look at me, "because if I remember correctly, he was big jerk who tried to rape you. Twice."

Was Jason jealous of everyone suddenly? Good God. First Jude, now Toby? How could someone be jealous of a gay guy and a dead guy? What was next? Actors on TV?

"He *was* a jerk," said Lilith.

I looked at her witheringly. "The last time I heard the two of you talking, you said you loved him."

"I was an idiot," said Lilith. "I guess he told both of us that he loved us, didn't he?"

"Well, yeah," I said, "but he only said that to me because the coven forced him to date me so that I would stay a virgin for the ritual. I kind of don't think that counts. He really loved you."

"Which was why he took off after you right after you and Jason left, right?" said Lilith. "That was why he ditched me and got himself killed. Because he loved me?"

Okay, point. "Right, well, like Jason said, Toby was a jerk."

"So, it's stupid to be mad at Lilith about her relationship with him, then," said Jason.

Stupid? Did Jason just call me stupid? "I don't think it's stupid, exactly," I said.

Jason made another hands-off gesture. "Bad choice of words," he admitted. "I'm just saying that Toby was never really that important to you, anyway, right?"

Well . . . "I dated him for four years," I said. "So, I mean, he was kind of important."

"But not as . . ." Jason trailed off. "Not as important as me?"

"Of course not!" I said. "God, your insecurity is getting to me!"

"I'm not being insecure," Jason said, looking hurt. "I'm just trying to moderate this conversation between you and Lilith. So don't get pissed at me."

It was hard to be mad at Jason. I bit my lip. "Sorry," I finally muttered.

"Me too," he said. "Sometimes the Toby thing makes me defensive."

I was the first and only person Jason had ever kissed, but I'd kissed Toby before Jason. We'd talked about it a few times. Jason felt a little threatened by the specter of Toby, even though he'd been, as mentioned, a really big jerk. I crossed to Jason and squeezed his hand. He kissed me on the forehead. I looked up into his huge, brown eyes. I melted.

"Whoa," breathed Lilith.

I snapped around to look at her. For a minute, I'd kind of forgotten she was there. "What?" I said.

She shook her head. "You two are just . . . whoa." Her mouth was slightly open. "You're really in love, aren't you?"

What did that have to do with anything? I looked back at Jason. "She can't stay here," I said. "She just can't."

"Zaza, you have no idea how sorry I am about everything," said Lilith.

"Don't call me that!"

"Bramford's apparently pretty horrible since your parents died and we left," said Jason. "The coven has gotten oppressive."

31

"I don't care," I said. I didn't.

Jason kept going. "They're convinced that they weren't successful in killing me because they weren't worthy. So everyone's been forced to participate in really bizarre rituals. Lilith's lucky to get out."

That did sound kind of awful. "So what?" I said, not ready to back down. "You don't want to be a Satanist anymore?"

"I never wanted to be a Satanist," said Lilith. "It was just peer pressure, you know? Everybody else was doing it. I wanted to run off with Toby. You heard me in the bathroom the night of Homecoming."

She *had* said something like that, hadn't she? Damn it. I didn't want Lilith around. Here in Bradenton, I was my own person. I was crazy and free and fun. Lilith would just remind me of who I'd been. Naïve, sweet, innocent. I wasn't that girl anymore. And I didn't need Lilith around to remind me of her.

I sighed. "If she stayed here, it couldn't be forever."

"No, I know that," said Lilith. "Just until I find something else. Get established. Maybe a few weeks. A month."

"Fine," I said.

"Really?" said Lilith. "Thank you so much." She leaped off the couch and hugged me. I didn't hug her back.

Finally, she released me. She stepped back, looking embarrassed. I didn't care. Lilith could stay here, but it didn't mean I was going to forgive her. It didn't mean we were going to be best friends anymore.

"What's Hallam think about it?" I asked Jason.

"Um, Hallam hasn't been home," said Jason.

"So, it's just been you and Lilith here?" I asked. "Talking? For hours?"

"Yeah," said Jason, giving me a funny look.

Lilith used to think Jason was really attractive. She used to joke about trying to have sex with him. Lilith was, well, promiscuous. I narrowed my eyes.

"Let me handle Hallam," said Jason.

* * *

Hallam wasn't pleased with the idea of Lilith crashing on our couch, but he eventually gave in. He said Lilith wouldn't have much privacy in our living room. I offered to give Lilith my room and stay with Jason. Hallam, of course, vetoed that idea immediately. Given the option of Jason and I "living in sin" or Lilith not having privacy, he decided her privacy was the lesser of two evils.

Truthfully, I didn't want to share a bedroom with Jason because I wanted to have sex. Not *just* because I wanted to have sex, anyway. I liked falling asleep with him. Snuggling in his arms, feeling his smooth skin against mine. I liked waking up with him. I just longed to be as close to Jason as I could, whenever I could.

We got Lilith some sheets and made up the couch for her to sleep on. By this time, it was pretty late, and we all had to be up early the next morning. Hallam had his early class on Mondays, Wednesdays, and Fridays. He also had early office hours on Tuesdays. On Thursdays, he didn't go in until ten. Sometimes, on Thursdays, Hallam slept in, and Jason and I would sneak into the shower together. But more often than not, Hallam just woke up early anyway. He said it was habit.

We all went to sleep. The apartment was quiet, and I could hear Lilith shifting around on the couch, trying to get comfortable. We'd gotten the couch at Goodwill, because it had been cheap. It was less than comfortable. I tried to feel a little sorry for Lilith, but I just couldn't do it.

I was exhausted, and I fell asleep almost immediately after that. I dreamed.

In my dream, I was in the basement of my parents' house, wearing a silky black robe. The hood was over my eyes. The room was lit only with candles, and they flickered eerily. My hands were tied together. I was drunk. I stumbled as I tried to run away, but I was surrounded by other people, similarly clad in black robes. They caught me. They held me. I struggled, but they were stronger than me. Their hoods were over their faces, so I couldn't see who was who.

I elbowed random robed people. They fell back, but there was always someone else to take their place, holding me fast. They were chanting, intoning something in another language that sounded ancient and evil.

"Stop," I slurred. "Stop. I think I'm going to throw up."

Lilith was in front of me, lowering her hood. "Zaza," she said, "we have to finish the ritual."

Someone grabbed me from behind. I twisted, trying to wriggle out of his grasp, but I couldn't break free. "Hold

34

still," said the person holding me, and I recognized his voice. Toby.

I struggled harder, my heart racing. But Toby was pulling me, dragging me down on the ground. Toby was on top of me, the weight of his body smashing my bones, suffocating me. I really thought I was going to throw up. I was so drunk.

"Toby, stop," I pleaded.

Toby didn't listen. His legs were between my legs, forcing them open.

I screamed. "Jason!" I yelled. Where was Jason? Jason always saved me. I needed him. Where was he?

I pushed Toby's hood out of the way, but when I looked at him, it wasn't Toby under the hood. It was Jason. He was leering at me as he fumbled with the buttons of my robe.

"No!" I screamed and with all of my might, I pushed Jason/Toby off of me and I ran.

I scrambled up the steps in the basement, and flung open the door at the top.

Outside the basement, I was on the beach in Bradenton. I wasn't wearing anything except my bikini, and the breeze from the ocean whipped around me, pulling goose bumps out of my skin. I looked around, confused.

Jude was waiting for me. He took my hand. "Let's get you home," he said.

I woke up out of breath, my heart beating out of my chest. Well. That was a new nightmare.

For a few minutes, I just lay still under the covers, the fear paralyzing me. I wanted to get up and go crawl in bed with

Jason, but I couldn't move. So I didn't. I stared at the ceiling until sleep pulled me under again.

The next morning, my alarm woke me at 6:15. I slapped it off and lay back on the bed. I didn't want to get up. But I dragged myself out of bed and into the shower. I got the first shower every morning, because I had to blow dry my hair, which I did in my bedroom while Jason was showering. Hallam's class wasn't until eight, so he showered after Jason. He grumbled a lot, because he ran out of hot water at the end of his shower.

Lilith was asleep on the couch, so we tiptoed around her as we left for school. Jason and I walked the five blocks to Bayshore High School every morning. In the morning, it was fine, but sometimes, in the afternoon, when we walked home from school, it was eighty-five degrees and humid. I often arrived home sweaty and gross. Whenever I could, I asked Jude for a ride home.

Bayshore High School was much bigger than my old high school. Nearly every day that I walked inside, I felt a little overwhelmed by its size and by the amount of people that went there. It was also strange to go to a school that was landscaped with palm trees. It made me feel like I was living on a television show or something. Of course, all the schools on television shows were in California. Florida definitely wasn't California.

Everything was different in Florida than it had been in West Virginia. We were still on block scheduling, but Bayshore was on an AB schedule, which meant we had different classes every other day. In West Virginia, I'd been in Honors classes, but due to the fact we hadn't requested our transcripts from Bramford, Jason and I were in general classes at Bayshore. General classes were very, very different. It was hard to learn anything, because our teachers spent most of their time trying to get the class to be quiet and listen. No one seemed particularly interested in doing that. Also, I felt like there was more work assigned in general classes, but it was all busy work. It was like the teachers had given up on us and just wanted to keep us from making trouble.

I was making good grades, though. So was Jason. Sometimes, Hallam asked us questions about college, but neither of us had really done anything on that front. At this point, it was practically too late. Back in Bramford, I'd sent in my application for WVU in the fall. I'd been so sure that I'd end up in Morgantown. Toby and I would both be there. And Lilith. My life had been all planned out then. Simple. Easy. Now, with the Sons and the Satanists and Michaela Weem, things like college didn't seem that important. I was alive, wasn't I? That was all that was important.

Jason and I arrived at school at 7:35, ten minutes before first period. We walked each other to our lockers, dropping off our book bags and getting our books for first block. Then we parted ways (without kissing, because PDA was strongly frowned upon) because we had different classes on different sides of the school.

It was an Odd day (or an A day), so my first class was

history with Mr. Sutherland. Jason had Mr. Sutherland too, but on Even days (B days). I couldn't figure out why they called the schedules Odd and Even. They didn't coincide with the day of the week. It didn't make any sense at all. Mr. Sutherland also taught AP History, but neither Jason nor I had any AP classes. Still, Mr. Sutherland seemed to expect a little more of his general classes. Maybe it was because he was from England, and they had higher standards there.

Mr. Sutherland really liked me, to the point that Jude was always teasing me about being a teacher's pet. Jude had first block with me on Odd days. Mr. Sutherland thought that I was "brilliant" and "talented," and he couldn't understand how I'd ended up in a general history class. I appreciated that he had such a high opinion of me, but sometimes, the way he fawned over me was really, really annoying. I blamed him for single-handedly making everyone in my history class hate me.

I met Jude at the door to Mr. Sutherland's class. We made our way to our seats the back corner. Mr. Sutherland wasn't much for seating charts, which was good, as far as I was concerned. If I got separated from Jude, this class would be unbearable.

"Tell me all about this Lilith chick," said Jude as we sat down.

God. How could I? There were some things I just couldn't share with everyone. It made me sound nuts to say that my family had turned out to be Satanists. No one would believe me if I said that Jason and I had been chased across the country by a secret society bent of global domination. I shrugged. "She was my best friend in West Virginia," I said.

As far as Jude knew, I'd moved here because my parents died. That was it.

"Was?" asked Jude.

"Well, she was sleeping with my boyfriend, so I kind of wasn't speaking to her anymore."

"She was sleeping with Jason?" Jude asked.

The bell rang.

"Excuse me," said Mr. Sutherland in his British accent.

No one listened to him. "No," I said. "Not Jason."

"Class!" said Mr. Sutherland. "Quiet down for announcements."

The room still didn't get quiet.

"A different boyfriend?" asked Jude.

"Yeah," I said.

"Who you're not dating anymore," said Jude. "So what's the big?"

Why didn't anybody understand this? "She betrayed me," I said. "I don't trust her."

"Next person to speak loses free time," said Mr. Sutherland.

Free time was Mr. Sutherland's way of keeping his classes in line. Everyone got five minutes to chat at the end of class, unless they misbehaved. Losing free time meant you had to do menial tasks for Mr. Sutherland like passing out papers or cleaning up trash from the floor or emptying the pencil sharpener.

Everyone got quiet.

"Thank you," said Mr. Sutherland.

The loud speaker beeped. "Good morning Bayshore High. This is your principal, Mr. Dingle."

He started out announcements like that every day. Like we didn't know who he was. And if you dealt with teenagers every day, would you really advertise the fact your last name was *Dingle*?

Mr. Dingle was a strange man. He was young, blonde, and tan. He always seemed very excited, and he carried a bell around with him, one of those silver ones with a wooden handle. If students were doing something he didn't approve of, he would ring the bell in their faces and say, "Now, now. Let's make a better choice, okay?" He'd rung the bell at Jason and me many times for kissing in the hallway. I really didn't like him.

A soft murmur began in the classroom as students began to talk again.

"You think she'd do it again?" Jude whispered to me. "Are you worried about Jason?"

Was I – ? That was silly. "Of course not," I said. Jason would never do that. He was devoted to me.

"Jenna, that's your free time," said Mr. Sutherland.

I shut my mouth.

Mr. Dingle continued, "The most important announcement this morning is that my bell has been stolen."

Really? That was great! Awesome. I hated that bell.

Other students seemed to share my sentiment, since a few

laughed and one guy emitted a whoop.

"Class!" warned Mr. Sutherland.

"Anyone with any information about the whereabouts of my bell should contact me or your teachers. When I find out who has taken the bell, he or she will be punished severely."

I rolled my eyes. Everyone in class laughed.

"That rocks," said Jude.

I grinned. "Yeah."

The entire classroom had erupted in conversation.

"Quiet!" yelled Mr. Sutherland, but it was a lost cause. Any further announcements were drowned out by the rest of the class talking.

"So," Jude said, "why is Lilith here?"

I sighed, picking up my purse to look for a pen. "She ran away from home. She's staying with us for a few weeks."

"Aren't her parents going to be looking for her?"

I shrugged. "She's eighteen. I don't know what they can do."

I couldn't wait until Jason and I were both eighteen, which wouldn't be until the late spring. Jason's birthday was soon, but mine wasn't until May. When that happened, we wouldn't need Hallam anymore. We could move out and be on our own.

I searched through my purse with my hands, not really looking at it. I felt for the small cylindrical plastic of my pen. Instead, my hand brushed cold metal. What was that?

I pulled it out of my purse to look at it, and everyone got quiet suddenly.

Dammit. It was Mr. Dingle's bell.

How had it gotten in my purse?

I looked at Jude, confusion and surprise all over my face.

He grinned at me. "Way to go, Azazel!" he said, applauding.

The rest of the class joined in, cheering. Well. On the plus side, maybe they wouldn't hate me anymore.

Mr. Sutherland was staring at me, slack-jawed. He looked crushed. After all, here I was, his star student, a delinquent. Except for the fact that I hadn't taken the bell! How had it gotten in my purse in the first place?

Mr. Sutherland smiled. "Well, Azazel, I guess we'll be spending some afternoons together." And he actually looked excited at the prospect. Eew. Mr. Sutherland ran afterschool detention.

I stared at the bell in my hands. Where had this bell come from?

"I'm going to have to write you a referral," said Mr. Sutherland.

Great.

CHAPTER THREE

michaela666 (6:33:02): You're going to see her today, right?

aird92 (6:33:44): everyday, u know that.

michaela666 (6:34:12): It worries me. If she figures out what you've done, there could be bad repercussions.

aird92 (6:34:53): u worry about everything. she doesn't suspect anything.

michaela666 (6:35:33): And Jason? Does he suspect anything?

aird92 (06:35:48): stop worrying. geez!!!

Mr. Dingle turned the bell over and over in his hands. "This is very simple, Azazel. Just tell me how you got the bell."

He didn't believe me. I didn't blame him. It sounded like something stupid that a kid would say to get out of trouble. "It just showed up in my purse, I swear," I said.

Mr. Dingle's office was covered in pictures of him holding a surf board. Where in God's name did he go surfing? We were on the Gulf. There weren't any waves here! Sometimes he was with other guys with surfboards. Sometimes he was with different blonde, pretty girls. Weird.

"You can't expect me to believe that," he said.

"I know it sounds stupid," I said. "And I really hate your stupid bell. But I didn't take it. I've been framed."

Mr. Dingle shook his head. "Why would someone do

that?"

Why would someone do that? As I'd been walking up the office, I'd had time to really look at the bell. It was silver, with a wooden handle. Nothing weird about that at all. But there was something about the bell I'd never noticed before. On the front of the bell, engraved into the metal was a picture of the sun, rising over the ocean.

The Rising Sun.

Someone was trying to give me a message. The Sons. But I couldn't very well tell Mr. Dingle that, now could I?

We went round and round for over an hour, which was kind of cool, because it meant that I missed the rest of Mr. Sutherland's class. On the other hand, I was freaked out, expecting the Sons to bust through the windows of Mr. Dingle's office at any second. They'd be in black. The glass would shatter, flying out, cutting our skin. It would be quick. One gun shot in Mr. Dingle's head. One in mine. We'd slump dead over his desk, blood seeping into his papers. The Sons would use silencers, so no one else would ever even know. At some point, one of the secretaries would come in. She'd scream.

But that didn't happen. Instead, Mr. Dingle assigned me a week of detention, starting tomorrow, so I could arrange transportation if necessary. He told me he was going to call my parents.

"My parents are dead," I told him.

He looked a little taken aback when I said that. Sorry for me. That pissed me off. How dare Mr. Dingle feel sorry for me? But after checking my records, he promised he'd call Hallam. Wonderful. Like Hallam needed another reason to hate me.

I returned to my 2nd/3rd block class. Apparently, word had spread. I was like a celebrity or something. Whenever I walked in, everyone started clapping and cheering. Our teacher, Ms. Ritter, calmed everyone down as best as she could. I sat down in my regular seat and tried to concentrate on the math lesson. All I could think about were the Sons. They'd put that bell in my purse for a reason. Why? What were they planning? Why were they messing with me?

After 2nd/3rd, Jason and I had lunch. It was 10:30 at that point. We had the earliest lunch shift in the school. I was never hungry at 10:30, so I usually just bought some yogurt from the vending machine. Jason, however, being the growing boy that he was, ate lunch. It kind of pissed me off, but I was used to it. I'd grown up in house full of teenage boys. They ate. A lot. And they never got fat, they just got taller. And taller. When I'd first met Jason, he'd been about 5'10". Now he was pushing six feet.

Jude and I didn't share a lunch shift, but I'd see him in 6th/7th block. That meant that I sat alone, waiting for Jason to come back with his tray every day. Except today, everyone in school was stopping to congratulate me on stealing Mr. Dingle's bell. At first, I tried to explain that I didn't know how I'd got it, but no one believed me, so eventually, I just started smiling and shrugging like I was proud of myself.

Jason sat down with me, carrying a tray loaded with chicken fingers and corn. "What the hell?" he greeted me.

"I didn't do it," I said. "It just appeared in my purse."

"Really?"

Did he think I would lie to him? "Really," I said. "But I think I know who did do it."

"Jude?" he asked.

"What?" I glared at him. "Jude didn't do it. Why would you even think that?"

Jason shrugged. "So who did it then?"

"The Sons," I said.

"What?" said Jason. "Why would the Sons steal Mr. Dingle's bell?"

"Have you ever looked closely at that bell? It's got a picture of a rising sun on it. They're sending me a message. I don't know what it means, but it's not good."

Jason took a bite of a chicken finger. "You're paranoid."

"You don't believe me?"

"It doesn't make any sense. Sorry. The Sons wouldn't steal a bell to send you a message. They'd just . . . I don't know . . . kill you."

"But the sun – "

"Coincidence."

"So how did the bell get in my purse?"

"I don't know," said Jason.

"Someone set me up. Who would do that?"

"I don't know."

"It's not like anyone hates me around here. No one even

knows I exist."

At that moment, two girls stopped by my table. "You're Azazel, right?" one asked.

"You stole the bell?"

I rolled my eyes. "That's me."

"Awesome," said one.

"Yeah, you rock," said the other.

"Thanks," I said.

They walked away.

"You were saying?" asked Jason.

"Well, no one knew who I was before this," I said. "I'm telling you. The Sons are the only thing that makes any sense."

Jason shook his head. "I know you're always freaked out about them, but you're wrong. And it doesn't make any sense."

I couldn't believe it. I had clearly been given a message from the Sons. A warning. And Jason didn't believe me. "It does make sense."

"No," said Jason, "it doesn't. Look, the Sons know to leave us alone. The minute they try anything, Hallam will go public with the information that Edgar Weem is my father. Weem would never take that chance."

"What if someone's working without Weem's knowledge?" I said.

"Impossible. He's too high up in the Council for something like that to happen. And he protects his own interests." Jason reached across the table and took my hand.

"Hey, Azazel, I know it's hard for you. If there was any way that I go back in time and protect you from all of this, I would. I'm so sorry that any of this ever happened to you. And I know it scares you. But it's over. Okay? It's over. The Sons aren't chasing us. The Satanists are dead. We're safe. Okay? We're safe now."

I squeezed his hand. I wanted to believe him. I really did. But . . . "What if we're not?" I asked.

"We are," he said.

I pulled my hand back. I hugged myself. "I want you to take me to the shooting range again."

Jason put down his chicken finger. "Jesus, Azazel, not this again."

"You haven't taken me in weeks," I said.

"Because you don't need to know how to shoot a gun," he said.

"I do so," I said. "I need to, even if no one's after us, so that I can feel safe."

"We went twice a week for a month," said Jason. "You know the basics. You're fine. We don't need to go again."

"What if I get out of practice?" I said. "And my aim still isn't very good. I need to shoot more or else I'm going to lose everything I know."

Jason sighed. "All I want is for us to be normal kids. But you can't let this go. You keep living like we're still being chased. We're not."

"Jason . . ." I trailed off. He made me feel bad. I knew that all Jason had ever wanted was a normal life. I didn't want to be the person who was ruining that for him.

We were quiet for a while. Jason shoveled corn into his mouth. I opened my yogurt and began to eat. A few more students stopped by to congratulate me on my stealing of Mr. Dingle's bell.

"I have detention," I said when they were gone. "For a week."

"That sucks," commented Jason.

"Yeah, it really does. Because I didn't do it."

Jason shook his head. "Why would someone frame you like that?"

I kept my mouth shut. I knew why. If Jason didn't want to believe me . . . But maybe he was right. Maybe I was being paranoid. After all, I was the only one who had nightmares. Jason was fine. He was well-adjusted. He loved living in sunny Florida and going to class every day. For him, our life was like paradise. For me, it was . . . Well, it wasn't paradise.

* * *

After school, I found Jude and asked if he minded giving Jason and I a ride home. He didn't mind. I met Jason at our regular meeting spot in the front of the school. Jason smiled when he saw me, but his smile faded when he saw Jude.

"Hi Jason," Jude greeted brightly.

"Hi," Jason muttered.

I wished Jason wouldn't be so blatantly rude to Jude.

"Jude's going to give us a ride home," I said.

"We can walk," said Jason.

"It's too hot," I said.

"It's not a problem," said Jude. "Really."

Jason shrugged his backpack further up on his shoulder. "Fine," he said. "Let's go."

The three of us trudged silently to the student parking lot and Jude's car. Jude drove an old Ford Aspire, which he'd painted bright purple. I offered to sit in the back, but Jason shook his head at me. He didn't want to sit up front with Jude. So Jason squeezed into the back seat of the car, and I sat up front. Jude turned on the car and blasted the air conditioning. He backed the car up, and we pulled out of the student parking lot.

"So, what did I miss in Mr. Sutherland's class?" I asked.

"Not much," said Jude. "Everyone was so excited about the fact you stole the bell that not much got accomplished. How'd you do it, anyway?"

"I didn't," I said. "Someone set me up."

"Did you do it, Jude?" Jason asked pointedly from the back.

"Me?" asked Jude. "Why would I get Azazel in trouble? She's my BFF."

In the backseat, Jason snorted.

I turned around and glared at him.

"Why would someone set you up?" Jude asked.

"Yeah," said Jason. "Why, Azazel?"

I ignored Jason. "I don't know," I said. "Probably because they didn't want to get in trouble for doing it." It was a message from the Sons! Why didn't Jason believe me?

"That's screwed up," said Jude. "Sometimes people are idiots."

"Yeah," I said.

"So, anyway, everybody was really excited about it," Jude continued. "And Mr. Sutherland barely got to talk about the kidnapping of the Limburger baby or whatever."

"Lindbergh baby," Jason corrected.

"Right," said Jude. "So, did you tell Dingle that you didn't do it?"

"Yeah," I said. "But he didn't believe me. I have detention for the rest of the week."

"Oh no," said Jude. "That totally sucks. What about Thursday? You're supposed to work right after school."

"I'm just going to ask Mindy to trade shifts with me," I said. "Think she will?"

"Probably," said Jude. "I'm really sorry that you have detention. Especially for something you didn't do. And I'm going to miss you on Thursday. Dammit."

"Yeah, it blows," I agreed. "So who's the Lindbergh baby?"

"Charles Lindbergh's son," said Jason from the back.

"Who's Charles Lindbergh?" I asked.

"I don't know," said Jude.

"We've been talking about him in class all week," said Jason.

"Really?" I asked. "It's hard to concentrate in that class. Everyone's so noisy. They always get Mr. Sutherland off topic by asking him about his life when he lived in

England."

"Oh, right," said Jude. "Lindbergh like flew a plane over the Atlantic in the 1930s, right?"

"Right," said Jason, sounding disgusted with both of us.

"So what happened to his baby?" I asked.

"It got kidnapped," said Jude.

"Oh," I said. "That sucks. Did they get him back?"

"I don't know. Mr. Sutherland didn't get to that," said Jude. "Apparently, at first, they thought it was a practical joke, because Lindbergh liked to hide the baby in the closet and pretend he didn't know where he was."

"That's kind of messed up," I said. "Who would hide a baby as a joke?"

"The guy flew across the Atlantic after six other people had died trying to do it. Maybe he was just crazy," offered Jason.

I laughed. Jude didn't.

Hmm. Maybe this dislike was a two-way street.

"I always thought," said Jason, "that would be a good way to pull off a kidnapping."

"What do you mean?" I asked.

"I mean, kidnap someone in their own house," said Jason. "Tie them up and knock them out, and keep them in their own attic."

"How would you get in and out of the house?" I asked.

"I don't know," said Jason. "Never worked that part out. But it would be super cool, after you got the ransom money, to be like, 'Yeah, they were two stories above you the whole time.'"

"That would be impossible to pull off," said Jude. "Besides, why would you want to kidnap someone?"

"I wouldn't," said Jason. "Not really."

We had arrived at our apartment. Jude parked the car in the parking lot. I wanted to invite him in, but I knew Jason wouldn't be cool with it. So I just said goodbye to Jude, and Jason and I got out of the car.

When we got inside, Lilith wasn't there. She'd left a note that she was off job hunting. Hallam was still at work, so we had the apartment to ourselves for a while. Usually, I got right to work on my homework after school. I should have today, especially since I was working later. I had to go in for about four hours that evening. But I wasn't feeling like doing homework. I was frustrated and confused about the turn of events at school. I wanted to talk to Jason about it, but after what he'd said at lunch today, I felt like it would be a bad idea. Instead, I hunted through the refrigerator for a snack.

Jason dropped off his books in his bedroom and joined me in the kitchen.

"Hey," he said. "I'm sorry about the way I reacted to what you said at lunch."

I closed the refrigerator. "You mean you think I could be right about the Sons?"

"Well," said Jason, "no. I don't think they're after us. But I'm sorry if I made you feel stupid for thinking it. After everything that's happened to us, I can see why you'd be jumping at shadows."

"I don't think that's what I'm doing," I said. "There was an engraving of a rising sun on that bell."

"And that's a weird coincidence," said Jason. "It's understandable that you'd freak out. And it is weird. That bell ending up in your purse."

"Why do you think it happened?" I asked.

"Somebody's idea of a practical joke, I guess," said Jason. "Like you said. Maybe that guy from the party that I beat up."

"You think?" I said.

"He'd be holding a grudge against you."

"Who was he? Does he go to our school?"

Jason shrugged.

"Jude said you put him in the hospital. Would he have even been at school today?"

Jason shrugged again. "Maybe he got one of his friends to do it. There were a bunch of people at that party."

Maybe Jason was right. There was probably a better explanation than the Sons of the Rising Sun being after us. "You really think we're safe?" I said.

"I'm sure of it," he said.

I sighed. He was probably right. I was overly excitable. That dream I'd had last night hadn't helped things either. "I had a nightmare last night," I said.

"The one about your parents?" Jason asked.

"No," I said. I explained it to him. But I left out the part where Toby turned into Jason. I didn't want Jason to think

54

that any part of me, even subconsciously, was ever afraid of him. "It was probably just because Lilith showed up," I said.

"It sounds horrible," he said. "I'm sorry I wasn't there."

"I wanted to come crawl into bed with you," I admitted, "but I was so scared. And I knew it would just piss Hallam off."

Jason folded me into his arms. "Screw Hallam," he whispered into my ear. "If you need me, you come to me. Don't let him stop you."

I hugged him back, liking how safe I felt with arms around me. His strong, strong arms. I snuggled against his chest. Jason stroked my hair. He kissed my forehead.

I looked up at him, into his eyes. My breath caught in my throat. He was so beautiful. Looking at him, close like this, I was so overwhelmed by how gorgeous he was. And he was mine. My beautiful, strong, wonderful Jason. His head dipped down and our lips met.

His lips were soft, supple against mine. But his arms held me close against him, pulling me tight against his body. I touched his neck, followed the outline of the muscles in his shoulders with my fingertips. He ran his hands over my back, my waist. His hands around my rib cage, I felt so small. I kissed him harder, parting his lips with my tongue.

Jason made a little noise in the back of his throat. He broke away for a minute. "How long do we have until Hallam comes back?" he whispered.

"Almost an hour," I said.

"Your room or mine?" he asked, gazing into my eyes

hungrily.

Less than fifteen minutes later, we were in my bedroom when we heard the front door opening. We tensed against each other. Jason clenched his jaw. "I'm going to kill him," he muttered.

I sighed and kissed him again. "Maybe," I said, "if we're just really quiet . . ."

Jason kissed me. "He'll kill us," he said.

"Yeah," I said. Stupid Hallam.

A voice called out my name from the living room. But it wasn't Hallam.

It was Lilith.

Stupid Lilith. Grr. Jason and I *never* had any time alone together. And here she was, ruining everything.

"Augh," I groaned. "It's Lilith."

Jason sat up. "Guess we need to see what she wants."

Lilith was moving through the house, calling my name. She knocked on my door. "Azazel?" she asked.

"Yeah?" I said, trying to sound as annoyed as I felt, but finding that there was no tone of voice quite strong enough.

"It's me," she said.

"One second," I said. Jason and I put ourselves back in order, and I opened the door. "Hi, Lilith." I glared at her.

"Oh," she said. "Was I interrupting something?"

I didn't answer.

"I'm so sorry," she said.

"It's okay," said Jason from behind me, straightening the edge of his shirt. "You didn't know."

56

Why was Jason telling her it was okay? It was not okay. It was anything but okay. I wished like hell that Lilith was not in my house. "What do you need?" I asked her.

"I just . . ." she trailed off. "You know, maybe I should go watch some TV or something."

"No," said Jason, "don't be silly."

Don't be silly?! What was wrong with him?

"It's too late," I said. "Besides, it would be weird with you here. Just tell me what you need."

"I was wondering if I could use your computer?" she asked. "To check email and stuff?"

"Fine," I said. "It's in the living room. Knock yourself out." She could see the damned thing. Why come ask me about it?

Lilith looked at the carpet. "Um . . . I don't know the password."

I sighed heavily, but I gave her the password.

"Thanks," said Lilith. "You guys go back to what you were doing." She pulled the door closed.

What we were doing? Not bloody likely. I looked at Jason. He looked at me. He shrugged. "Soon," he said.

"It's been like three weeks," I said.

"I know that," he said. He kissed my forehead. Then he left my bedroom.

I plopped down on my bed.

"Azazel?" called Lilith from the living room.

"What?" I demanded.

"Do you mind if I sign on to the AOL Instant

Messenger?"

"No," I said. "No, that's fine. Do whatever you want."

Clearly, she would anyway.

CHAPTER FOUR

To: Renegade Son <settingsun007@yahoo.com>
From: Edgar Weem <eweem@risingsun.org>
Subject: Re: Monthly update
Hallam,

I appreciate the update. I know you have a soft spot for Jason, but you must realize that the boy is not what he appears to be. Please continue to keep an eye on him. If the situation escalates, especially the violence, it may be necessary for us to step in. Of course, we'll try to avoid that at all costs.

Edgar

I waited until the last possible second to get to detention, so I was almost late. Mr. Sutherland met me at the door to his classroom. He smiled at me. "Hi Azazel," he said. "I was beginning to think you wouldn't show up."

I looked past him into the classroom. Several other students were sitting inside at the desks. I didn't recognize any of them. None of them looked particularly like people I wanted to get to know either. There was a burly guy with a bandana tied around his head. He was wearing several large gold chains. One guy was wearing a white tank top which showed off his tattoo-covered arms. Another guy had greasy hair pulled into a ponytail at the nape of his neck. There were two girls as well. They both wore large hoop earrings and lots of makeup. None of them looked at me as I came inside and sat down.

This was stupid. I did not belong in detention. I hadn't done anything wrong. I was a good kid. I made good grades. I did not belong here with all these delinquents.

Mr. Sutherland shut the door to his classroom. "Well," he said, "today in detention, one of you will be alphabetizing my books by author." He gestured to a large bookshelf which was groaning under the weight of all the books on it. Mr. Sutherland had to be kidding. "The others will be scrubbing down my desks."

Ugh. Why did Mr. Sutherland have to make detention into work?

The burly bandana guy raised his hand. "Hey, isn't there some law that you can't make us do manual labor?"

Mr. Sutherland shrugged. "I'm not really familiar with your American laws," he said, smiling.

"Bullshit," said the tattooed guy.

"Watch your language," said Mr. Sutherland. "Anymore of that and I'll have you after school for another day." He smiled. "Now. Would anyone like to volunteer to alphabetize?"

No one said anything.

"Fine," said Mr. Sutherland, "then, Azazel, I think that's a good job for you. I'm certain you know the alphabet. I don't know about the rest of these guys."

Thanks, Mr. Sutherland. Insult the rest of the people in detention at my expense. That would make this a great,

great experience for me. What a jerk!

But I got up and went to the bookshelf. While Mr. Sutherland instructed the other students in the technique he wanted them to use to wash the desks off, I began pulling all of the books off the bookshelf. Within a few minutes, I was surrounded by stacks of books. I sat down Indian style on the ground and began going through them, looking for authors whose last names were at the beginning of the alphabet. I was astonished when one of the books I picked up was *Holy Blood, Holy Grail*, by Michael Baigent, Richard Leigh, and Henry Lincoln. I'd read this book sometime last year, in the wake of my literary love affair with Dan Brown and *The Da Vinci Code*. It was the book on which Dan Brown had based his book. The book was extremely intriguing, all about the Holy Grail, secret societies, and conspiracy theories. That kind of stuff used to really interest me. Until I met Jason, and I found out that the Sons were the real thing. Secret societies were interesting when I didn't have to intimately interact with them. It was weird that Mr. Sutherland had this book.

I held it my hands, turning it over and staring at it, memories rushing back to me. It had only been a few years ago that I'd read it, but it seemed like forever. I'd been so young and silly then. I remembered having passionate conversations with my dad about the book, trying to convince him that there really were secret societies behind the scenes, pulling hidden strings. He'd just laughed at me. Everyone had. In the end, it had turned out that I was right.

I half-wished I hadn't been.

"Would you like to borrow that book?" Mr. Sutherland asked.

He was standing directly over me.

I looked up at him, startled. "Um, no," I said, "that's okay. I've read it already."

Mr. Sutherland crouched down so that he was on my level. "You have?" he asked, sounding pleasantly surprised.

"Yeah," I said. "I used to be really into that kind of thing."

"That kind of thing?"

"Secret societies and stuff," I said.

"Oh," said Mr. Sutherland. "Well, it happens to be one of my interests as well." He began searching through the stacks of books I'd made. "I have several books on various similar subjects. A few on the Knights Templar, some on Freemasonry. I'd be happy to let you borrow them."

I shook my head. "That's okay, Mr. Sutherland," I said. "It was just kind of a phase. I'm not into it anymore."

"Really?" he said.

I nodded, going back to the books.

"Is that why you took the bell?" he asked.

"What?" I said, looking back up at him.

"The bell," said Mr. Sutherland. "It has an engraving on it. Very intriguing. It reminded me of something . . ." He began paging through the book he was holding. "In here somewhere . . . Yes. Here it is." He showed me the book. On the page was a picture very similar to the engraving on the bell. It was a picture of the run rising over water.

My heart started to beat faster. "What is that?" I asked.

"It's a picture associated with an ancient secret society from the Renaissance," said Mr. Sutherland. "They've long since died out. There were called the Rising Suns or something like that."

I swallowed. "Really?" I managed.

"Did you see the resemblance as well?" he asked. "Quite remarkable, really. I wonder where Mr. Dingle acquired that bell."

"I didn't . . ." I trailed off, shaking my head.

Mr. Sutherland smiled. "Oh, of course. You told Mr. Dingle you didn't take the bell, didn't you?"

"I didn't take the bell," I said. I felt like I was strangling. I could hardly breathe, let alone speak.

"Of course you didn't," said Mr. Sutherland. "Would you like to borrow this book?"

I nodded.

He offered it to me. "Anytime that you'd like to talk conspiracy theories, just let me know," said Mr. Sutherland. "You're a very intriguing young lady, Azazel. Very intelligent."

I snatched the book out of his hands. "Thank you," I said, my voice shaking.

Mr. Sutherland's lips curved into a deep smile. "Certainly," he said.

He stood up and went back to supervising the other students.

I looked down at the book he'd given me, my hands trembling. Oh my God. Why hadn't I seen it before? I was so stupid. Mr. Sutherland. He was from England. I'd found the bell in his class. And he was interested in secret societies?

Mr. Sutherland was a member of the Sons. It was so obvious to me now. He was after me. And now I had to spend every day this week in his classroom for detention. Surely he wouldn't hurt me in front of these other students. Would he?

It made sense. He was here to watch both Jason and me. That was why we both had him as a teacher. And he had planted that bell in my purse himself. He'd wanted to get me into detention somehow. He was planning something. What was he planning? Why had he done it? What were the Sons going to do to me?

He'd even mentioned the Sons. He'd gotten the name slightly wrong, of course, but that hardly mattered. He'd sent me the message loud and clear. I knew what was going on. He must know that I knew. I stared at the books I was supposed to be alphabetizing, too terrified to move. At any second, I expected Mr. Sutherland to whip out a gun and shoot us all. Any second.

But detention just dragged on. Mr. Sutherland didn't do anything else suspicious. And eventually, I even went back to alphabetizing. By the time it was time for me to leave, I had even gotten all of them back on the shelf, in alphabetical order.

Mr. Sutherland dismissed us from detention, but as I was

heading for the door, he said, "Azazel, would you stay a second?"

No. I wouldn't. I couldn't. This was it. If I stayed, he would take out his gun. Calmly shoot me between the eyes. Step over my body. Leave the school. No one would ever hear from him again. "Okay," I said.

Mr. Sutherland handed me a slip of paper. "This is my address," he said. "I wouldn't give it to just anyone, but I feel like we have a little bit of a connection. You're a special girl. I have more books like the one I lent you at home. Stop by sometime. I can let you borrow them."

Go to his house? Was he crazy? Did he think I was stupid? If I went there, he'd kill me for sure. I wasn't going anywhere near his house. He should realize that. Luckily, at that second, my cell phone rang. That was probably Jude, who was waiting to take me to work. "I have to go, Mr. Sutherland," I said. "Someone's waiting for me."

"Okay," said Mr. Sutherland, smiling easily. "Just hang onto my address though. Drop by anytime."

It took all my will not to run out of the room. Instead, I walked. I took very large steps, and I got out of there as soon as I could. I got into Jude's car, still clutching the slip of paper that Mr. Sutherland had given me.

"Hey," said Jude. "You look freaked. What happened?"

I shook my head. I couldn't talk about this with Jude. I wanted to beg off work and go see Jason immediately. Jason would have to believe me now. And he'd know what to do. "Nothing," I said.

I'd be safe at work, though. It was a public place. There were lots of people there. The Sons wouldn't risk trying to kill me in such a populated building. I could go to work. I would. If I didn't, it would look weird. Jude might get suspicious. I couldn't put Jude in danger.

"What are you holding?" Jude asked. "Looks like you've got a death grip on it."

"Mr. Sutherland's address," I said. "He asked me to go to his house."

Jude made a face. "Eew," he said. "Why'd he do that?"

I shrugged. "He wanted to give me some books."

"Oh," said Jude, looking disappointed. "I thought maybe he was like a pedophile or something. It would have been fun to get him fired."

If I thought getting Mr. Sutherland fired would have made any difference, I would have been all for it. "Let's just go to work," I said. "I hate detention."

* * *

When I got home from work, it was after midnight, so I knew that both Jason and Hallam would be asleep. I was planning on waking Jason up anyway, though. What I'd found out was too important. He needed to know. After I'd told him, he'd probably want to wake up Hallam as well, but for now, I'd just tell Jason. I didn't know what was going to happen. Were we going to have to go on the run again? I didn't want to. I'd been happy here in Florida. We'd been settled. Still, it clearly wasn't safe here. We'd have to do what we had to do.

I was shocked when Jude dropped me off, and I saw that the lights were still on in our apartment. When I walked in the door, I heard the sounds of laughter. Jason and Lilith were sitting next to each other on the couch. Lilith was laughing so hard that she was resting her forehead on Jason's shoulder.

I couldn't believe it. Why were they still awake? Jason knew we had school in the morning. I cleared my throat.

Jason and Lilith both looked up at me.

"Hey Zaza," said Lilith, her voice still full of laughter.

God. Why couldn't she stop calling me that? I glared at her.

"You two look like you're having fun," I said.

"What time is it?" said Jason.

"It's after midnight," I said.

"Really?" said Jason. "Wow. Lilith and I have been talking. I guess we lost track of time." He smiled at her. "I should probably go to bed."

She grinned back. "I didn't mean to keep you up."

"It's okay," said Jason.

"Actually," I said. "I have something to tell you, Jason."

"Okay," he said. "What's up?"

"I don't want to tell you in front of Lilith," I said.

"How come?" asked Jason.

"It's about the Sons," I said.

"Oh, that's cool," said Jason. "I told her all about that stuff."

"You did?"

"She wanted to know what happened after we left Bramford. I filled her in," said Jason.

Lilith shook her head, horror all over her face. "Wow, Zaza. That shit was crazy. I can't believe Jason's mother is such a bitch."

He told her about Michaela Weem? He'd been talking to her all night? They'd been laughing together? I remembered what Jude had asked me the day before in Mr. Sutherland's class. Was I worried that Lilith would sleep with Jason? I hadn't been. I wasn't. I trusted Jason. But I didn't trust Lilith. Not at all.

"Yeah," I said. "I can't believe it either."

"So, it's cool," said Jason. "Sit down. Tell me what you need to tell me."

I really didn't want to tell Lilith about this. It was none of her business. And if we did go on the run, Lilith was *not* coming with us. The Sons would leave her alone. She would only slow us down.

I started at the beginning, telling Jason everything that had happened in detention. I showed him the picture in the book that Mr. Sutherland had given me. When I was finished, I sat down on the couch. "So, you think we should wake up Hallam?" I asked.

Jason didn't say anything.

"Zaza, you're paranoid," said Lilith.

I was not paranoid! I didn't respond, however, waiting for Jason to defend me. He'd see the seriousness of the situation. Lilith couldn't understand.

"That's not how I'd put it," said Jason. He turned to Lilith. "She's been through hell, Lilith. She saw her parents murdered right in front of her face."

Wait. Why didn't this sound entirely like he was defending me?

"Azazel," said Jason, "I don't think Mr. Sutherland is a member of the Sons."

"But the book," I protested. "And the bell. And I found it in his classroom."

"So, he's into secret societies," said Jason.

"And he's British," I said.

"That doesn't mean he's a member of the Sons," Jason said.

"You don't believe me?" I said. I was incredulous.

"It doesn't make sense," said Jason. "It's not how the Sons work. If they wanted me back, they wouldn't have some guy pose as a teacher to watch me. They'd just come for me. They're not subtle when it comes to me. You must remember that, don't you?"

"He knows things," I said. "He smiled at me in the creepiest way."

"He sounds like he was just trying to be nice," said Lilith. "He probably thinks you're a gifted student. He wants to help you."

I turned on Lilith. "You don't know what you're talking about."

She shrugged. "Sorry," she said. "But Jason told me about the deal you made. Edgar Weem would have to be stupid to go back on that."

"Don't you see?" I said. "Edgar Weem is trying to find some way of getting Jason back. He's not going to do it in the normal ways. He knows that we'd make his secret public. He's being stealthy."

"The Sons would not plant a bell in your bag, Azazel," said Jason. "Why would they want you in detention?"

"So that Mr. Sutherland could watch me," I said.

"Oh come on," said Jason, "that's really farfetched. You can't really think this."

I shook my head. Why didn't he believe me? It was obvious that we were in danger, and Jason didn't see it. What was I going to do? No one was taking me seriously. "Maybe if you weren't so busy making jokes with Lilith, you'd actually listen to what I'm saying," I said.

"Lilith doesn't have anything to do with this," said Jason. "Now, I know you're mad at her about what happened in Bramford, but honestly, Azazel, she was just as much a victim as you were. Why can't you let it go? She's trying to make amends here."

"You're right," I said. "Lilith doesn't have anything to do with this. So let's just leave her out of it."

"You're so stubborn," said Jason.

I stood up. "You used to like that about me," I murmured.

"Azazel – " said Jason.

"No," I said. "Don't." And I walked back to my room, feeling defeated, frightened, and confused. What was going on here?

* * *

Jason cornered me. "Look at me," he said.

I glared up at him. We were just a few feet from the school building. We'd been walking for the past few blocks in silence that morning. After our discussion last night, I just hadn't felt like talking to him.

"You can't just keep ignoring me," he said.

The hell I couldn't. I was good at ignoring people. Jason should know that. He'd witnessed me ignore my ex-boyfriend Toby for an entire day. Of course, Toby and I didn't live in the same house, which had kind of made it easier. Also, I wasn't nearly as in love with Toby as I was with Jason. That made it hard too.

"I'm not mad at you," he said.

I shrugged.

"Talk to me," Jason ordered.

I focused on a spot of the sky just above his head.

"That's it," he said, taking my hand and leading me away from the school.

"But—" I said, then cut myself off. I wasn't going to speak to him.

"We're skipping Chem," said Jason.

"I've already got detention," I protested.

"We'll sign in late," he said. "We were sick. You can't get in trouble for that."

We walked for blocks, neither of us speaking. But I knew where Jason and I were headed now. We were going to a

71

park that was near our apartment. It had a playground, complete with swings and a sandbox. Jason and I sat down on the swings. I stared down at my feet, swinging idly back and forth, tracing lines in the sandy soil with my toe.

"Azazel," said Jason. "What's wrong?"

I shrugged, concentrating on burrowing my toe in the sand underneath the swing.

"How long are you planning on ignoring me?" he said.

I shrugged again. I could ignore him forever. He should realize that. I was good at ignoring him.

Jason got up off the swing. He put his foot in the seat of it and clutched the chains. "You're acting like a six-year-old," he muttered, gazing past me out at the playground.

Insulting me wasn't going to get me to talk. It would just make me angrier and make me less likely to talk to him.

"Azazel," said Jason. "Come on."

I shook my head.

Jason sighed. "Fine," he said. "At least we're getting out of Chemistry." It was an Even day, so Jason and I had the same 1st period. He sat back down on the swing.

I glared at him. That was it? He was just going to give up? Didn't he want me to talk to him? How could he just stop trying to get me to talk? "Even Toby didn't give up that fast," I said to my shoes.

Jason vaulted out of the swing. "You did not just say that," he said.

Instantly, I felt guilty. I knew that Jason felt threatened by Toby. I really shouldn't have said that. "I'm sorry," I said.

"No, you're not," Jason said. He folded his arms over his chest. "Sorry I'm not Toby."

"Oh hell, Jason, you know that's not what I meant," I said.

"Do I know that? Because it sounded to me like you just compared the two of us and said he was better than me."

"I – " I broke off. "I didn't mean it."

Jason shook his head. "So why'd you say it?"

I shrugged. "I don't know," I said.

"You meant it," Jason said.

"No, I didn't," I insisted. "I'm sorry, really."

"Lilith said you weren't over him," said Jason.

"Lilith?" What did Lilith know about me and Toby, anyway? "Why are you and Lilith talking about me behind my back?"

"We're not talking about you behind your back," said Jason. "We were just talking. That's all."

"God," I said. "She's trying to sabotage me. I just knew it. I should never have trusted her again." Lilith was saying things about me to Jason that weren't true. It was making the little issues that Jason and I had into bigger ones. She was such a bitch. I hated her.

"She's not trying to sabotage you," said Jason. "She's trying to be your friend. She's worried about you."

"Oh, she would want you to think that, you know," I said, standing up to face Jason. "Otherwise, she wouldn't be able to manipulate you quite so easily."

"What?" Jason was incredulous. "I don't know what is up

with you, but every time I talk to you, you just sound more and more paranoid. Jesus, isn't there anyone who you don't think is out to get you?"

I folded my arms over my chest too. We squared off. "I'm not paranoid," I said.

"But everything's fine. Can't you see that everything's fine? Why won't you just let things be? Why do you have to keep looking for trouble?"

"And why do you have to keep pretending like there isn't any trouble to be found, when at any second, we could be just like we were a few months ago – running in fear for our lives?"

"Let it go, for Christ's sake! We're safe."

"What if we're not?"

Jason unfolded his arms. He put his hands on my shoulders and looked deeply into my eyes. "I'd never let anything hurt you. You have to know that. If I thought there was any chance that something bad could happen to you, I would fight until – "

I ripped myself away from him. "Maybe that's just it," I said. "Maybe I've been spending too long waiting for you to protect me. Maybe I need to protect myself."

"From the Sons? Azazel, most trained police officers couldn't hold themselves against the Sons."

"You killed five of them, though," I said.

"Yeah, but the Sons trained me," said Jason.

"So, you could train me."

Jason sighed heavily. "No," he said.

74

"Why not?"

"I just . . ." Jason clenched his hands into fists. "I don't want to think like that anymore. I don't want you to think like that. I want to move on. I want to put all of this behind us."

"I know that's what you want," I whispered. "But that doesn't mean that just because you want it, you'll get it."

"Well, just because you think everyone's out to get you doesn't mean they are either," said Jason. "You really need to give Lilith another chance. She's trying so hard. If you could hear the way she talks about you – "

"Which you hear since she's like your new best friend."

"You don't like me spending time with Lilith?"

"That's not what I said."

"Well, get used to it. I just got her a job as the new hostess at my restaurant," said Jason.

My mouth dropped open. "So you'll see her all the time. More than you'll see me."

"She's going to be around us, Azazel. It would just be so much easier if you could get along with her."

I was stunned. Jason was going to be spending half of his life with Lilith. And what was worse, he was taking her side instead of mine. Was Jason right? Was I paranoid?

I didn't think so. Somehow, this was all Lilith's fault.

* * *

When we got back to school, 2nd/3rd block had already started. Jason and I signed in at the office, telling the secretary that we'd been sick during the night, but felt better now. "Food poisoning," said Jason, a painful expression on his face. The secretary nodded at us sympathetically and wrote us passes to class. Jason and I parted ways. Even though we'd been arguing, I didn't want to be away from him. Jason and I lived together, but I felt like too many things kept us apart sometimes. School. Work. Detention.

If it hadn't been for that stuff, I wouldn't even have had to worry about Lilith and Jason hanging out, because I would actually be with the two of them. It wasn't that I really thought that Jason would do anything with Lilith. I trusted him. But Lilith was so . . . experienced. She was thin and curvy, with flaming red hair and big pouty lips. When she walked down the hall at Bramford, she was the kind of girl who turned boys' heads. I wasn't that kind of girl. Sure, I was sort of pretty in my own way. But I wasn't remarkable. Jason made such a point of bringing up the fact that I had more experience than him. What if he wanted to . . . even things up or something? And I was the only girl Jason had ever dated. Maybe he'd just settled for me because I was there. Maybe if he had a choice, he'd pick someone else. Someone prettier. Someone with less issues. Someone who wasn't constantly worried about being found and killed by the Sons. If Jason really wanted to be normal, maybe he wanted to date a normal girl. I had so much baggage . . .

I could hardly concentrate on the lecture in my English class. I tried to take notes, but my mind kept wandering. I didn't want to worry about Jason and Lilith. It felt tawdry and stereotypical. I felt like a stupid girl. But no matter how much I tried to put it out of my mind, I didn't seem to be able to. I pictured Lilith laughing as she sat next to Jason on the couch. The laughter racked her body, making her breasts bounce. She collapsed against his shoulder, still giggling. I saw it again and again, in slow motion. It was driving me insane.

I didn't even hear it when someone called me to the office over the loudspeaker. Ms. Call, the English teacher, had to come to my desk and touch me on the shoulder.

I started, staring up at her wildly. Had she asked a question? What were we even reading in English class?

"They just called you to the office," she said gently.

"Oh," I said.

"Are you sure you're feeling well?" she asked me. "Your admit slip said you were sick this morning."

I shrugged. "I'm fine," I said.

Ms. Call made a sympathetic face. "You're a good student, Azazel," she said. "I know you don't like to miss school, but your health is important."

I nodded. She was concerned for me. Cool. I wasn't paying attention in class, and I didn't even get in trouble. I excused myself and went to the office, convinced that I was in trouble for skipping Chemistry. But when I got there, they directed me to Mr. Dingle's office, where both Mr. Dingle and Hallam were waiting for me.

Great. What was going on, now? *Was* this about skipping Chemistry? Why was Hallam here?

"Sit down, Azazel," said Mr. Dingle, gesturing to a chair

in front of his desk.

Sullenly, I did. I stole a look at Hallam. He didn't look happy.

"We're just waiting for Jason," said Mr. Dingle.

Jason? What was this about?

Right then, Jason came into the office. I looked up at him, feeling a swell of happiness at seeing him. I smiled at him. Jason didn't look at me. Great. He was still pissed about the conversation we'd had earlier. Come to think of it, so was I. I turned away, the smile dying on my lips.

Mr. Dingle directed Jason to sit down next to me. "When I discovered your living situation," said Mr. Dingle, "I decided I wanted to have a conference with your guardian."

Great. Perfect. Hallam was probably pissed at having his schedule interrupted.

"Azazel, Mr. Wakefield tells me that your parents were killed in November and that he is legally responsible for both you and your boyfriend Jason," said Mr. Dingle.

I nodded. Did he want a prize for correctly describing my living situation? I hated Mr. Dingle. I wished I *had* stolen his bell. I tried to catch Jason's eye and roll my eyes, but he wasn't looking at me.

"So," said Mr. Dingle, "you've had a lot of upheaval in your life recently. My concern is that you're acting out in order to garner some attention. Certainly, living in a house with a young guardian must be different than living with your parents."

Hallam surprised me by saying, "Azazel's not the

problem."

What? What did he say? Hallam hated me. He'd never liked me.

Jason turned to Hallam. "What's that supposed to mean?"

Hallam folded his arms over his chest. "Honestly, Mr. Dingle," he said, "I'm surprised you've called me in about Azazel. Hasn't Jason been in at least two fights since the two of them started attending school here?"

Jason shook his head. "Hallam, this is low. If you've got an issue with me, you should talk to me about it yourself, not with the principal."

Hallam ignored him.

"Well," said Mr. Dingle, "yes, he has. But Azazel stole my bell and continues to lie about it. I know that you aren't a parent, Mr. Wakefield, but you have to see that this kind of behavior is inappropriate."

The bell was sitting on Mr. Dingle's desk.

Hallam picked it up. "Is this it?" he asked.

Mr. Dingle didn't look happy about the fact that Hallam was holding his bell. He nodded.

Hallam turned the bell over in his hands, looking at the engraving on the side. He raised his eyebrows. "Where did you get this bell?" he asked.

"I bought it at a rummage sale," said Mr. Dingle. "I liked the picture of the water. As you can see, I like to surf." He gestured to the myriad of pictures that decorated his office.

Hallam set it back down. "Interesting," he said.

"Stealing my bell was clearly an act of defiance," said Mr. Dingle. "And it has to be punished."

"So, you gave her detention, right?" asked Hallam.

"Well, yes."

"So, then what did you want to see me for?"

"I was hoping," said Mr. Dingle, "that you would support my disciplinary efforts at home."

Hallam shook his head. "Discipline?" he repeated. "We're talking about two very mature seventeen-year-olds, here. Before they became my legal charges, they were living on their own. I don't discipline them. I do my best to point them in the right direction, but that's all I can do."

"They aren't adults yet, Mr. Wakefield."

Hallam smiled tightly. "Sometimes I think they're more adult than most of the adults I interact with." He sighed. "Listen, Mr. Dingle, I'm as concerned about Jason's behavior as you are. But I don't think Azazel's as much of a problem as you think she is."

"If you're so concerned about my behavior," said Jason to Hallam, "why aren't you saying anything to me about it?"

"I'm saying things to you about it," I said. "I wish you wouldn't fight so much."

Jason didn't look happy. He pointed at Mr. Dingle. "This is none of his business," he said.

"If the two of you can't behave," said Mr. Dingle, "I'm going to have to recommend that neither of you live with Hallam anymore."

"For four months?" Jason demanded. "We'll both be

eighteen by May. Why would you do that?"

Was Dingle serious? He'd try to get us taken away from Hallam?

Jason and I both looked at Hallam, trying to see how he'd take this.

Hallam just looked frustrated. "Well," he said to us both, "it sounds to me like you've got a choice. Either stop hitting people, or get separated for months in the foster system. Shouldn't be too hard for you to figure out, should it?"

Jason and I looked at each other. I didn't want to be separated from him. I reached out to take his hand, but Jason turned away. Slowly, I retracted my hand.

CHAPTER FIVE

michaela666 (04:31:43): If it worked so well, what kind of results are you seeing? Does she seem different at all?

aird92 (04:32:01): shes alot more angry and paranoid. that count? idk, r u sure we did it right?

michaela666 (04:32:15): My instructions were correct. I only have your word that you followed them properly.

aird92 (04:32:30): i did follow them!! look i can't watch her every second of everyday so i don't know what shes doing all the time

michaela666 (04:32:50): find a way to watch her every second.

aird92 (04:33:04): doing my best here, k?

I didn't have time to talk to Hallam after our meeting with Mr. Dingle, but I wanted to thank him for sticking up for me. I also realized that I wanted to talk to Hallam about the bell and Mr. Sutherland. I wasn't sure why it hadn't occurred to me before. Maybe the fact that Jason was repeatedly shooting down my ideas had kind of worn on my confidence. But Hallam was clearly the person to talk to about this. He'd worked for the Sons in an official capacity. He knew exactly what they were capable of. He would see that what I was saying was true. Plus, he'd seen the picture on the bell. So he would know why I was so paranoid. He'd definitely looked interested in the engraving on the bell.

Hallam was going to help me out. I just knew it.

The rest of the day passed without much incident. I wasn't looking forward to detention, but I knew that I needed to just get it over with. I also wasn't looking forward to whatever menial task Mr. Sutherland was going to assign to us, either.

I spent the afternoon washing Mr. Sutherland's windows along with two other girls, both of whom smelled like cigarette smoke and swore a lot. I really didn't like detention. I tried to stay as clear of Mr. Sutherland as I could. I didn't want to talk to him now that I was convinced he worked for the Sons. But Mr. Sutherland seemed to hover around me, asking me about my schoolwork or showing me how to wash the windows without leaving streaks.

He *was* watching me. Jason could say what he wanted, but it was obvious that Mr. Sutherland was very, very interested in me. And I didn't like it. Not at all. I couldn't wait to get out of detention .Unfortunately, Jason was working, and Hallam taught a night class on Wednesdays, so I'd be alone when I got home.

I didn't have to work that night, so after detention, I walked home. I had expected Lilith to be there, so I hadn't been too worried about having an evening at home by myself. However, Lilith was apparently at work with Jason, so I had the house to myself. I didn't like that. I really, really hated being by myself.

When I'd left detention, I'd made a point of having a completely fake conversation on my phone with Jason, chatting with him about what we were going to do together when I got home. I didn't want Mr. Sutherland to think that I was going to be there by myself. If he really did work for the Sons, he'd know where I lived, and he might come in and attack me. Mr. Sutherland didn't seem to pay any attention to my conversation. I wondered if I *was* being paranoid. But it didn't matter. It was better for me to play it safe. I couldn't afford to take risks.

Once back in the apartment, I locked all the doors. I tried to work on some homework for about a half an hour, but I couldn't concentrate. Instead, I got out the book I'd borrowed from Mr. Sutherland. I paged to the picture of the rising sun emblem and read the copy underneath it.

"This picture," it read, "is believed to be associated with a society entitled The Rising Suns. Little is known about this society except that several of its members were executed as witches in the seventeenth century."

Hmm. Bust. I looked through the index, but there weren't any other mentions of The Rising Suns. The book offering no more information, I got on the internet. A google search for rising sun yielded pages on the Phoenix Suns, the Animals Song "House of the Rising Sun," and an obscure music video on youtube. Nothing. I searched through the search results a little longer and finally found a reference to the same book I was holding. Weird. If this book had referenced the secret society, then where were its sources? Had they made The Rising Suns up? Or was it just that the Sons had taken great pains to eradicate any trace of their existence?

Idly, I did a search for "bell secret society." I found out that there was a made-for-tv movie from 1970 called *The Brotherhood of the Bell*. It was about Skull and Bones. It didn't seem to have anything to do with Mr. Dingle's bell. Jason was right. It didn't really make any sense for the members of the Sons to steal this bell if it wasn't associated with them. The picture on the side of it – was it actually an old symbol for the Sons? Why had Mr. Dingle acquired it then? And why would the Sons want to let me know they were watching me? It was too confusing. The more I thought about it, the more confused I got. What was I supposed to do with this information? I'd decided that I would take care of this without Jason's help. What was I going to do?

It was starting to get dark outside. I really didn't like the dark. I walked around the apartment, checking the doors and windows, making sure they were locked and secure. I thought about my conversation with Jason earlier. I'd asked him to train me to fight the Sons. Jason had said no.

When Jason and I had first settled down in Bradenton, he'd been happy to teach me stuff. The origin of that had been back when we were on the run. In New York, I'd wanted to let Jason go out on his own, because I thought that I was in the way. He could fight better than me. I felt like I slowed him down. Jason had told me that he could teach me to take care of myself. When we'd gotten settled, Jason had started to take me shooting. He figured that if I knew how to shoot a gun, I'd feel much safer.

He was right. I liked it. We went to a shooting range in

Sarasota. We had to use fake IDs to get in since we weren't 18, but those were easily obtained, considering most kids have fake IDs for the purpose of buying alcohol. We went twice a week at the beginning. Jason taught me all kinds of things. He'd practically grown up with a gun in his hand and had been shooting since he was about five years old. I got better and better. We started to go less. Work got in the way. We had different schedules. Soon it was once a week. Then it was once every two weeks. Pretty soon we weren't going at all. When I asked Jason about it, he said that I was fine. I could shoot well. And besides, why did I really want to know how to do that? The Sons weren't after us. I was paranoid.

I kept asking about it, but we hadn't been there in a very long time. I really missed it. When I came home from the shooting range, I always felt better. More sure of myself. Less worried that the Sons of the Rising Sun were going to get me. More assured that if they did come after me, I could at least take a few of them down with me.

Wandering around my empty apartment, I realized that I wanted to go shooting again. And I didn't see why I had to wait and go with Jason. I was just going to go. By myself. Why not?

For one thing, I didn't have a car. Hallam had the car. Jason had gotten a ride to work with a co-worker. The shooting range was at least a twenty-minute drive from my apartment. I certainly couldn't walk. Dammit. I was going to have to wait for Jason after all.

Then my phone rang. It was Jude.

"What are you doing?" he asked.

"Trying to do homework," I said. "But I can't concentrate."

"Wanna hang out?" he asked. "I'll come pick you up."

I only considered for a half a second. "You wanna shoot guns?" I asked.

* * *

When Jude picked me up, (twenty minutes later, since he had to scramble to find his fake ID) there was a car in the parking lot near my apartment with the lights on. I didn't pay much attention to it, even when they pulled out behind us. When I realized the car was following us into Sarasota, I began to feel a little nervous.

Was Mr. Sutherland in the car?

It was bad for me if I was being trailed by the Sons, but it was even worse for Jude, who had nothing to do with any of the crazy stuff I was mixed up with. I already felt a little guilty for taking Jude to a target range. Jude was excited about the prospect of going shooting, but curious as to why I suggested it. When I told him I'd gone a bunch of times, he was even more curious. Why did I do that? I told him I just liked doing it. Shooting was fun. He was intrigued. He'd never known this about me. "Girl, you've got all these layers!" he exclaimed. "Are you sure you didn't steal that bell?"

I worried that letting Jude further into my life would make him too curious about me. And I didn't want Jude to get hurt. He needed to stay out of the messy business of my circumstances. I needed to protect him. Still, going to shoot guns seemed harmless enough. And Jude didn't seem to think it was too weird.

I didn't want to mention the fact that the car behind us made me nervous. It made me sound paranoid. We were going from Bradenton to Sarasota on Route Forty-One. It was a pretty standard route, and lots of cars used it. Maybe I was just being silly. Maybe nothing was wrong. Still. It was weird that the car didn't pass us. It was weird that it just hovered behind us. I watched it as Jude drove and chattered animatedly about stupid people at work. But I didn't say anything.

I was relieved when the car turned onto Fruitville Ave and didn't appear to be following us anymore. I *had* been paranoid. Nothing was wrong.

The hardest thing about shooting a gun for me was keeping my hand steady. When I first started, I wasn't very strong, and just a few minutes of holding the gun straight out would really, really hurt my arms. Think of holding a book straight out in front of you for hours at a time. Ouch. Anyway, after some time, my arms got stronger, and that helped a lot.

When Jude and I arrived,I was worried that it had been too long. That I wouldn't be able to shoot with the kind of accuracy I had before. But apparently, shooting a gun was something like riding a bike. I still knew how to do it, but in my muscles, not my head. My body remembered how it worked. My body remembered how to stand. My body remembered how to breathe. One of the mistakes I kept making in the beginning was to hold my breath while I aimed. It kept screwing me up. Jason taught me to breathe evenly and steadily, and to pull the trigger as I exhaled.

I didn't have much luck teaching Jude what to do. He was hopelessly horrid with a gun. He didn't even hit the target the whole time we were there, which meant that the both of us spent a lot of time laughing about how bad he was at shooting. Jude was also completely awed by my skill. He thought I was really good. Of course, I wasn't. If Jude had seen either Jason or Hallam handle a gun, he'd know I was a complete amateur.

But I did feel better. My aim was good. I was able to hit the target (mostly) where I wanted to. If I was on the run from the Sons, I'd have a fighting chance. I felt more confident. Less concerned for my safety. I was glad that I'd come to the range. And Jude seemed to like it too.

As we turned in the guns we'd rented, he said, "We've got to come back here and do this again sometime. This was too fun." (We rented guns because you could shoot guns owned by the range without a permit. Jason and Hallam had guns in the apartment, but they didn't have permits for them. We didn't bring those guns to the range. That would get us in a lot of trouble.) I assured Jude that we could come back whenever we wanted, feeling cheered. Maybe I couldn't go shooting with Jason, but I could get practice in with Jude. And Jude was fun to hang out with.

We burst out of the range and into the parking lot, talking loudly and laughing.

"How long have you been shooting?" Jude asked me.

"A few months," I said.

"That's all? You're like a pro."

"No, it's just not that hard. You can get that good too."

"That'd be kind of sexy, don't you think?" Jude asked. "Don't you think guys would dig it if I could shoot guns like really well?" He got his keys out of his pocket as we approached his car.

I shrugged. "I don't know. I guess."

"Does Jason think it's sexy that you shoot?"

"Um . . ."

Jude opened his car door. "He's totally threatened, isn't he? I knew it. He's such a tough guy. There's no way he could handle it if you were tougher than he was." He swung into the driver's seat.

I opened the passenger's side door and stood there thoughtfully for a second. "It's not that," I said, struggling for a way to explain what Jason thought about it without giving too much away.

Suddenly, strong arms grabbed me from behind.

I shrieked, twisting to see who had me. I couldn't see anything in the darkness.

One arm pinned my arms to my chest. Another swept my legs up so that I was being carried like a baby.

And then whoever was holding me was running.

I could hear Jude yelling my name.

I strained to look back at him. I could see him getting out of the car and running after me and my attacker.

Looking up, since I was closer, I tried to get a look at my attacker. My heart was thumping in my chest, but I felt an odd sense of calm radiating throughout my limbs. Maybe I'd been expecting this all along.

I couldn't see anything. The man had a black ski mask over his face.

For several seconds, I did nothing. I let the strange man who was cradling me run with me. I went limp.

Then it was like a switch went off in my brain. I was being captured. I wasn't going to stand for this.

I wished I still had a gun. At this range, I could have made a complete mess of the guy who had me.

But I didn't have a gun. I didn't have anything but my body. I struggled in his arms, digging my elbow into his rib cage.

He made an umphing noise, but kept running.

"Azazel!" Jude called from behind us.

I kept struggling, and with an effort that wrenched the muscles in my arm, was able to free the arm that wasn't against my attacker's body.

We thudded against the ground with the rhythm of his running feet. The jarring was making my stomach hurt.

I didn't have much time to think.

He was grabbing for my arm, attempting to pin it down.

I didn't know why I did it. Lots of other things made more sense. Going for his eyes. Clawing him with my nails.

91

But instead, I balled up my free hand into a fist and I drove my fist into the man's nose.

The man grunted. Stopped.

Blood gushed onto his ski mask, dripping onto me.

He dropped me, his hands going to his face.

Pain shot through my hip as I hit the ground hard. I winced, but rolled over as fast as I could and scrambled to my feet.

"Jude!" I yelled, running away from the man who'd grabbed me.

I could see Jude ahead of me, running towards me.

He paused, seeing me on my feet.

"Go, go!" I yelled, catching up to him.

Jude grabbed my arm and we raced towards his car. Both of the doors were still open.

As I threw myself inside the car, I looked back. The man who'd grabbed me was gone.

Jude started the car, and we screeched out of the parking lot.

* * *

Hallam paced in the kitchen of the apartment, looking anxious. "What happened, Azazel?" he asked.

Jason and Lilith were apparently still at work, even though it was late. I'd convinced Jude to go home after dropping me off, even though he'd wanted to call the police. I'd lied to him and told him that I'd be calling the police on my own. It was just me and Hallam in the house. I figured now was as good a time as any to talk to Hallam. I started at the beginning, telling him about my suspicions about the bell and about Mr. Sutherland. Then I explained what had happened at the target range that evening.

Hallam sat down at the table heavily when I finished. "It doesn't make sense," he said.

"I think it does," I said. "The Sons are after us again."

He shook his head. "No, they can't be."

I was flabbergasted. Why didn't he believe me? I'd been attacked. I'd nearly been carried off. And with all the other evidence I'd amassed, how could he say that I was wrong? Were he and Jason both incredibly blind?

"They can be," I said, "and they obviously are."

"No," he said again. "No, it's not the Sons style, Azazel. Why would they capture you? They don't care about you. They care about Jason. The only way they'd do anything to you is if you were in the way of Jason. And ski masks and parking lot assaults are not their style."

I thought about what he'd said. The Sons did have a tendency to come in shooting. Usually in mass numbers. One guy in a parking lot was a little sketchy. "Maybe he's not working with the full knowledge of the whole organization," I said. "Maybe he's just doing something covert. For Edgar Weem or something."

"No, that's not possible," said Hallam. "This has nothing to do with Edgar Weem."

"How can you be sure?" I demanded. "You and Jason both seem to think that Weem is iron-clad to this deal you made with him. But I don't think that deal made him happy.

93

And I can't see any reason why he wouldn't try to find some way around it."

"It's not Weem," said Hallam. "I'm certain of that."

"How are you certain?"

"I just am," said Hallam. "Trust me on this."

I didn't. But Hallam's tone of voice warned me not to press the point any farther.

"What else could it be?" I asked. "If it isn't the Sons, then who could have done it?"

"Someone crazy?" Hallam suggested. "People do get kidnapped, you know."

"Why would anyone kidnap me?" I asked. "I don't have money."

"Your grandmother does," said Hallam.

Oh. He was right. I shuddered. "Do you really think that's what it was?"

My grandmother was pretty rich. She lived in a multi-million dollar home. It was old money, but it had been augmented by the work my grandfather and Aunt Stephanie had done for the company my family owned. I had no idea how much my grandmother was worth, but it might be enough that someone would try to hold me for ransom because of it.

Had I been completely wrong? Had I assumed that if something bad was happening to me, the Sons had to be part of it?

But there were other things. Not just the kidnapping. "What about the bell?" I asked. "I saw you look at it today in

Dingle's office."

Hallam spread his hands. "I'll admit," he said, "that engraving does resemble an old Sons emblem. I've seen it on old documents."

"So, there could be a connection?"

"I don't know," said Hallam. "I'm inclined to think it's a coincidence."

"I didn't think you believed in coincidences," I said, remembering a conversation we'd had in November.

He sighed. "Well, it wouldn't make sense not to look into it," he said. "I'll do some digging. I'll even check out this Sutherland. But I've got to say, Azazel, his interest in secret societies seems to clear him entirely. If he were really a member of the Sons, why would he mention that to you? Why would he want to make you suspicious?"

I didn't know. If he was a member of the Sons, it seemed like he'd try to keep a low profile. He'd shown me the engraving on the bell. Why would he have done that? Still, something about Mr. Sutherland really gave me the creeps. I couldn't exactly put my finger on what, but I didn't trust him. And I felt like there was some kind of connection between the bell and Mr. Sutherland and the Sons. I just knew it.

"I'd like it if you checked into him," I said.

"I will," said Hallam. "I can't believe that he stole that bell and put it in your purse to get you into detention. He sees you every day as it is in class."

"Every other day," I said. "Maybe he just wanted to be

able to talk to me. He asked me to go to his house. Maybe he wanted to tell me something."

"Well," said Hallam, "until we know what's going on with this guy, I wouldn't recommend going to his house."

"I know that," I said.

Hallam sighed, looking at the clock. "Where's Jason?" he asked.

"At work, I guess," I said.

"You didn't call him?"

Huh. Weird. I hadn't. I'd nearly been captured, taken away by a scary man in a black ski mask, and I hadn't even thought to call Jason. Why hadn't I done that? "No," I said.

"I half-wonder if we should tell him at all," said Hallam.

"Really?" I asked. "Why?"

"He's erratic, Azazel, surely you've noticed. Especially when it comes to you. I don't want him out trying to hunt down this masked man. God knows what he'd do."

That was probably true as far as it went. Jason would be livid. He would want to protect me. "Well, he can't," I said. "Go after the guy. We don't even know who he was."

"Does he share your opinions of Mr. Sutherland?" Hallam asked.

"No," I said.

"Thank God for that. At least he won't be after Mr. Sutherland."

"I have to tell him," I said. I couldn't keep something this big from Jason. It would be like trying to keep a secret from some part of myself.

"I suppose you do," said Hallam, "but try to keep him calm."

"I will," I said.

"He's becoming increasingly violent," said Hallam. "I'm concerned."

This was weird, considering that Hallam had spent his time working for the Sons doing things like slaughtering sorority girls at their request. "*You're* concerned about his violence?" I said.

"Of course I am."

"But you . . ." How did I put this delicately? "You've done things that . . ."

Hallam raised his eyebrows. He stood up from the kitchen table. "Jason told you about that, then?"

I nodded.

Hallam shook his head. "That was a bad night," he said finally. "I don't think Jason's ever been the same." Hallam stared at the linoleum, not speaking for several moments. "But I wonder if there wasn't something . . . something within him . . . something that was always there."

"What do you mean?" I asked.

"What he did that night," said Hallam. "It was – "

And the door burst open. Jason and Lilith tumbled inside, drunk and laughing.

I wanted to ask Hallam what he meant by what *Jason* did that night. Jason had told me that Hallam had shot the girls. He'd said that Hallam had screamed while he did it, blood spattering his face. Jason had said that he hadn't done anything but watch.

I turned toward Jason, my brow furrowing. Hadn't he told me everything? I'd always trusted Jason, but lately things seemed different. We were at odds. He didn't believe me. And here he was stumbling into the house, late on a school night, clearly drunk. This wasn't the Jason that I knew.

Jason stopped laughing, but Lilith was still giggling.

"Who died?" Jason asked us.

"Where have you been?" Hallam asked.

Jason rolled his eyes, striding into the kitchen. He flung himself into a chair at the table. "Geez, Hallam, you sound like you think you're my mother."

Had I ever seen Jason drunk before? I tried to think. Sure, Jason drank at parties, but he usually didn't have more than a few drinks.

Lilith followed Jason into the kitchen and sat down with us. She was still grinning. "We went out for a couple of drinks with some of the people from work," she explained.

Really?

"Oh?" said Hallam, folding his arms over his chest.

"It was my idea," said Lilith. "I didn't know if Jason would go for it or not, but when I asked he said, 'Sure.' I think Jason needs to get out more. Don't you, Zaza?"

I glared at her. I couldn't believe her. I did think Jason should get out more. I'd said as much to him on numerous occasions. But when I asked him to come out with me, he always said no. Apparently, when Lilith asked, it was a completely different story. "Did you have fun, Jason?" I asked him.

He grinned at me. "I had a blast. Lilith was telling me this hilarious story about you freshman year. She said that you got lost your first day and you went into the wrong classroom . . ." He started laughing again and so did Lilith.

"That's great," I said. "Because while you guys were off having a blast, some guy picked me up and tried to carry me off."

Jason stopped laughing. "What?" he said, his eyes darting between Hallam and me.

"She's right," said Hallam.

We filled Jason in on the details of the evening.

"I can't believe you went to the shooting range without me," Jason said angrily.

I snorted. "I can't believe you went out drinking with Lilith without me."

"That's ridiculous," said Jason. "I wasn't in any danger."

"That's not the point," I said.

"It absolutely is," said Jason. "You went off to Sarasota with *Jude*, and you nearly got hurt."

"I'm fine," I said. "I took care of myself."

"Because I wasn't there," said Jason. "You're blaming me for not being there, but you snuck off without me. You could have asked me to go with you."

"I did the other day at lunch," I said. "You didn't want to go."

"But if you just had to go," he said, "you could have

called me."

"You were working!" I protested. "Besides, you didn't call me and ask if I wanted to come with you tonight."

"It was just people from work," he said. "I didn't think — This is not my fault."

"I'm not saying it is," I said.

"Yes, you are," he said. "If I'd been there, this wouldn't have happened."

I couldn't believe him. "Jason, are you listening? I hit the guy. He dropped me. I'm fine. Nothing happened. I didn't need you."

Jason jerked back, as if I'd slapped him. He didn't say anything for several moments. "I wish you would have called," he said finally.

"Well, so do I," I said.

"Listen," said Hallam, "it's over. There's no point in worrying about whether the incident would have been preventable or not. It happened. We just need to figure out who did it and why. So, I'm going to do some digging tomorrow. We'll get to the bottom of this."

"It's my fault, anyway," said Lilith. "I really shouldn't have encouraged Jason to come out tonight."

"It's no one's fault," said Hallam. "Let's go to bed."

But I kind of half-agreed with Lilith. Why had she asked Jason to hang out? What was more, why had he said yes? The two were awfully chummy these days. I didn't like it.

Hallam left the kitchen, leaving me with Jason and Lilith.

"I'm so sorry," said Lilith. "I'm sorry that happened to

you."

"I'm fine," I said. I didn't need her pity.

"You must have been so scared," she said.

I shrugged. I'd been terrified. Hadn't I? With all the worrying I did about the Sons swooping in and terrorizing me, I expected myself to be more jumpy about the entire incident. But I felt calm. I'd felt calm almost the entire time. It surprised me. Apparently I was tougher than I thought I was. "Not as scared as I thought I'd be, actually," I said.

Jason was shaking his head. "Well, I don't think you should be alone anymore."

"I wasn't alone tonight," I said. "I was before, in the apartment, but after that I had Jude with me."

"I don't think Jude counts for much," said Jason.

"Well, what do you want, Jason? You can't be around me all the time. We both work a lot. And we don't have the same schedule at school. Who else do you think is capable of guarding me?" I couldn't help but be a little sarcastic. Jason couldn't be mad at me about this. I wasn't the one being reckless tonight. I'd gone to the range because I wanted to improve my abilities to take care of myself. It had been a preventative measure. Jason was the one who'd been out having fun. He'd been irresponsible. It was ridiculous for him to be angry with me.

Jason heaved a huge sigh. "You're pissed at me," he said.

I rolled my eyes.

Lilith bit her lip. "Maybe I should leave you two alone," she said.

I stood up. "Thanks, Lilith, but I think I'll leave. It's late, and I'm tired. I was nearly kidnapped tonight. It took a lot out of me."

I stalked back through the apartment to my bedroom and began throwing off my clothes, letting them fall in a messy pile on the floor. I yanked open my dresser drawer, took out my pajamas and began forcing on pajama pants.

There was a knock on my door.

I jerked my pajama shirt over my head and flung open the door.

It was Jason.

"What?" I demanded.

"Can I come in?" he asked.

I moved out of the doorway wordlessly.

He walked past me.

"Well?" I said, folding my arms over my chest.

"Why are you mad?" he asked. "If it's not because I wasn't there, why are you mad?"

"I'm not mad," I said.

"Right," he muttered. He crossed to me, put his hand on my cheek.

I ducked away from him.

"I just feel like I can't do anything right anymore," said Jason.

I rolled my eyes. "I'm tired, Jason," I said. "I had a rough evening. I just need to rest."

"Because," he said, "if anyone should be mad, it should be me. I mean, you didn't say anything to me about going to the range by yourself, and then all of the sudden you're there. With Jude." He said Jude's name like Jude was a leper or a mass murderer.

I couldn't believe it. I glared at him. "Listen, Jason, there is no reason for you to be jealous of Jude. He's gay for God's sake, and I'm in love with *you*."

"I'm not *jealous* of him!" Jason said. "It's just that he doesn't look out for you. Look what happened at that party over the weekend. He can't keep you safe."

"No one can keep me safe," I said. "That's ridiculous. Jude's my friend. If anything, being around me makes it less safe for him, not the other way around."

"You spend an awful lot of time with him," Jason said.

"Because he's my best friend," I said.

"When I knew you in Bramford, you didn't spend nearly as much time with Lilith as you do with Jude now, and Lilith was your best friend."

"Sure I did," I said. "I hung out with Lilith all the time. And we talked on the phone like crazy!"

"No," he said. "You didn't. You spent a lot of time with Toby, but not with Lilith."

"Who's telling you this?" I asked. "Lilith?"

"It's my own observation," he said. "Which she happens to agree with."

"Why are you two constantly talking about me behind my back?" I demanded.

"We're just talking."

"You know who it seems like you're spending a lot of

time with?" I said. "Lilith. You and Lilith are really pretty friendly lately."

"What's that supposed to mean?" Jason asked.

"Well, it's not like she wasn't sleeping with my last boyfriend," I said. "How am I supposed to trust her?"

Jason's face twisted in disbelief. "What?" He took a step back. Ran his hand through his hair. "You're supposed to trust *me*," he said.

"I do," I said.

"So then why would you even say that?" Jason asked.

I was fuming inside. I clenched and unclenched my fingers. I looked away from Jason, at my bedroom wall. "She's not like me," I said. "She's all curvy and sexy and experienced. And you're always around her. And you're always taking her side, not mine. And I just think that she can be very manipulative."

"I can't believe you would think that about me," said Jason. "Look at me," he said.

I didn't.

Jason advanced on me. He snatched my chin between his thumb and forefinger and forced me to look at his face. His eyes were just a few inches from my own. They blazed at me, smoldering. I could feel his breath on my cheeks. "If you think that I would ever – that I *could* ever – do any-thing like that to you, or that I would ever want anyone but you, then you don't have any idea who I am."

He dropped my chin. Gave me one last fiery look, his eyes burning into mine. Then he left my bedroom.

I stood there for a second, too stunned to process what had just happened. Then I closed the door. Leaned against it, the back of my head thudding against its hardness. And I started to cry.

CHAPTER SIX

To: Edgar Weem <eweem@risingsun.org>

From: Renegade Son <settingsun007@yahoo.com>

Subject: Questions

Edgar,

Someone tried to snatch Azazel last night. That doesn't have anything to do with the Sons or you, does it? And you don't have any ties to a Liam Sutherland, do you? I'm willing to cooperate with you, but you need to be straight with me.

Hallam

Even though it was late, I couldn't sleep. I sat in my room with the door shut, picking at my bedspread. I felt so alone. I toyed with my phone, searching through the contact numbers. There weren't many names there. Jude. Jason. Hallam. Some people from work. I didn't know many of them well. I certainly couldn't call anyone for comfort. As I scrolled through them, I settled on my younger brother Chance's name. Chance lived in New Jersey with Grandma Hoyt. I hadn't talked to him since Christmas, when he'd come to visit us in Florida. I knew that I couldn't tell Chance what was happening to me here. I didn't want to worry him or endanger him. But suddenly, a longing welled up inside me to talk to someone who I'd grown up with. Someone who I'd known before all this mess had started. My brother.

I hit send on my phone, holding it to my ear as it rang. It

was late. He was probably asleep.

But Chance answered. "Zaza!" he greeted cheerily.

Geez. For the first time in months, the nickname didn't make my stomach turn over. "Hey Chance," I said, grinning from ear to ear. "Sorry I'm calling so late."

"It's no big deal," he said. "I'm up."

"So how are you, little brother?"

"Excellent," he said. "I'm going to Italy."

"What?" I said.

"Yeah," he affirmed. "I'm going to a boarding school in Italy for really rich American kids. It's going to be a blast."

"Whoa," I said. "When were you going to tell me this?"

"I was going to call you," he said. "Soon. I totally was. I have tons of crap to tell you. And Jason. Hey, is Jason there? I wanted to ask him if he got the new game for X-box."

"Um ," I said, "Jason and I are kind of fighting."

"Oh," said Chance. "So that's why you're calling me."

"Sort of," I admitted, fighting tears.

"Hey," said Chance, his voice full of concern, "it'll be okay. You two are awesome together. He really cares about you."

"Yeah," I said, trying to pull myself together. "So why are you going to Italy?"

"Well," said Chance, "I asked Grandma about it months ago, because my friend Palomino got shipped off at the beginning of the semester."

"Oh, right, your *friend*, Palomino," I said knowingly.

"She's not my girlfriend!" Chance said. "Anyway, she's

been in Italy for months. I barely get to talk to her except online."

"Sure, Chance. Whatever you say."

"She's not!" he said. "Anyway, Grandma said no. She said she wanted me close. But then, right after Noah and Gordon left a few weeks ago – "

"Wait," I said. "Noah and Gordon were there?" Noah and Gordon were my adopted brothers. No one had heard from them since November. They hadn't even come to my parents' funeral service.

"Oh, I forgot to call and tell you that," said Chance. "Sorry."

"Where have they been?" I said.

"I don't know," said Chance. "They didn't stay long. They just came by one day. They talked to Grandma Hoyt for hours in her office. Then we all went out to dinner. The next morning they were gone. And right after that, Grandma Hoyt said that it would probably be best if I went to Italy."

"So you'll get to go to school with Palomina, then," I said. "That's cool."

"I know, right?" I could tell he was smiling on the other end.

"That's weird about Noah and Gordon, though," I said. "I haven't heard from them at all."

"Really?" said Chance. "Because they told me they were planning to visit you."

* * *

I called Jude when I woke up and asked him if he could

give me a ride to school. The thought of facing Jason and walking to school with him was simply too much. I'd cried myself to sleep the night before. I felt guilty for practically accusing Jason of sleeping with Lilith. And I couldn't shake the look in his eyes when he'd left my room. He was right. There was no way that he could possibly be unfaithful to me. It wasn't like Jason. I was probably temporarily insane. But it didn't help that Lilith was always around.

I got ready as quickly as I could. Jason and I crossed each other when he was getting ready to take his shower, and I was leaving the bathroom. I looked down at the floor and not at his face. He didn't say anything to me. I didn't say anything to him either.

When Jude knocked on the door, I gathered my book bag and purse and went to meet him. Jude grinned at me as I slid out of the apartment.

"How come you're not walking to school with Jason?" he asked.

I sighed. "He came home late last night. Drunk. He was out with Lilith."

"Oh," said Jude, looking sympathetic. "I'm sorry."

I shrugged.

We started for his car. "So," Jude asked as we walked, "did you call the police?"

Right. Jude had been with me when I'd been attacked. Dammit. Being around him was probably a bad idea. "Hallam thinks that someone might have tried to kidnap me to collect ransom from my grandmother," I told Jude.

"No way," said Jude. "The rich one in New Jersey?"

As if I had another grandmother. My dad's parents had both died before I was born. I nodded. "Hallam's going to contact her and see if she wants to involve the police." This wasn't true at all. As far as I knew, no one was going to contact my grandmother.

I didn't really think that the person who'd snatched me was trying to get money from my grandmother. I didn't know what I thought anymore. I wasn't completely convinced that it was the Sons, exactly. But they seemed like the best option. Still, I did need to be careful. I scanned our parking lot quickly, looking for any suspicious figures or cars.

Not seeing anything, I got into Jude's car. We backed out of the parking lot and pulled onto the road.

"You aren't worried about it, then?" asked Jude.

I sighed. "I guess I should be," I said. "But all I can think about is Jason and Lilith."

Jude laughed. "Yeah, I guess that makes sense. I mean, being carried off like that was probably pretty traumatic. You'd want to focus on something else."

"Maybe that's it," I said. But it was odd. I hadn't found the experience traumatic at all. Maybe it was because so many other much more horrible things had happened to me. Or maybe it was because I'd been able to get out of the situation all by myself.

"It was cool how you just punched that guy in the face, and he dropped you," said Jude. "I didn't know you could punch so hard."

"Neither did I," I said.

"Really? So you think it was like adrenaline or something? Like when people lift cars?"

That was an interesting theory. "Maybe?" I said.

"How did you feel?" Jude asked.

"I don't know. Um, calm," I said. "Weirdly enough, I felt really calm."

"That's awesome. It's probably why you were able to deal so well with the situation."

"Yeah, but it's strange, isn't it?"

Jude shrugged. "Maybe you're just growing as a person," he said. "You're stronger now. You and Jason are arguing a lot. Maybe you're growing out of him."

"No way!" I said. "I'm never going to grow out of Jason! He's everything to me."

"And if he were sleeping with Lilith?"

"He isn't."

"Maybe not yet. But what if he does?"

I shook my head. "It won't happen."

"What if Jason had done something horrible?" Jude asked. "What if . . . I don't know, he killed someone or something?"

Ha. Jude didn't know it, but I'd already witnessed Jason kill five members of the Sons, saving my life. "That wouldn't make any difference," I said. "None of it would."

"So even if he cheated on you, you'd forgive him?"

I considered. When I'd found out Toby had been cheating

on me, all of my feelings for him had shriveled up. I'd felt nothing for him except disgust. There hadn't been any way I could have forgiven Toby. But if I found out that Jason had slept with Lilith, would he disgust me? No, I realized, he wouldn't. He'd still be Jason. It would hurt. I'd be devastated. But there would be nothing more devastating than losing Jason completely. "I think I would," I said.

"Wow," said Jude. "You really like him."

"I love him," I said. "More than anything else on earth."

Jude pulled the car into the parking lot at school and parked. We both got out and began walking toward the building. "So why do you think you two are having problems lately?" he asked me.

"I don't know," I said. Why were Jason and I arguing so much? We never argued much in the past. How had it started? I thought back to the beginning of the week. Lilith. The bell. Jude. At some point, Jason and I had stopped trusting each other. Jason didn't believe me when I said we were in danger. Jason didn't take my side when I didn't want to let Lilith stay with us. Jason didn't like Jude. It seemed like everything was spiraling out of my control. I didn't know how to make anything better. "If he'd just listen to me," I said. "If he'd just believe me, maybe . . ."

"He doesn't listen to you?"

"He was mad at me because I didn't call him last night when I went to the shooting range."

"But he was at work."

"I know," I said. "And he said that I was angry with him

because he wasn't there to protect me. But I wasn't. I took care of myself just fine, without him. I didn't need his help. But he wouldn't listen."

"He gets angry a lot," said Jude.

Did he?

"He's always beating people up. I don't want you to take this the wrong way, Azazel, because I know you really care about him, but are you sure he's, well, good for you?"

I glared at Jude as we entered the school building. "Of course I am."

He shrugged. "It's just that he seems kind of scary sometimes." He paused. "You wanna go to my locker or your locker first?"

"Yours," I said. "And he's not scary. Not to me."

Jude's locker was on the first floor. I watched as he dropped off his book bag and grabbed his History book. "Never?" asked Jude. "He's never scared you?"

"No," I said, even though that wasn't strictly true. There was one time, back in November, in a hotel room . . . But Jason had been really upset then. And he'd stopped when I asked him to.

We were climbing the stairs to my locker, which was on the second floor.

"Maybe I'm out of line," said Jude.

"Jason is all I have," I said to Jude as we stopped in front of my locker. I opened it. Stared inside at my books.

"That's not a good reason to date someone," said Jude.

I chewed on my lip. Opened my book bag. Exchanged a

few books. "That's not why I'm dating him."

"Okay," said Jude. "I'm sorry. I won't say anything else. I just worry about you sometimes. Jason isn't like other guys, you know. He's . . . intense."

Yeah. Jason was intense. And after I'd met him, my life had gotten really dangerous, really fast. But that wasn't Jason's fault.

We started down the hall to 1st block. It was an Odd day, so Jude and I were heading to Mr. Sutherland's class. My heart sank. I really didn't want to see him again. And I wasn't looking forward to having two more days of detention with him either. Even if Mr. Sutherland wasn't a member of the Sons—and I wasn't convinced that he wasn't—he was kind of creepy. I could live a happy, fulfilled life never seeing him again, ever.

But when we arrived at Mr. Sutherland's classroom, he wasn't there. Instead, there was a different woman, who'd written her name on the board: Mrs. Clearing. She introduced herself as Mr. Sutherland's substitute.

* * *

I knew exactly why Mr. Sutherland wasn't at school today. He'd been the man who'd grabbed me in the parking lot last night. He wasn't at school, because I'd punched him in the nose. He probably had two black eyes. He knew that if he showed up today, I'd know it was him. I'd been right! Mr. Sutherland was mixed up in this somehow, and something weird was definitely going on.

I wanted to tell Jason about it at lunch, but I wasn't sure if we were speaking yet. Of course, maybe he wouldn't believe me, anyway. I didn't know what else to do, so I bought my yogurt out of the machine and sat down at our usual table. I waited, eating my yogurt, to see if Jason would show up.

It seemed like a very long time passed. No Jason.

Geez. He was really angry with me, wasn't he? So angry he wouldn't even sit with me at lunch? Of course, I hadn't walked to school with him this morning. Maybe I deserved the cold shoulder.

I finished eating my yogurt and stared into the empty container, running my spoon around the edges, trying to scoop up the last bits of yogurt.

"Did you ride to school with Jude?"

My head snapped up. Jason was standing over me, carrying his tray. He had a large helping of spaghetti with meat sauce and a salad covered in ranch dressing.

"Hi," I said.

"Did you?" he asked.

"Yeah," I said.

He nodded.

"Do you want to sit down?" I asked.

Jason hesitated. He looked around the cafeteria as if he were trying to find some other place to sit. Then he sat down.

We were quiet for several minutes, neither of us saying a word. I fiddled with my empty yogurt container some more, feeling very uncomfortable. I wondered if I should just leave. Maybe Jason wanted to be alone.

"I heard detention was cancelled since Mr. Sutherland isn't here," said Jason.

"Yeah," I said. I wanted to tell Jason why I thought Mr. Sutherland wasn't here, but I didn't. He wouldn't believe me anyway. What was the point?

"This morning, Hallam told me that he was going to be out late looking into some stuff," said Jason. "I've got to work tonight. So does Lilith."

So? "Okay," I said.

"I told him it wasn't a big deal, because you had detention, so I figured you'd only be home by yourself for an hour or so. But now . . ."

Oh. Jason was worried about my safety. At least that was something. I guessed. "I'll be fine," I said. "I know where the guns are. I know where the bullets are. I'll lock the doors."

"I might be able to get someone to cover my shift tonight, if you want," said Jason.

Jason wanted to stay home with me? "Well, would that be hard for you to do?" I asked.

Jason shrugged. "It might be. It's short notice. I don't know if I could convince anyone to work for me."

"Never mind, then," I said. "I'll be fine."

"You're sure?"

"Yeah," I said.

Jason nodded. "Just be careful, okay?"

I nodded.

We were quiet again. I picked up my purse and rummaged through its contents. I felt awkward sitting next to Jason and not talking to him. There were a bunch of old receipts in my purse. A few tampons. A slip of paper . . . What was this?

Huh. It was Mr. Sutherland's address. I still had that, did I?

Finally, the bell rang. Both Jason and I got up. I started away from him, heading to my 6th/7th block. Jason caught me by the elbow. I turned to look at him.

"Hey," he said, "I just wanted to let you know that I thought you did a good job taking care of that last night."

This was different than the Jason who always wanted to protect me. He was actually acknowledging that I could handle myself.

"Thanks," I said.

"Just make sure you do the same thing tonight if something happens, okay?" Jason asked.

"I will," I said.

"You better. I don't want anything to happen to you."

* * *

I knew that it was a stupid idea to go to Mr. Sutherland's house. I was convinced he was the man who'd attacked me in the parking lot, and that meant he was dangerous. I'd promised Jason I was going to be careful. If I went there, I'd probably be in a lot of danger, and there would be a strong chance that I'd end up getting hurt. I knew that I really shouldn't go.

But after I found Mr. Sutherland's address, I just couldn't let the idea go. Jason walked me home after school. We didn't say much. Things were still awkward between us. I wanted to say something. To apologize maybe. But just as I was screwing up my nerve to say it, we got back to the apartment. Lilith was there. She was on our computer, and she smiled when we came inside. "Hey!" she said.

I didn't say hi to her. She'd put me instantly in a bad mood. How long was Lilith going to stay here, anyway? I didn't think I could handle it for much longer. We needed to find someplace else for Lilith to go. She'd only been here for four days, and already she'd managed to practically destroy my relationship with Jason.

"Zaza, I thought you had detention," she said.

"Can you not call me that?" I asked.

She made an apologetic face. "It's just habit. I'm sorry."

"Mr. Sutherland wasn't there, so detention was cancelled," I said.

"Cool," said Lilith.

Jason was walking through the living room towards his bedroom.

"Jason, where are you going?" Lilith asked. "We've got to be at work in fifteen minutes."

"I'm going to change," he said. "I'll be back in second."

Jason disappeared into his room. I was left with Lilith. We gazed at each other for a few seconds.

"Well," I said, "I'm gonna go to my room too."

"Wait," said Lilith. "I, um, I couldn't help overhearing you and Jason last night."

Really? Dammit.

"I mean," she continued, "not everything. It was muffled. But I was sure I heard my name. Were you two arguing about me?"

I shrugged.

"You want me to leave, don't you?" asked Lilith.

"I . . ." I did want her to leave. But how could I say that? "No, Lilith. You can stay as long as you need to." God. How had she gotten me to say that? She really was manipulative, wasn't she?

"Really?" Lilith looked so relieved. She threw her arms around me. "Oh, thank you so much. I really need this. Thank you."

I didn't hug her back. "It's fine," I said. "It's really fine."

After Lilith and Jason left, I went and found the gun, just like I'd told Jason I would. I loaded it with bullets. Then I stalked around my house, locking the doors and windows, telling myself it was very, very stupid idea to go to Mr. Sutherland's house.

If I did go, I told myself, I'd bring the gun. I'd fight him off if he tried anything. After all, I'd fought him off the night before. Who was to say that I couldn't do it again, if I needed to? I could do it. I knew how to use the gun. I wanted to confront Mr. Sutherland, anyway. I wanted to know who he was and what he wanted. He'd given me his address because he obviously wanted me to come to his house. He'd tried to drag me off last night. He wanted to see me. Alone. How was I going to find out what he wanted if I didn't do what he asked?

119

And if I was wrong, then I'd know it immediately. If I got to Mr. Sutherland's house, and he didn't have a swollen, purple nose, then I'd know it wasn't him last night. I'd know if my paranoia was getting away with me, the way Jason and Hallam claimed it did.

But if his face was mangled, then I'd have proof. Mr. Sutherland had attacked me in the parking lot last night. And I could use that proof to intimidate him. I could wave the gun in his face. Force him to talk. Force him to tell me who he was working for and what he wanted with me. I imagined Mr. Sutherland cowering in a darkened corner in his apartment, begging me to spare his life. Telling me everything I wanted to know.

I knew I shouldn't go, but the advantages to going seemed to outweigh the risk. If I could get enough information from Mr. Sutherland, then maybe we could stop anything bad from happening. Then maybe Jason and I could stay here. I could relax. He could too. We could be together again, without all the things that had come between us lately. I knew, even though it was a bad idea to go to Mr. Sutherland's house, that I was going to go anyway. I couldn't help it. I had to.

I brought bullets with me. I brought the gun, tucked into the inside pocket of my jacket. I brought my purse, which contained the slip of paper that had Mr. Sutherland's address on it. I locked the door to the apartment behind me, and I set out to walk to see Mr. Sutherland.

His house wasn't too far from mine or from the school.

Actually, he lived in an apartment as well. It took me about twenty minutes all told, because I made a wrong turn and had to double back. But finally, I was standing at Mr. Sutherland's door. I double-checked the address one last time, and then I knocked on his door.

There was no response.

My heart was thumping, and I was squelching the desire to put my hand inside my jacket and feel the gun. Maybe he wasn't home. Maybe I was crazy. Maybe Mr. Sutherland hadn't been at school today because he'd gone on a trip. Maybe he had nothing to do with anything.

I knocked again.

I was ready to walk away when the door opened.

CHAPTER SEVEN

To: Renegade Son <settingsun007@yahoo.com>

From: Edgar Weem <eweem@risingsun.org>

Subject: Sutherland

Attachment: sutherlanddossier.doc

Liam Sutherland?! This isn't good, Hallam. Not at all. Sutherland is a very dangerous man who's managed to find out far more about our organization than is good for him. We've been on the hunt for him since before Jason's birth. Since we hadn't heard anything in years, I'd almost hoped he was dead. Pass on any information that you can to me about his whereabouts. The organization would be very grateful.

I've attached a document containing all our intel on Sutherland.

Finally, of course we're not after Azazel. Let me know if you need to use any of our resources to track down her attacker, however. Honestly, my money's on Sutherland.

Edgar

Mr. Sutherland stood in the doorway, his nose swollen and red. There was a huge greenish-blue bruise spreading from the bridge of his nose over his cheekbones. I gasped. I'd been right.

"Azazel," said Mr. Sutherland. "What are you doing here?"

"What happened to your face?" I said.

He smiled. "Would you like to come inside?" He stepped aside from the doorway. I walked past him. He shut the door behind me.

"I assume you're after some books?" he said.

I turned on him, my hand going inside my jacket, brushing the cold metal of my gun. "Let's not play games, Mr. Sutherland," I said. "I've got a gun."

He raised his eyebrows, then winced at the movement. "All right," he said. "You've got quite a right hook, I must admit. I wasn't expecting that."

So, he was going to admit it, then? Good. That would make things considerably easier.

"I wasn't expecting to be jumped in a parking lot," I said.

He chuckled. He took a step toward me.

I whipped out the gun, flipping the off the safety as I did. "No quick moves, okay?" I said.

Mr. Sutherland put his hands in the air. "That's really not necessary, Azazel. I don't intend to hurt you."

"Right," I said. "That's why you attacked me and tried to carry me off last night."

"I just wanted to talk," he said. "I asked you to come over here, but you didn't seem interested in that idea. In fact, you seemed frightened of me. I didn't know how else I'd get the chance to speak to you alone."

"I'm here now," I said. "Talk away."

"Might we talk without a gun in my face?" he asked.

"No," I said. "I don't trust you."

He shrugged. "Fair enough. But it would make me a lot more comfortable."

"You can say whatever you have to say with the gun out," I said. "It makes me more comfortable."

"Really?" he said.

My arms were starting to tremble a little bit. The gun seemed to be getting heavier with every second I held and aimed it. I ignored the trembling. "You work for the Sons, don't you?"

Mr. Sutherland laughed. "The Sons? Heavens, no. I don't work for anyone, Azazel."

"Why should I believe you?"

"If I worked for the Sons, would I talk to you about secret societies? That would blow my cover, wouldn't it?"

Funny. That was what Hallam had said. "Maybe," I said. "Maybe not."

"If I worked for the Sons, I would never have spoken to you. I would have watched. Undetectable. You'd never have even known I existed. That's the way the Sons work. You don't see them until they're about to kill you. No one sees them. No one alive anyway."

"You know about the Sons, though," I said. "And you know about me? About Jason?"

He nodded.

"So what do you want then?" I didn't know if I believed him, anyway. But I could play along.

"I told you. To talk. I have information you might find interesting. Helpful."

So we were back here again, were we? "And I told you to go ahead and talk."

"Not until you put away the gun."

Dammit. What was I going to do? I could just leave, I guess. If Mr. Sutherland didn't want to talk, I could just leave. I could put the gun to his temple. Demand that he tell me, or I would blow his brains out. I shuddered at the thought. I didn't think I could really blow Mr. Sutherland's brains out. Not at close range. I'd shot a lot at targets, but I'd never actually shot a person. I swallowed.

What if he were telling the truth? What if he didn't work for the Sons? What if he really did just want to give me information?

Slowly, I lowered the gun. "I'm not putting it away," I said. "But I won't aim it at you. And the safety stays off."

Mr. Sutherland sighed. "Very well," he said. He gestured behind me to a leather couch. "Would you like to sit?" he asked.

I guessed sitting was okay. I was beginning to feel like I was doing a very bad job at this. I should have brought Jason or Hallam along. But since neither of them believed me . . . I crossed to the couch and sat down. Mr. Sutherland did as well.

"So," I said, "if you're not working for the Sons, then why are you here?"

Mr. Sutherland tilted his head, as if he were thinking about how to put what he was about to say. "You could say that I find the Sons intriguing," he said. "I am a Watcher, if you will."

I arched an eyebrow. "What? Like *Buffy the Vampire Slayer*?" When I was a kid, I used to watch reruns of that show in the afternoons.

Mr. Sutherland looked confused. "What?"

"Nothing," I said. "What do you mean, you're a Watcher?"

"I study secret societies. Chart their movements. Try to get close to them. Try to figure out what it is they're doing."

"So you study the Sons?"

"The Sons are the most secret and the most powerful secret society in operation. No one knows about them. Unlike the Knights Templar or the Illuminati, their name does not appear on websites all over the world or in popular fiction."

"Wait," I said, "the Illuminati are real?"

Mr. Sutherland laughed. "Not anymore," he said. "Not really. No, the only secret society with any active power these days is the Sons. And they jealously guard their identity and cover up their actions quite well. Finding out information about them is difficult at best."

"And why do you do it?" I asked. "For kicks?"

Mr. Sutherland chuckled. He seemed to be finding me quite amusing. That was not really my intention. I'd wanted to threaten him. Scare him. "The Sons have their enemies," he said. "The information I provide is valuable, to certain people. Certain rich people. I sell what I find."

"I thought you said you didn't work for anyone."

"I don't. I'm a gun for hire, if you will, although I don't actually shoot anything. I work for the highest bidder."

"And who are you are working for now?"

"I'm hoping to work for you," he said.

What? "I don't have any money," I said.

He smiled. "I know that."

"And I can't get money from my grandmother, so don't even think that – "

"I don't want money."

"What do you want?"

"As I've already said, information is very valuable to me. I thought perhaps we could trade."

"Trade?" I said. "What do you mean?"

"I have things I want to know about the Sons. I think you know them."

"I don't know anything about the Sons," I said. "And I don't have any idea what you could know that I'd want to know."

Mr. Sutherland smiled. "Someone very close to you," he said, "has completed an invocation. Does that mean anything to you?"

I was stunned. The invocation of Azazel? My parents and the rest of the Satanists had attempted to imbue me with the spirit of the ancient Jewish demon I was named after. It was supposed to give me the power to kill Jason. However, the invocation had never been completed, because it was supposed to end with my losing my virginity to a member of the coven. I'd lost my virginity to Jason. Even though

Michaela Weem had said that I had the spirit of Azazel within me, I knew that the other members of the coven had believed that the ritual needed to be finished. "Who is it?" I said.

"Not so fast," said Mr. Sutherland. "You need to agree that we'll trade. I give you a name, and I'll also throw something else in. Something that has come up over and over again in certain messages I've intercepted from various members of the Sons, something that I believe has something to do with Jason. In return, you answer some questions for me."

I considered. What was the harm? Mr. Sutherland might be lying and his information might prove to be completely false. He might not be who he said he was. Also, he might use the information I gave him to sell to someone who would use it for nefarious purposes. On the other hand, he said he sold information to enemies of the Sons. How did that saying go, "The enemy of my enemy is my friend"? Could it really hurt anything?

It didn't matter anyway. I was too curious. Who could be trying to complete the invocation? Who was close to me? I had to know. "Okay," I said.

He smiled. "Good." He stood up and walked to one of his bookshelves, where he removed a small stack of paper. "Just to show you my good faith, I'll go first. These are the intercepted messages from the Sons. Look through them. They're yours."

He handed me the stack of papers.

It was four different email messages, each from names I didn't recognize. Mr. Sutherland had highlighted various passages. Because I was scanning through them quickly, I just read the highlighted portions.

They read as follows:

"The Rising Sun is ultimately considered a benevolent force of unification, but there is extensive association to Shiva in some of the later prophecies. Why is the Rising Sun associated with Shiva the destroyer?"

"Have not received any commentary from Weem on the Shiva aspect of the prophecies. Odd, because he usually communicates quickly with me about these issues. When I spoke to him about it over the phone, he seemed defensive."

"Could it be that the solitary nature of our order will protect the Rising Sun from the destructive tendencies of Shiva? Shiva uses the power of his Shakti, the goddess Kali, to accomplish his destruction. If the Rising Sun is celibate, perhaps this power is neutralized?"

"Also noticing the dual nature of certain gods associated with the Rising Sun: Balder has Hoder, Jesus has Lucifer, Apollo has Artemis, and on and on it goes. Does our Rising Sun have a twin or a dark force?"

I looked up at Mr. Sutherland. "What does this have to do with me? And who's Shiva?"

"Shiva is a Hindu god who is the destructive aspect of their greatest god. Shiva's consort is Kali, the goddess of destruction. The two are inextricably bound," he said. "As for what it has to do with you, that actually leads directly into my first question. Can you confirm that the Sons do believe Jason is the Rising Sun?"

He didn't know that? "Yes," I said. "They do."

Mr. Sutherland grinned. "I thought so! I was ninety percent sure."

"I still don't see what it has to do with me," I said.

"They think you're Kali," said Mr. Sutherland. "They think your presence will cause Jason to be destructive."

I furrowed my brow. "What?"

"I conjecture, at any rate," said Mr. Sutherland. "I can't prove that."

I shook my head. That didn't sound good at all. Maybe I was in more danger than I'd thought from the Sons.

"But that doesn't make sense," said Mr. Sutherland.

"What doesn't?" I asked.

"Why aren't they chasing Jason anymore? Why is he allowed to live here in Florida, away from the Sons, with you?"

We'd discovered that Edgar Weem had engineered Jason's birth, purposefully impregnating Michaela Weem himself, so that she would give birth to what he thought would become the Rising Sun. We were using this knowledge to blackmail Edgar Weem into leaving us alone. But since this knowledge was so valuable, I didn't think it was worth telling Mr. Sutherland, so I simply said, "We know some information about Edgar Weem that he doesn't want out. We're blackmailing him to let us be."

"And what information is that?" Mr. Sutherland wanted

to know.

I hesitated. "I can't say," I said.

Mr. Sutherland's mouth settled into a firm line. "We made a deal, Azazel. You can't withhold this information from me."

"I have to," I said. "If you know this information, and you sell it to someone who leaks it, it will ruin everything. We'll have no power over Weem anymore, and the Sons will come after Jason and me."

Mr. Sutherland shook his head. "I gave you information in good faith. Do you have any idea how difficult it was to find those email messages I've given you?"

"I-I'm sorry," I said. "I can tell you other things, but I can't tell you that."

"You've given me nothing at this point, except to confirm what I already knew about Jason," said Mr. Sutherland. "You owe me."

"Ask me something else," I said.

"No," he said. "It doesn't work that way." Then he smiled suddenly. "But there is something, perhaps, that you could do to even things up a bit."

"I could . . . do?" I asked. This deal was supposed to be an information exchange. I wasn't supposed to have to do anything.

Mr. Sutherland scooted a little closer to me on the couch. I backed away, tightening my grip on my gun. "What are you doing?" I managed. My voice, to my chagrin, sounded high-pitched and breathless.

Mr. Sutherland moved fast. He leapt forward, one hand going to the hand which held my gun. In a swift movement, he wrenched my wrist. I cried out, dropping the gun.

Twisting my arm, he pulled it above my head. His other hand grasped my other wrist, which he pulled into the same position. And his hips settled against mine so that he pinned me to the couch.

I panicked. I struggled against his body, but he held me fast. I kicked as his legs with mine. He just laughed.

What the hell was going on here?

"I used to be a teacher, actually," said Mr. Sutherland, his bruised face inches from mine. "I mean, a real teacher. In England. You know why I lost my job?"

I shook my head. How was I going to get my gun back? What was I going to do?

"Linda Thames," he said, a wistful look in his eyes. "She was so intelligent. So beautiful. So young. Flawless skin." He smiled, as if savoring a particularly nice memory.

I renewed my struggles. I didn't like the sound of his voice. I didn't like what he was saying.

"She made the loveliest noises," mused Mr. Sutherland. "And her tears . . . But strangling her was by far the best part." He looked me in the eye, his smile wide and maniacal.

Oh God. Oh no. Oh, no, no, no.

And to think, I'd come here voluntarily. Why was I so stupid?

Mr. Sutherland lowered his face to my neck. I felt the dry pressure of his lips, the wetness of his tongue.

I made a face, but I didn't make any noise. After that comment about the other girl's noises, I didn't want to give him the satisfaction.

Maybe . . . maybe, I just needed to keep him talking. If he was talking, he couldn't . . . hurt me.

"So you killed one of your students?" I squeaked. "That's why you lost your job?"

"I didn't just kill her," said Mr. Sutherland. "I kept her locked in a cellar for weeks, and I raped her repeatedly. When I finally did kill her, she was begging for it."

Oh. I made another face. Could I really keep him talking about this?

"So how did you get caught?" I asked.

"I was sloppy back then," he said. "Too many people knew I liked Linda. She was my favorite student."

"People know you like me," I pointed out.

"Yes, but I'll be long gone from the U.S. before they find your body," he said.

My . . . body? He was going to kill me? Oh, Christ, what had I gotten myself into? I needed my gun.

I could see it. It was lying on the floor next to the couch, barely two feet away from my body. How was I going to get it?

"So," I said, "if they caught you, how come you're not in jail?"

He grinned. "I told you I find good information. I've made my share of bargains."

Wonderful. Wonderful. "So you aren't scared of the law,

then?" I said.

"Not a bit."

"Or the Sons?"

He laughed.

"When Jason finds out that you did this, he will hunt you down and kill you," I said. I was serious. It was true.

"I'm not afraid of Jason either," he said.

Of course he wasn't. "Jason will know that," I said. "He'll use it to his advantage. You've never seen when he's angry. He's unstoppable. He killed five members of the Sons in the span of two minutes. I watched him do it."

Mr. Sutherland looked a little taken aback. "Five?" he asked.

His grip on my hands loosened a little bit. I kept talking.

"Five," I said. "And Jason and I took out an entire church full of them in Shiloh. Did you hear about that?"

"I always wondered about that incident," said Mr. Sutherland. "What did he do?" His grip was a little looser still.

I yanked my hands away from him as hard as I could. "We did it together," I grunted as I freed my hands. I clenched them into fists and forced them up into Mr. Sutherland's body, right below his rib cage.

He made a strangled noise in the back of his throat and his eyes got wide.

I rolled away from him, off the couch, feeling for my gun.

Mr. Sutherland recovered quickly. He was behind me, his arms reaching around me, trying to pin me down.

I elbowed behind me as hard as I could. I made contact with some part of his body. Some soft part.

Mr. Sutherland let out a cry of rage. "Maybe you are imbued with the spirit of demon," he growled.

Where was my gun?

Well, there was no time. I scrambled to my feet. "Think about that the next time you plant a stolen bell in a girl's purse," I said, running for the door.

Mr. Sutherland was right behind me.

I tugged open his door, threw myself through it and ran out into the street. I didn't look back, and I didn't hear Mr. Sutherland running after me.

But I did hear him calling after me from his doorway, "Azazel, I didn't put that bell in your purse!"

* * *

I ran and ran. There were no footsteps behind me, but I ran anyway. I ran, taking streets at random, hoping that if he were following me, I'd lose him. My breath went ragged and quick. My lungs started to hurt. The joints in my knees ached each time my foot hit the pavement. Eventually, I stopped, looking around me. There was no one there. And I wasn't entirely sure where I was.

I tried to catch my breath.

Damn.

What was wrong with me? Was there a big sign on my head that said, "Please attempt to violate me sexually"? First there was Toby. Then there was the veiled threat of that guy on the beach. Now Mr. Sutherland?!

I wasn't even that pretty. I wasn't ugly or anything, but if anybody should be getting all this negative sexual attention, it should be someone like Lilith. Not someone like me.

But I couldn't ponder that. I was lost on the streets of Bradenton, out of breath, and I'd lost both my purse and my gun. That really sucked. I'd lost my fake ID. I'd lost my driver's license. And I'd lost my check card. I was going to have to get that cancelled immediately. On top of everything else, I'd lost my phone.

And just when I really, really, really wanted to call Jason, too.

What was I going to do?

If I could find my bearings, I guessed I should go back to my apartment. Luckily, my keys were in my pocket, so I could get in.

But Mr. Sutherland knew where I lived. Was there any reason that he wouldn't have just gotten in his car and driven there? He was probably waiting for me.

I rubbed my face with my hands. I wanted to cry, but I couldn't. My eyes were dry. My chest was loose. I wandered to the end of the street to look at the street signs.

Oh. Well, I wasn't that far from home after all. A few blocks.

I didn't have anywhere else to go, so I guessed I'd go home. I'd be very careful. Look around for Mr. Sutherland's car. Then, as quickly as possible, I'd get inside, find the other gun, load it, and hide in a closet somewhere until Jason or Hallam got home. We didn't have a landline phone, so I couldn't even call anyone.

I walked the few blocks to my apartment and cautiously approached, looking around for Mr. Sutherland.

And then I saw Jude. He was standing outside my door, his phone to his ear.

Dammit. Jude was probably calling me. What was he doing here, anyway? Well, if Mr. Sutherland was around, he might go after Jude. Jude could be in danger.

I broke into a sprint again, snatching my keys from my pocket and feeling for the one to the front door as I ran.

"Jude!" I yelled as I approached.

He looked up and half-waved, confused because I was running towards him.

"Azazel?" he said as I approached. "Why are you – "

"Don't move," I said, fitting the key to the lock of my door and swinging it open. "Inside," I ordered.

Jude obeyed, his eyes wide.

Once we were safe in the house, I slammed the door after us and locked it.

"What's going on?" Jude asked.

I shook my head. I dashed back the hallway and went into Hallam's room. He kept his gun under his pillow, and the bullets in his top bedside drawer.

"Azazel?" said Jude, following me.

I didn't answer. I just got the gun, got the bullets, and methodically loaded the gun.

"Jesus!" said Jude. "Why do you have a gun?"

I turned on him, angry now. "Why are you here?" I

asked. "You're gonna get yourself killed."

"Why?" he said. "Is someone after you?"

I strode out of Hallam's bedroom, more confident now that I had the gun. I didn't think that Mr. Sutherland could have broken into our apartment, but I wanted to make sure. I went from room to room, checking closets and under beds. No one was there.

"Azazel," said Jude, "you are freaking me out! What's going on?"

I looked at him, finally. What was I going to tell him? What kind of lie would keep him safe, but keep him from being so curious that he'd keep wondering what was going on? I guessed I'd better stick as closely to the truth as possible.

"I went to Mr. Sutherland's house this evening," I said.

"Why?" said Jude.

"I don't know. I got this weird idea that maybe he was the guy in the parking lot last night. Because he wasn't there at school today, and because he seemed so weirdly into me."

"So you went to his house?" Jude said. "Why would you do that?"

"I don't know!" I said. "I guess I just thought . . . I wanted to tell him to leave me alone."

"What happened?"

"When I got there, his face was bruised and messed up," I said.

"So it was him," said Jude.

I nodded. "Yeah. And then he . . ." I trailed off. I didn't

138

really want to talk about what Mr. Sutherland had tried to do to me.

"I was right," said Jude, "he *is* a pedophile."

I remembered Jude's joke in the car earlier that week. I laughed bitterly. "Yeah," I said. "He told me that he did this to a girl at his last job. He said he kept her in a room and . . . over and over. And then he strangled her." I swallowed.

"Jesus!" said Jude, looking disgusted and little terrified. "How'd you get away?"

I shook my head. "I don't know, really. I struggled, and hit him and I ran, and . . ." I looked around again, half-expecting Mr. Sutherland to jump out at me, his bruised face twisted into an expression of psychotic glee. "He knows where I live, because he followed us to the shooting range the other day. I was afraid he'd be here, waiting for me."

Jude looked around too. "He's not, is he?"

"I don't think so. I left my purse there. All my money was in it, and my phone and – " I broke off. "Jude, do you have your phone?"

"Sure," he said, taking it out of his pocket and handing it to me.

"Thanks," I said. "I want to call Jason."

I flipped Jude's phone open and stared at the numbers. I started laughing.

"What?" said Jude.

I couldn't stop laughing. The laughter rolled out of me. I doubled over from the force of it. Could hardly catch my breath.

"Azazel?" said Jude.

I tried to squelch the laughter. I handed the phone back to Jude. Between giggles, I said, "I don't know his phone number."

It was programmed into my phone. I'd never dialed it. I just always searched through my address book and selected Jason.

"Oh," said Jude. "Maybe I have it."

"You've never called Jason," I said, still laughing.

Jude searched through his phone anyway. "You're right," he concluded. "I don't have his number."

Suddenly, it didn't seem so funny anymore. The laughter caught in my throat, where an enormous lump was forming. And before I could help it, I was sobbing.

It was just too much. Everything that had happened to me, and now not being able to call Jason. If he knew, he'd drop everything. He'd leave work. He'd come home. He'd wrap me in his arms. And then, I'd feel safe again. But I couldn't call him, because I didn't know his phone number! It had seemed so utterly ridiculous before, but now it seemed tragic. Cruel.

"Oh God, Azazel," said Jude. "I am so sorry."

As if he'd been reading my mind, Jude put his arms around me. I'd never noticed it before, but Jude had very strong arms. He was nearly the same height as Jason, and they had a very similar build. I buried my face in Jude's shoulder, and it felt so much like Jason's shoulder that I started crying harder.

We stood like that for a long time – Jude holding me, and me crying onto his shoulder, clutching Hallam's gun like it was my lifeline.

Finally, I quieted. I pulled back from Jude, feeling embarrassed. I scrubbed at my eyes. "I got your shirt wet," I said.

Jude shrugged. "What's a little wetness between friends?" he said. He cringed. "Okay, I didn't mean that like it sounded."

I laughed. "Well, that's the closest you'll probably ever get to wetness, anyway."

He snorted. "Right."

Jude and I went into my bedroom and sat down on the bed.

"When will Jason be back from work?" he asked.

"A little after eight," I said.

It was six o'clock then.

"I'll stay here with you until he comes back," said Jude. "You shouldn't be alone right now."

"Thanks," I said. "You're a good friend, Jude."

Sensing I'd had enough of talking about what had happened, Jude breezily changed the subject to something ridiculous. For over an hour, he and I critiqued Britney Spears' latest video, which Jude thought was "tasteless."

He sighed dramatically. "I used to love her so much," he said, "but I don't know what's happened to her lately. She's just betrayed her roots."

Since I'd never liked Britney Spears at all, not even when

I was a kid, I found this hilarious, and we spent another fifteen minutes debating whether Britney had any actual roots to betray. I didn't think she did. She was a product of marketing and record companies. She didn't have anything personal to say.

By this time, Jude and I were laying on my bed. I lay flat on my back and Jude lay on his side, propped up on his elbow.

He looked shocked. "What about when she did 'My Prerogative'? That was personal."

"That was a cover!" I said.

"Still, she made it her own," said Jude, shaking his head solemnly.

I threw a pillow at him.

He caught it, laughing, and checked the clock. "It's almost eight," he said. "Jason will be back soon."

"Good," I said.

"He's going to be pretty pissed off at Mr. Sutherland, isn't he?"

Oh. Yeah. He was. I hadn't thought about that before. I nodded. I thought about what Hallam had said the night before about Jason becoming more and more violent. I looked up at Jude.

His eyes were dark and large like Jason's, but they didn't have the intense luminosity of Jason's. In Jason's eyes, there were depths. Layers and layers of pain and anger. Jude just looked kind. Safe. Happy. I wondered if Jason's eyes would look like Jude's if nothing had ever happened to him.

"Jude?" I said.

"Yeah?"

"You remember this morning when you asked me if Jason ever scared me, and I said he didn't?"

"Yeah."

"I lied. Sometimes he does scare me."

Jude was quiet. He just looked down at me, his expression concerned.

"Not because I'm afraid he'll hurt *me*," I said. "He'd never hurt me. But other people . . . He just gets so, so mad. That guy at the party he beat up is just one guy. There have been others."

Jude nodded, still not speaking.

"You asked me if I'd forgive him if he murdered someone," I said. "I know Jason, and if something bad happened to me, he would. He'd kill someone." He has, I thought, but I didn't say that out loud.

"Azazel – " started Jude.

But at moment, the door to the apartment burst open, and I heard Jason hurrying back the hall to my bedroom. "Azazel, where are you?" he called. "I called your phone three times – "

He broke off as he entered my bedroom. He looked at me and Jude, lying together on my bed. I watched emotions flit across Jason's face. Disbelief. Hurt. Anger. And then he put his hands in the air and backed out of the room.

Jude shot me a look. "Um," he whispered. "He knows I'm gay, right?"

"He knows," I said.

Jude nodded. "All the same, I think I'm gonna go." He got up and walked out of my bedroom.

"Be careful," I called after him.

"I will," he called back. "Hi, Jason," he said as he walked through the hall. Jason didn't respond. "Oh," came Jude's voice, echoing through the house, "you must be Lilith. Nice to meet you."

"Hi," she said. "You're Jude?"

"Yeah. I'm actually on my way out."

"Too bad," said Lilith.

And then the apartment door opened and closed.

I got up and went to my door. "Jason, come in here. I need to tell you something."

His face was stone, but the rest of his body was twitching. His hands were clenched. His jaw was set.

"Jason, come on," I said. "This is a big deal."

He shook his head. "No," he said. "I don't want to hear it."

"You don't even know what it is," I said.

"I know what it is," he said.

"No, you don't."

He wouldn't look at me. "I worried," he said, "I always worried, because I knew that you kissed me while you were still dating Toby. But I told myself that didn't matter. I told myself that what we had was different than that. I told myself — "

"You worried about what?" I demanded.

144

"But you haven't changed," he said. "And right in our house."

"I haven't changed?" I repeated, my voice steadily rising. "What the hell?"

"I don't believe you, Azazel," Jason said quietly. "You have no idea what you mean to me. If I meant half as much to you as you do to me — "

"What is your problem, Jason? Why are you leaping to conclusions? And how could you throw Toby in my face like that?"

"You cheated on him with me," said Jason.

"But he had been cheating on me for four years before that," I said.

"But you didn't know that when you kissed me," he said. "And you said you loved him. You told me you loved him so many times. So many times that I almost believed it. I didn't think I had a chance."

"Oh my God, Jason, how can you possibly think that about me?"

"You have a pattern. You find your next boyfriend before you've dumped the other one. Well, I'm not going to give you the pleasure of dumping me, because I'm going to beat you to it. It's over, Azazel."

What?!

"You idiot!" I growled. "You stupid, stupid, idiotic bastard. How dare you say I have a pattern? I don't have a pattern. And if you were so worried about this, why didn't you tell me you were worried? How could you have such a

145

low opinion of me that you would think that I would do anything behind your back? You said that I didn't know you, but you clearly don't know me. And how dare you even think about breaking up with me?"

"Stop it," said Jason. "I just caught you – "

"You caught shit!" I screamed. "Fuck you!" And I was so angry that I slammed the door in his face.

I stood there fuming for several seconds. I could not believe that Jason thought such horrible things about me. And that he'd thought them for so long. He'd been waiting for me to be unfaithful to him, something he apparently thought I was capable of doing at any time for any reason. And I loved Jason more than I loved myself. I loved Jason more than life. I didn't want to imagine a world where Jason didn't exist. I was devoted to him, body, soul, and mind. And he thought –

Wait. I loved him.

I opened the door.

Jason was still standing there, but he looked a little bewildered.

"Listen," he said. "You and Jude were lying together in bed – "

"Jude is gay!" I yelled. "Do I have to say it a thousand million times?"

"Bullshit, he's gay," Jason shouted. "I see the way he looks at you. That guy is about as gay as the Rock."

"He likes Britney Spears. And he *paints his fingernails!*"

"So?" said Jason.

"So, he's gay."

Jason shook his head.

"Oh, fine, whatever," I said. "The point is, nothing happened. Nothing happened at all. And if you'd shut up for a second and stop thinking stupid, horrible, unfounded things about me, I'd explain to you why he was even here in the first place."

Jason pursed his lips. "Nothing happened?" he asked.

"Nothing at all. He's gay!"

Jason ran a hand through his hair. "I just thought – "

"I know what you thought. You made that abundantly clear."

"Well, it's not like I don't have reason, Azazel," he said. "You have to admit that."

"Because of Toby?"

"Yeah."

"Toby is dead, Jason. How long do we have to live under the specter of Toby? And I never felt even a thousandth of the things I feel for you for Toby. I worship you, you dumbfuck. I can't live without you." I bit out the last words and folded my arms over my chest.

Jason hung his head. "I'm sorry," he mumbled. He turned to walk away.

"Where are you going?" I shrieked. "Mr. Sutherland tried to rape me!"

Jason whirled, his eyes wide. "What?" he said. And there was an edge to his voice. A tinge of threat that terrified me.

CHAPTER EIGHT

aird92 (08:12:45): what the hell is going on? do u have anything to do with what happened to her?

michaela666 (08:13:08): What happened?

aird92 (08:13:22): sutherland. is he on our payroll or not?

michaela666 (08:14:02): Oh, no. Don't tell me that he did something.

aird92 (08:14:12): i thought he was under control. u said that he wouldnt mess everything up. or is this part of some plan u havent told me about?

michaela666 (08:14:37): I should have known that bastard couldn't keep his dick in his pants. Dammit! Tell me everything.

By the time Hallam got home, I was nearly frantic. Lilith had a cell phone, and she had Jason's number. We'd called it fifty times, but Jason wasn't picking up. Every time we called, it just went to voicemail. We left messages, each one more desperate, but it didn't seem to make any difference.

Once I'd told Jason what had happened with Mr. Sutherland, he'd taken Hallam's gun from me and left the house. He'd been angry. He hadn't said anything, but I could tell from the way he walked.

I'd begged him not to leave. I didn't want him trying to tangle with Mr. Sutherland. I didn't want Jason to get hurt. And I didn't like the look in Jason's eyes. It scared me. It reminded me too much of the look Mr. Sutherland had gotten in his eyes when he'd described strangling that girl named Linda. Jason had swept out of the house, fierce determination written all over his face. And . . . something else. He looked . . . I don't know. Insane.

Lilith had been frightened too. "Jason's kind of intense, isn't he?" she'd said in a small voice.

Hallam got back soon after Jason did. I feverishly filled him in on what had happened. He wasn't happy with me.

"Azazel, if I'd thought there was a chance in hell that you'd go to see that man, I would have contacted you sooner," he said. "Liam Sutherland is a wanted criminal in seven different countries. He's a rapist and murderer, and he has powerful friends. How stupid could you be?"

"I know," I said. "I'm sorry."

When I told him that Jason had gone after Mr. Sutherland, Hallam got nearly as frantic as I was. "How could you let him go?" he demanded.

"We tried to stop him," said Lilith.

"We have to find him," Hallam said.

The three of us piled into the car. We went to Mr. Sutherland's house. Hallam made us stay in the car, because he didn't have a gun. (I'd lost one in Mr. Sutherland's apartment, and Jason had the other one.) When he returned, he told us that the apartment had been broken into and searched, but that there was no sign of Jason or Mr. Sutherland.

"Mr. Sutherland probably went on the run after I left," I

said. "He knew that I knew where he lived."

We checked the airport, to see if Mr. Sutherland was there. The airline personnel wouldn't disclose the names of passengers, and we weren't sure that Mr. Sutherland would even be travelling under his own name. Hallam bought a ticket for a plane, but he had to go through security to search the airport. It didn't take him too long. The Sarasota-Bradenton airport was not that large, and it didn't take too long to get through security. But they weren't there. Then we had to wait for Hallam to get a refund on his ticket.

By this time, it was getting pretty late. We checked some bus stations, but couldn't find anything.

"He might have just driven out of town, anyway," Hallam said. "Or maybe he went to Tampa to get a flight out."

"Well, Jason probably didn't find him, did he?" I asked.

Hallam didn't know. "Jason had a head start. Maybe he pulled him out of the airport. I don't know."

Finally, we went back home. It was after midnight. Hallam and Lilith were both exhausted and went to bed. Hallam told me that I should do the same. I tried. I put on my pajamas and lay awake in the dark. But I couldn't sleep. I couldn't stop worrying about Jason. Just because I'd been able to get away from Mr. Sutherland didn't mean that he would. I'd mostly been lucky. A few good shots. And Mr. Sutherland had underestimated me. He'd thought I was an easy mark. I didn't know how much of a match he'd be for Jason.

And even if Jason didn't get hurt, what if he . . . ?

I didn't know why it bothered me so much. But the wild look in Jason's eyes when he'd left the apartment was just scary. I didn't know why Jason got like that. Why he felt that he had to protect me so much. Why he felt the need to punish anyone who hurt me.

The hours crawled by. It was dark outside. I lay in bed, staring at the ceiling, squeezing my eyes shut every time an image of Jason broken and bleeding appeared in my head. But it didn't work, because I could see the images even with my eyes closed. Nothing worked.

At around four in the morning, I heard the door to the apartment open. I jumped out of bed and raced into the living room. Jason stood in the living room in the darkness. He dropped his keys on the floor.

Lilith was sleeping on the couch, and she stirred faintly, mumbling something incoherent.

I didn't want to wake her up.

I took Jason's hands to lead him out of the living room. They were wet, but not with water. It was too thick for that. Too warm.

It was blood. I knew it.

Jason was bleeding. My worst fears realized, I led him to the bathroom. I closed the door after us and flicked on the light.

Jason's hair was plastered to his forehead with blood and sweat. There were red streaks on his cheeks and chin. His clothes were spattered with it. And his hands . . .

His hands were covered in blood.

Jason looked up at me from under his stringy, matted hair. His eyes were dull. He looked through me.

I put my hand to my mouth to stifle the little cry that was threatening to escape my lips.

"Jason, what happened?" I whispered.

He didn't answer. Didn't acknowledge that I'd spoken.

What had happened to him?

Shaking, I wet a washcloth in the sink and began to gently wipe away the blood, looking for his wounds.

There weren't any.

I swallowed. This wasn't Jason's blood.

Jason wasn't hurt.

Oh God. What had he done? And if he'd done it because of me, was it my fault?

Jason picked up his hands. It was the first real movement I'd seen him make. He looked at them. I'd tried to wipe away the blood, but it gathered in the creases of his palms. Underneath his fingernails.

"So much," he murmured. "So much blood."

Oh. Oh, God.

I didn't know what to do. "We'll get rid of it," I said finally. "We'll wash it off."

But there was a lot of it. It was all over him.

I stripped off his ruined clothes and started the shower. I got him inside, but once there, he wouldn't move. He just stood unmoving under the water. I needed to help him, so I got in the shower with him.

I scrubbed him and scrubbed him. Scrubbed away every trace of blood. Washed his hair. Watched the blood wash down the drain, red and pink, swirling away from us like it had never existed.

"Azazel," Jason said suddenly, as if he'd just recognized me. He caught my head with both hands, looked deeply into my eyes like he was lost, and he didn't know how to find himself.

"I'm here," I said.

"I'm sorry," he said. "I don't know what I . . ."

"It's okay," I said. "Whatever it is. It's okay. I love you."

"I need you," he said, and he kissed me.

His mouth was on mine insistently. I felt like he wanted to devour me, like he was pulling strength from my mouth.

I broke away. "Jason," I said breathlessly. "Jason, what happened?"

He looked at me. He looked away. "Nothing can ever happen to you," he told the shower walls. "Without you, I'm nothing."

He looked back at me, and his eyes were filled with tears.

I pulled him close, pressing my body against his. He put his lips on mine again. I felt his hands move on my skin, stroking me through the streams of water that rushed over us.

And because I didn't know what else to do, because his hands were urgent, because I felt vulnerable and frightened, I touched him back.

The water poured over us, pounding against our naked

skin. And we did the best we could to comfort each other the best we knew how. Jason gave me his hurt and confusion and fear and guilt, and I took it into my body. And as we crashed into each other, I gave it all to the water. I let it wash down the drain with Jason's tears.

* * *

My alarm went off at 6:15 the next morning. Jason stirred and then sat straight up in bed. "What?" he said, his eyes searching the room.

I reached over and turned the alarm off. "It's just the alarm," I murmured to him sleepily.

Jason lay back down. He drew me into his arms. He was wide awake, even though we'd only been asleep for a little over an hour. Jason could always be alert at a moment's notice, no matter how little sleep he'd gotten. "Are you getting up?" he asked me.

"Skipping school," I mumbled. I fell asleep again almost immediately, snug and safe in Jason's embrace.

When I woke up again, it was 9:30, and Hallam was standing over my bed. His arms were folded over his chest. He wasn't saying anything. I was still in Jason's arms, and Jason was still asleep.

I looked at Hallam. He looked pissed. "Good morning?" I said.

"When did he get here?" Hallam asked. Damn. He sounded pissed too.

"Four or so," I said.

"You know I don't like it when the two of you sleep in

the same bed," said Hallam.

How could he possibly be concerned about Jason and I having sex after what had happened last night? It seemed like the least important thing to focus on.

"He was . . ." I searched for a way to explain what Jason had been like last night. "He needed me," I finally settled on.

"Wake him up," said Hallam.

"We didn't get to sleep until nearly five," I said.

"Oh, spare me the details of your adolescent lust," Hallam said.

I glared at Hallam. "He needs to rest," I said.

"Wake him up," said Hallam. "And then get dressed and meet me in the kitchen."

"Hallam," I protested.

But Hallam was already going out the door to my bedroom.

I sighed. I looked at Jason, sleeping next to me. His face looked so peaceful. I didn't want to wake him. Lying next to him like this, I could hear his heart beating, steady and warm against my ear. If we just stayed like this, I could pretend that everything was normal and safe. I could pretend that Jason hadn't come home covered in blood last night. We could just be . . .

What could we be? There was nothing normal about Jason and me. Normal kids didn't live together with a twenty-two-year-old ex-member of a secret society. Normal kids didn't deal with death and danger as much as we did. And normal kids didn't feel the way about each other that we felt about each other.

I stroked his cheek. He stirred slightly, his lips parting. I kissed his temple, his forehead. His eyes fluttered open.

"Azazel," he whispered.

"Hey," I replied, kissing his lips.

He held me close. "This is nice. Waking up with you."

"Mmm," I agreed.

He gazed into my eyes, a small contented smile on his lips. I smiled back. Was there any reason that we had to move? Couldn't we just stay here, this close?

Hallam pounded on my door. "I mean it, Azazel!" he said. "Both of you get out here."

I sighed. "Hallam wants to talk to us."

"Yeah," said Jason. "Sounds like it." He started to push the covers aside, then stopped. "Can you get me some clothes from my room?"

I laughed. "Sure," I said. I shrugged into my pajamas and opened the door to my bedroom. Hallam was standing outside my door.

"I'm getting some clothes for Jason," I told him.

Hallam pushed past me into my bedroom. As I ducked into Jason's room to grab him a t-shirt and some pants, I heard Hallam yelling at Jason.

"This is the second time this week I've caught the two of you in the same bed," he was saying.

I sighed, rushing back with the clothes as quickly as I could. Just when I thought Hallam was starting to be kind of cool, he turned into the same prudish, overbearing jerk he'd always been.

"Jesus, Hallam," Jason was saying as I reentered the room, "can you give me a second to put on some pants?"

"Don't act like that," Hallam said. "You were off doing God knows what last night, and we were all quite concerned. Beside ourselves, really. Just because Azazel's forgiven you doesn't mean that I have. So, don't pretend for a second that this isn't serious."

I handed Jason his clothes and sat down on the bed. Hesitantly, I said, "What did happen last night, Jason?"

"Oh," said Hallam sarcastically, "so you didn't ask him that before the two of you started screwing then?"

Screwing? That wasn't a word I'd heard Hallam use before. He must be pretty angry.

"It wasn't like that," I said, studying my hands. "I had to . . ." It wasn't any of Hallam's business.

Jason was holding his clothes. "Can you give me a second, Hallam?" he asked.

"A second?"

"Yeah. To get dressed. Or are you jealous that Azazel got to see my penis, and you didn't?"

I stood up, throwing a confused look at Jason. He didn't sound like himself. He usually wasn't so flip.

Hallam rolled his eyes. "Oh, by all means, if you need your privacy." He stalked out of the room, leaving the door open.

"Jason," I said.

"What?" he said, yanking his pants over his feet.

"Where were you?"

He shook his head.

"You have to tell me," I said. "I washed all that blood off of you. Why did – "

"Not yet," Jason interrupted me. "I don't want to talk about it. Yet."

I watched him for a minute. He wasn't looking at me. Then I followed Hallam out of the bedroom.

I found Hallam in the kitchen. He was sitting at the table with his head in his hands. I stopped in the doorway, feeling a little like I was intruding. "Where's Lilith?" I asked.

Hallam dropped his hands and looked up at me. "I sent her out for a few hours when I realized Jason was back."

"But is that safe?" I asked.

"I assume whatever threat Mr. Sutherland presented is neutralized," said Hallam. "Isn't that right, Jason?"

I looked over my shoulder. Jason was standing behind me. His hands were shoved in his pockets. He was staring at the floor.

"Well?" Hallam prompted. "Isn't that right?"

Jason raised his eyes to meet Hallam's. "Look," he said, "do we really have to do this right now? I mean, I'm kind of hungry. Maybe we should get breakfast or something."

Hallam snorted. "Breakfast," he repeated. He gestured to the other chairs at the table. "Both of you come in here and sit down."

As we did so, I was oddly reminded of sitting down with my parents in October. They'd found out that Jason and I had snuck out to a party and that Jason had beaten someone up. I'd been so certain they were going to punish me, but instead, Jason had turned their own words against them. I remembered how I'd realized in that moment that Jason was different. He wasn't like other guys. He was more serious, more intelligent, more sure of himself. I looked at him now, and I still saw all of that. I reached for his hand. He squeezed my fingers briefly and then dropped my hand.

"You two are too young to be having the kind of sexual relationship that you seem to want to have," said Hallam.

Oh God. Not this again. "What's the big deal?" I said. "Most kids our age are having sex."

"Most kids your age are not living together," said Hallam.

"If they are," I said, "I bet they're sleeping in the same bed."

"Besides," said Jason, "we might be young, but we've been through a lot together. You can't tell me that we behave like normal seventeen year olds."

Hallam shrugged. "I believe that Sunday morning, you were telling me that the reason that Azazel was drinking so much was because you were normal seventeen-year-olds."

I rolled my eyes. "I don't understand why this bugs you so much, Hallam," I said. "I know that you were part of the Sons, and that they were all celibate or whatever, but why do you care so much what we do?"

"I'm your guardian," said Hallam.

"But you aren't our parent," I said. "And we'll both be

eighteen in a few months."

"We were together before you were even part of our lives," said Jason. "We don't need this kind of interference."

Hallam shook his head. "You don't understand. It's not about the sex. I couldn't care less what the two of you are doing. It's about how close the two of you are. It's not healthy."

What? I tried to look at Jason and see his reaction that statement, but Jason was still staring at the table. "We're in love," I said to Hallam. "Of course we're close."

"No," said Hallam. "You two aren't in love. You're obsessed with each other. When I look at you, it's like seeing two parts of one entity or something. It's disturbing."

Disturbing?! "You know, I don't think you're really qualified to talk much about love," I said to Hallam. "When have you ever witnessed it?"

"I know that the way Jason reacts to threats to your safety is very, very frightening. It's not normal. It's dangerous. For all of us."

I didn't say anything. Jason didn't either.

"Look at me, Jason," said Hallam.

Jason didn't.

"Jason," said Hallam.

Jason looked up. "What?" he asked.

"I need you to tell me what you did last night."

Jason shook his head. "I don't want to talk about this."

"I don't care," said Hallam. "We have to talk about this. Incidentally, where is my gun? Did you leave it somewhere with your fingerprints all over it?"

"I lost it," Jason said again.

"*Lost* it?" said Hallam.

"Jason," I said softly, "you do need to tell us what happened. I can't handle you running off like that."

Jason buried his face in his hands.

"Did you find Sutherland?" asked Hallam.

"Yes," said Jason.

"Where was he?"

"In his apartment," said Jason. "He didn't even try to run."

"And then what happened?" asked Hallam.

"I don't –" Jason said. "Does it really matter?"

"Fine," said Hallam. "Then tell me this. What did you do with it?"

The gun? What did Hallam mean, "it"?

"Hallam, it's confusing," Jason said, dragging his fingers over his face. "It's all blurry, okay?"

Hallam stood up. He leaned across the table. "I need to know. I need to know, because I need to know if anyone's going to find it. You forget, Jason, that we don't have the Sons to clean up our messes anymore. If you're going to run off all half-cocked, and you don't clean up after yourself, then we're all going to have problems. All of us. Azazel included, you understand that?"

Jason ran a hand through his hair. "Hallam, please don't – "

"Jason," Hallam interrupted, his voice even and low,

"what did you do with the body?"

I gasped, sitting back in my chair. Body?

Jason got out of his chair. He walked out of the kitchen.

Hallam went after him. I didn't move. I couldn't move.

"Answer me, Jason," he said.

Jason came back into the kitchen. He sat down next to me. He took both of my hands in his.

"Is it true?" I asked him. "Did you . . ."

"No," said Jason. "No, I didn't."

"Don't lie to her," said Hallam, clapping a hand onto Jason's shoulder.

Jason dropped my hands. He didn't look at Hallam. He didn't look at me.

"You saying you didn't kill him?" asked Hallam. "Then where is he? If he's alive, he's more of a problem than if he's dead."

Jason shook his head, still staring into space. "I remember that he had a gun, and that I kicked it out of his hands. I remember that I hit him. I hit him a lot. I remember that he was bleeding. He was bleeding everywhere. I just kept hitting him."

"Is he dead?"

"I don't . . ." Jason started shaking, all over.

I looked up at Hallam. "Don't make him — "

Hallam silenced me with a look. "Pull yourself together. I taught you better than this."

Jason stood up abruptly, knocking over his chair. He advanced on Hallam. Hallam backed up. "That's right, you

162

did, didn't you?" said Jason. "You taught me how to do this. You showed me." As he talked, he kept moving forward. Hallam kept backing away from him until he was against the counter over the kitchen sink. Jason just kept talking, angrily spitting his words into Hallam's face. "That's why you're so angry with me now, isn't it? Because you think it's your fault. You think that if you hadn't ever showed me what to do, I'd never have done any of this."

"I'm not responsible for your actions, Jason," Hallam said quietly, but he looked alarmed. "You're the only one who's responsible for what you've done."

"What I've done, huh? Because whatever it is that I've done is so dangerous to all of us?"

"Yes," said Hallam.

"Three things, Hallam," said Jason. "First of all, Sutherland's not a problem anymore. He's taken care of."

I felt a little chill run through my body. What did that mean?

"Second," Jason continued, "while you're going on about how horrible it is that I'm behaving the way I am, you seem to be forgetting one important thing. I saved your life. You remember that?"

"Jason — " Hallam sounded a little nervous.

"*Remember* that?"

"Yes."

"And you promised me that you'd always have my back too. Remember that?"

"Yes."

"Good," said Jason. "Third, you can't tell me where to sleep."

Jason didn't look at me as he swept out of the kitchen. I heard the door to our apartment slam. I winced.

Hallam was still standing against the counter. His face was white. I swallowed, looking at him.

"Well," I said. "That went well."

* * *

Hallam left the house pretty quickly after Jason did. He didn't say much. He just gathered his things and took off. Jason hadn't taken the car when he left, so I didn't think that he'd gone far. I was worried, but not as worried as I had been the night before. I didn't have a cell phone, so I couldn't call Jason. I ate some cereal in the kitchen, wandered around the house. I didn't know what to do. It felt like lately, all I did was worry about things. I was exhausted. I hadn't gotten much sleep the night before either.

I lay back down, finally. And within a few minutes, I went back to sleep. My sleep was dreamless. I felt like I'd been pulled into a black hole. When I woke up, I could hear voices floating down the hall from the living room. It was Lilith and Jason.

I stirred. Opened my eyes. Jason was home. I should go to him.

Then I heard my name.

"I don't know what to do about Azazel," Jason was saying. "I love her so much, but I don't know if she loves me as much as I love her."

What? I froze on my bed, unable to believe he doubted my feelings for him.

"Why don't you know?" Lilith asked.

"I don't feel like she really had a choice," Jason said. "Her entire world got destroyed. I was all she had. I don't know if she really loves me or if she's just clinging to anything she can cling to."

"You think she's clingy?"

"No," said Jason. "No, just the opposite, really. She's very independent. She wants to party all the time. She wants to protect herself. Wanting to go shooting and all of that. It's like she's trying to make sure she doesn't need me. Like she's preparing to leave or something."

No! It wasn't that at all. It was that I didn't want to slow Jason down. I didn't want him to become hurt because he had to protect me. Why did Jason doubt me? Had I ever given him cause?

"The partying bothers you, huh?" asked Lilith.

"No, not really," said Jason. "I understand that she wants to have fun."

"I always felt like Zaza was a powderkeg," said Lilith. "Back in Bramford, I got the impression that the only thing holding her back was Toby and her family. If she could have let loose then, I think she would have. Big time."

That wasn't true. I wasn't a powderkeg.

"So, it's good that she's doing it now, then," said Jason. "She's free."

"Is it good?" Lilith asked.

165

"Yeah," said Jason. "It's fine. I just worry about her, you know. I worry about her a lot. She's very important to me."

"You don't worry that she might explode?" Lilith asked.

"Explode?"

Explode?!

"That it might end up being too much. That she'll go overboard with the partying and drinking. She'll self-destruct," said Lilith.

I wasn't anywhere close to self-destructing.

"Why?" said Jason, sounding concerned. "Do you think she might?"

"I haven't really been able to talk to her," said Lilith. "But she is sneaking around a lot, isn't she? To the shooting range, and then to Mr. Sutherland's?"

"That's true," said Jason.

"She's lying. She's trying to hide her behavior, because she knows it's erratic," said Lilith.

Bull. Lilith was full of crap.

"Maybe you're right," said Jason.

God. I should get up right now and let them know that I was listening to their conversation. I wanted to shut Lilith up. But for some reason, I was driven to keep listening. Some kind of morbid curiosity, maybe.

"And have you noticed that both of those times, she ended up alone with Jude?" Lilith asked.

What was she doing? Was she trying to make Jason jealous of me? Was this why he was acting the way he was? Was Lilith poisoning him?

"You met him," Jason said. "Do you think he's gay?"

"No way," said Lilith. "That boy's eyes settled on my tits for like five whole seconds. He's not gay."

Jason laughed. "Well, I don't know if that's conclusive, Lil."

Lil?! He was calling her by a nickname?

"Gay guys don't like tits," she said.

"Maybe not," he said, "but I think it's tough for anyone not to . . . stare at you."

"Stare at me?" Lilith giggled.

"You're kind of . . . well-endowed," Jason said.

Oh. My. God. Jason was talking to Lilith about her breasts? Now I *couldn't* move. I was beginning to feel very, very sick.

"Maybe," said Lilith, "but the look that Jude gave me was a very ungay look."

"I know what you mean," said Jason. "I really don't like the way he looks at Azazel."

"Do you really think that Azazel would do that to you, though? Do you think she'd cheat on you and not break up with you?"

"Where would she go? If she didn't want to be with me, she'd probably feel trapped here. She has to live here."

I did not. Was everyone forgetting the fact that I had a very rich grandmother? I stayed with Jason by choice. And I couldn't believe that after last night, he could possibly still be questioning my fidelity. If I didn't want to be with him, he should realize that showing up covered in blood would

167

have probably sealed the deal.

Besides, when we'd made love last night, it had felt, to me anyway, like something very, very real. Like Jason and I had connected on a level we'd never connected with. Like it wasn't just our bodies touching, but our souls . . .

Clearly, he hadn't felt that.

"Wow," said Lilith, "that's true."

"But," said Jason, "she cares about me. I just think she realizes that I'm holding her back. That being with me makes her life dangerous. I think she wishes she could have a boyfriend like Jude. Someone fun. Someone who she can just go crazy with."

Why was Jason so jealous of Jude?

"Someone normal," said Lilith.

"Yeah."

Augh. She couldn't have picked a worse word to say.

"So," said Lilith, "when you found them on her bed yesterday, you don't think anything was going on?"

Jason hesitated. "I don't think she thinks anything was going on. I think she thinks Jude is really gay. But I think Jude was loving every second of it. When he walked past me in the hall, he gave me this look." There was a long pause. "But, she couldn't be. Last night, when she took care of me when I came back, she was so . . . I can't believe that I could have been so close to her, that she could make me feel the way she made me feel, and be doing anything behind my back."

So, he had felt something then?

"Can't believe, or don't want to believe?"

"She couldn't have faked that," said Jason.

"Girls can fake all kinds of things, Jason." Lilith's voice dropped. It sounded sultry. Suggestive. "For instance, are you sure that she's completely, well, satisfied?"

She wasn't asking this, was she? She couldn't be.

"What do you mean?" Jason asked.

"You know what I mean."

"I . . ."

"You know," said Lilith in her seductive voice, "I used to be very, um, frustrated myself. I guess I thought that guys would know how to please me without me telling them anything."

"And they didn't?" Jason sounded concerned.

"The female body is a mysterious thing to men," Lilith said, her voice going breathy. "There's no way they could have fully understood what it was I needed."

"Oh."

"You think you understand what women need?"

"I . . . well . . ."

"It's okay. It's not your fault. Someone needs to show you."

Show him?

And then it was quiet.

My heart raced. What was going on? Why weren't they talking? What was Lilith doing? And why couldn't I move?

I fought with myself. Fought against the images that were flashing through my mind. Images of Lilith and Jason, just a few rooms away. They were sitting on the couch, probably. Was she close? How close was she? What could she possibly be showing him?

I could think of several possibilities. All of them made me sick to my stomach.

I needed to get up. Throw aside the covers on my bed. Jam my feet into slippers. Tear into the living room. Scream at them to stop.

But try as I might, I couldn't will my body to move.

aird92 (07:22:43): idk i think it might be working. she and jason seem to be fighting a lot.

michaela666 (07:22:55): fighting isn't enough, and you know it. we need to step in. There's a lot at stake here. We can't risk things going wrong.

aird92 (07:23:12): is there really that much of a rush? couldnt we give it like another week or so?

michaela666 (07:23:32): Absolutely not. And by the way, are you getting enough to eat?

aird92 (07:23:40): geez. im not answering that.

Finally, I heard Jason's voice.

"Lilith, what are you doing?" he said. He sounded embarrassed. He sounded guilty.

Oh God, what had just happened?

Lilith didn't say anything.

"You know I think you're very attractive," said Jason, "but I'm in love with Azazel. I don't want to . . ."

"For all you know, Azazel is banging Jude," said Lilith. "Even the score."

Even the score?!

"Azazel isn't doing anything like that," Jason said.

"Are you sure?"

"I . . ."

He wasn't *sure*?

"It doesn't matter," said Jason. "Whatever she did, it doesn't matter. She's all I want."

"You'd stay with her if she was sleeping with someone else?" Lilith demanded.

"I'd stay with her if she was the devil incarnate. I can't be without her. She's everything to me. Without her, I don't know if I can exist."

My heart swelled. I felt the same way. And it was good, because I wasn't cheating on Jason, and I never would. But we were going to be okay. Because he loved me, and I loved him. And no matter what happened, we'd always have that. And that was all that mattered.

And then, I could move! Finally. I burst out of my room, making as much noise as I could. When I appeared in the living room, I saw Lilith sitting on the couch. Jason was standing on the opposite side of the room from her, his hands thrust into his pockets. He was staring at the carpet.

I looked at the both of them.

Lilith smiled at me. "Hi, Zaza," she said.

"I don't want you to stay here anymore," I said to her.

She raised her eyebrows.

"God," I said. "What is it with you and my boyfriends, anyway? There are thousands of men on earth. Pick someone else for Christ's sake."

Jason snorted.

I turned to look at him. "What?" I said.

"Nothing," he said, "it's just funny that when it's about me, Toby means nothing to you, but when it's about Lilith, he's still important."

I felt hurt. Jason had just said that he couldn't exist without me, but was angry with me. About Toby. About Jude. "He's *not* important," I said.

Jason shrugged. "I don't know what to think anymore," he said.

"You just said I was everything to you," I said.

"Were you eavesdropping?," said Jason.

"I heard you two talking," I said. "I wasn't eavesdropping."

"How much did you hear?" said Jason. "If you heard us, why didn't you come into the room? Why did you wait in there and listen?"

"Lilith shows up and suddenly you're hanging with her twenty-four/seven," I said. "She takes you to parties. You guys go out drinking. Whenever I ask you to go out – "

"You don't ask me, Azazel," Jason interrupted. "You call me plastered from the party and ask me to pick you up. You don't want me to come along."

"I do so ask you," I said. "But you work later than I do, and what do you want me to do? Wait around for you to get off work before I go to the party?"

"Well, that would be horrible, wouldn't it?" Jason said sarcastically.

"I'm sorry," I said. "I didn't know you minded."

"How could you not know? No, you just want to spent time alone with Jude."

"I don't," I said. "Jude's my friend, that's all."

"You guys looked real friendly yesterday, lying on your bed together," Jason said.

"I'd just gone through something pretty traumatic," I said. "I needed someone. You weren't there."

Jason looked stung.

"And then," I said, "the minute I told you, you just ran off again, and God only knows what you did while you were gone. You could have died. Or you could have . . ." Killed someone. "Maybe you did. I don't know. But you came back. And I had to clean you up. I had to clean it up. And I was the one who was . . ."

"I did it for you," Jason said, sounding agonized.

"What did you do, Jason? God help me, what did you do?"

Jason looked away. When he turned back to me, he'd gotten a stony expression in his eyes. His face was carefully controlled mask. "I protected you," he said. "I *can* protect you, Azazel."

"I don't want you to *have* to protect me," I said.

"Then don't go running off without me," he said. "Don't do things like that."

"You don't go running off without me either," I said, my voice shaking.

I reached out for him, and he took my hand, pulling me over to him. Against him. His arms went tight around me, like he was grabbing onto me for dear life.

"So you're just going to forgive her?" asked Lilith.

Dammit. I'd forgotten she was even there. I yanked

myself away from Jason. "Why are you still here?" I asked. I turned on Jason. "What was she trying to 'show' you, anyway?"

Jason's eyes darted away from mine.

I glared at Lilith.

She crossed her arms over her chest. "I was just trying to help you out, Zaza. I figured that even if you'd gotten enough courage to find your clitoris, you'd be too scared to help Jason find it."

I blushed to the roots of my hair. "That's really none of your business."

Lilith shrugged. "Well, what are you doing, anyway? I mean, you've got this amazing guy, and you're blowing him off for parties and some guy who you think is gay?"

"He is gay," I said, exasperated.

Lilith shook her head. "Not gay, sweetheart. Definitely not gay."

"And I'm not blowing Jason off," I said.

"He thinks you are," she said. "Let me tell you a little secret about men, sweetie. Men like to feel like they're needed. They like to be able to do things. You make Jason feel like he's useless. He can't party with you. He can't save you. And he can't even give you an orgasm. You keep that up for too long and even the best guy will start looking for someone who wants him."

"I want Jason," I said. "And I'm not talking about our sex life with you."

Lilith laughed. "Well, there's not much to really talk

about, now is there?"

"Just shut up," I said.

"Did I strike a nerve?" she asked.

I looked at Jason. "I don't make you feel useless, do I?"

"No," he said, but he didn't sound very convinced.

I didn't know what to say. Lilith had tried to seduce my boyfriend, and he wasn't helping me get rid of her. He'd rejected her, sure, but how long would that last? Lilith wasn't on my side. She was out to get me. She could claim she was trying to help, but you didn't help someone by flirting with her boyfriend.

"I don't want Lilith to stay here anymore," I said.

"Azazel," said Jason.

"No," I said. "No more excuses. I don't trust her with you."

"Then you don't trust me," he said.

I didn't say anything.

Lilith sighed. "I've got to go to work," she said. "But I've got enough cash that I can probably afford a hotel for a few nights."

"No," said Jason, "you're not going to a hotel. I've got to work tonight too. We all need to cool down, and we'll talk about it later."

* * *

I was alone again. For hours, I tried to distract myself. I made food. I watched television. I messed around on the internet. But finally, I couldn't distract myself anymore. It was getting dark outside my house. Jason and Lilith would be getting off work soon. I paced around the house, angry and frustrated. I felt like everything in my life was disintegrating. This wasn't a new feeling for me. I'd felt it before, when Jason and I had driven out of Bramford. I'd left my family, my best friend, my boyfriend, everything I cared about. Everything had been ripped away from me. Things weren't that dire yet.

Yet.

Jason was right about one thing when he was talking to Lilith. He was all that I had. He was my lifeline. He was everything that I lived for. We'd worked so hard to try to have a normal life together. Here, in Florida, in paradise, everything was supposed to be better. It was warm here. We could walk on the beach. We could finish high school. We could be what we'd always wanted to be, two normal kids. It seemed that the world had different plans for us, however. We could run as far as we wanted. We could set up our lives to appear as normal as possible. But something lurked within both of us that made us different. We were trapped. We'd never be free of it.

In just the past few days, everything had gotten crazy. I'd been nearly raped on a beach, carried off from a parking lot, and assaulted on a couch. All of those things were bad. I wished like hell they'd never happened to me. But it was worse than that. It was worse than that because I felt like I was losing Jason.

I thought of his face when I'd told him about Mr. Sutherland. The way he'd been overtaken by anger. How single-minded he'd been as he left the apartment. And then I thought of his returning, covered in blood, staring through me in the bathroom. He hadn't looked like the Jason I'd fallen in love with. He'd looked so haunted. What had Jason done? Why had he done it?

If Jason had killed Mr. Sutherland, it wouldn't be the first time he'd taken a human life. But the first time Jason had killed a person, it had been to protect me. And he'd said, as we stood in the living room, that he'd done what he did to Sutherland because of me. How could I handle the responsibility of that? It felt like I'd murdered people myself. I hadn't pulled the trigger, but I'd been the trigger. If Jason was driven to kill because of me, then what was it that Jason was becoming? And was he becoming that because of me? What was I doing to him?

Jason was jealous. Jason was always accusing me of things I didn't do. Jason didn't trust me. And Lilith wasn't helping matters either. The two of them had been quiet for several moments before Jason had spoken. What had they done in those moments? Had Lilith kissed Jason? Had she touched him? Had she showed him her body? Had he touched her? Where had he touched her?

It was agony. I couldn't handle the thought of it. What was worse, I couldn't believe that Jason didn't agree that Lilith needed to leave. Just a few days with Lilith around, and he was spending lots of time with her, and he was having conversations with her about our sex life? I couldn't believe it. I had a right to be jealous when he was doing that.

It was stupid for Lilith to interfere anyway. Jason and I were having great sex. Really. Not that we got to do it very much with Hallam around, but when we did, I enjoyed it. Tons. I was satisfied. Really. I guessed I'd always worried a little about . . .

Well, I didn't worry that much about it, considering I couldn't even think the words. But I'd always heard that it was harder for girls than it was for guys to do that. Especially girls my age. So, I didn't think it was that big of a deal. Sometimes, I guessed I felt a little jealous of Jason, because sometimes, when we had sex, afterwards, I felt kind of unfinished. Like I'd been building up to something, and instead I just hung there, trying to deal with the fact it was over. But I didn't know what to do about that. I didn't know how to talk to Jason about it. It seemed like we had to work so hard to find time to have sex as it was. I didn't want to create problems.

Still. I thought about the way Jason's voice had sounded when he'd asked Lilith whether or not guys had known how to please her. He'd sounded worried. Was this a big deal? If I couldn't do it, did it make Jason feel useless?

Did Jason feel useless?

I hated Lilith. Before she'd shown up, Jason and I hadn't been fighting about this stuff. In fact, before Lilith had shown up, everything had been fine.

Sort of. The bell had shown up in my purse. That had really started everything, actually.

But wait. The bell had appeared in my purse after Lilith

showed up.

Hold on. I didn't really think . . .

Truthfully, I'd been so caught up in worrying about Jason hurting Mr. Sutherland and our domestic issues that I hadn't thought much about the bell or anything else in some time. Which was pretty strange, I realized, because Mr. Sutherland had said something very important to me. He'd said that someone close to me was trying to complete an invocation. That could only mean the Satanists.

This whole time, I'd been concerned about the Sons. I'd never even considered the fact that the Satanists might not be down for the count. And actually, it made more sense, considering everything had happened to me, not Jason. The Satanists would be interested in me.

Somebody had put a bell in my bag, framing me for stealing it. And then Mr. Sutherland had been weird, but Mr. Sutherland hadn't even really been connected to any of it. So really, the only thing that had happened had been the bell. Hmm.

If the Satanists were responsible for putting a bell in my bag, why would they have done that? Would they have wanted me in detention? That didn't make much sense. Did it? I wandered into the living room and turned on the computer.

Mr. Sutherland said something about the invocation. If the Satanists were trying to complete the invocation, what would they have done?

I pulled up google and typed in, "Invocation to Azazel."

I didn't come up with much. There were several websites describing silly incantations, telling the reader to visualize the nature and modern civilization and to focus on the "gods of this world," while repeating a bunch of junk about the "Queen of Hell" and other such things. There was also a website about the mythical Azazel, claiming that Azazel was the scapegoat for the Jewish people, or the being who was punished for their sins in place of them. Darkly, I wondered if this was why my life was so screwed up. Was I being punished for the sins of the world, even though I'd done nothing wrong?

Abandoning the search, I tried another query. Was the bell related? I searched for "invocation bell."

I hit a few unrelated websites at first. One was actually for a role-playing game which instructed the player to "ring the bell of invocation" and descend into the pit of Moloch or something. There was another that was a news item about a Lions Club meeting.

Then I found a website entitled, "The Beast: Satanic Rituals and Spells." It took me to a site within the larger site that was headed, "Invocations to Satan." There was a description of something very similar to the first invocation I'd been part of, instructing the performer of the invocation to drink from a sacred chalice and chant in Latin. Beneath that, there was another ritual.

"If the first invocation fails, or if the desired object of the spirit of the demon is an unwilling participant (though this kind of magic is highly dangerous and not encouraged by

181

the creators of this website), try this instead. Gather several large candles, a chalice consecrated to the demon in question, a bell, and an object that will symbolize the demon himself (or herself.) This object should be something that embodies or symbolizes the spirit of the entity you intend to invoke. For example, if you are invoking Lilith, a sexually charged item or talons of some kind might work well.

"This object needs to be anointed with some kind of body fluid from the person hoping to be filled with the spirit of the demon. Blood, semen, and/or vaginal fluid are the most effective, but saliva or sweat will work as well. Ring the bell to focus the demon on the spot you wish him to concentrate on."

The website went on to describe the various chants and spells one had to say over the person who was invoking the demon. It all sounded pretty gross to me. However, it was proof that someone might use a bell to invoke Azazel. And that the Satanists might have put the bell in my bag as a warning or something.

Mr. Sutherland had said that someone close to me had completed an invocation, and, when I'd elbowed him in the ribs, he'd grunted, "Maybe you are imbued with the spirit of a demon."

Someone had already performed this ritual on me. Who was close to me? Who had ties to the Satanists? Who'd shown up just before the bell did?

There was only one person who fit the answer to all those questions.

Lilith.

And she slept in my house, for God's sake. She could have come into my room as I slept, performed the ritual over me, and then placed the bell she'd used in my purse.

And it made sense that she was trying to seduce Jason. The Satanists wanted me to kill Jason. Perhaps they thought that if Jason slept with Lilith, I'd be so angry with him that I'd destroy him.

Augh. I couldn't believe I'd allowed Lilith into my house with her stupid story about wanting to get away from the Satanists. She didn't want to get away from the Satanists at all. Instead, she was working for them! And Jason had told her it was okay to sleep in our house tonight! I couldn't believe that. I had to get away from her. I had to get her away from Jason. Who knew what kind of damage she'd already inflicted?

I needed to call Jason. Tell him what I'd figured out. But no. I couldn't call Jason. I didn't have a phone. Hallam had a phone, but I didn't know where Hallam was. I guessed I should tell Hallam too. Maybe he'd know how to help. Or what to do.

I thought about Hallam and Jason earlier. Hallam screaming at Jason. Hallam demanding to know what Jason had done with Mr. Sutherland's body. Hallam was angry at both of us. Who knew if he was even on our side anymore? Should I wait for Hallam to come back?

No. I should just go to Jason. But I didn't have a car. Hallam had the car. Jason and Lilith had caught a ride with a co-worker. It wasn't too far to walk, but it was dark outside, and after what had happened over the last few days, I didn't feel quite comfortable walking around in the dark.

How was I going to get there?

Well. I could ask Jude for a ride.

Of course, I didn't think that would make Jason particularly happy. And it wasn't smart to get Jude anymore involved in this mess than he already was. Still. We had to stop Lilith.

I signed onto AOL instant messenger. With my luck, Jude wouldn't even be online. It was a Friday night, and he probably had something exciting to do, like a party or something. If he wasn't, it was a sign, I told myself. I'd just wait for Hallam to come home. Or for Jason and Lilith. I'd get Jason alone and tell him what I'd figured out. He'd believe me. He'd have to. Wouldn't he?

But Jude was online.

He messaged me immediately. "u didnt come to school today. u okay?"

"Fine," I typed. "Can you come pick me up?"

He could. He would. As I signed off, I mused over his AOL handle. It was weird, because I couldn't figure out why he'd picked it. It wasn't his name, like mine was. Of course, Jude was a much more common name than Azazel. Maybe he wanted something more original. Still. His handle wasn't that original. It reminded me of something. I couldn't remember what, but I knew I'd heard it somewhere. Like a last name or something?

184

Where had I heard the name Aird?

* * *

"You're kidding," Jude gasped. "She said somebody needed to *show* him and then it was quiet?"

"Yeah," I said. "And Jason has the nerve to be jealous of me and act like it's my fault."

Jude was pulling into the driveway of the restaurant where Lilith and Jason worked. He shook his head as if he couldn't believe it. "So the two of you had another fight then?"

"I guess so."

"Girl, is it just me, or are the two of you arguing a lot lately?"

"It's Lilith!" I said. "She's ruining everything. I just want to get rid of her."

"So that's why we're going to Jason's work? So you can confront him about Lilith?"

I couldn't explain to Jude why exactly I was going, so I guessed his interpretation worked as well as any other. "Yeah."

Jude parked the car in the parking lot and turned it off.

"Thanks for driving me," I said. "I know I must not seem like the safest person to be around lately."

Jude shrugged. "I got your back, Azazel. Really. Whatever you need to do."

I was glad he hadn't asked any questions about Mr. Sutherland. It made everything much easier. Jude was a good friend. I didn't care what anyone thought. I was glad

185

to have him. And there was nothing going on with him beyond that.

"So," said Jude. "You want me to wait in the car?"

I nodded. That would be easier. I need to talk to Jason privately. Jude might get in the way.

"Okay," said Jude.

"Thanks," I said. I put my hand on the door handle.

"Azazel?" said Jude.

I stopped and looked at him. "Yeah?"

"If you ever feel like . . ."

"What?" I said.

"It's not important."

Trailing off drove me crazy. "Tell me," I said.

"It's just that if you feel like you have to stay with Jason because he's all you've got, I want you to know that's not true."

"Jude –"

"I know you think you love him. Maybe you do. But just because you love someone doesn't mean that you two are good for each other, you know? Anyway, I just want you to know that if you ever need anything, you have me, okay?"

I just smiled. "Thanks Jude. That means a lot. It does. But nobody else really gets Jason and me. What we have goes beyond being good or bad for each other." We're each other's oxygen. But I didn't say that out loud.

I went up to the restaurant. The door was locked, because they were closing, so I went around back to the kitchen entrance. A few guys were outside, dumping large garbage bags into the dumpster behind the restaurant. I recognized them because I knew they worked with Jason, but I couldn't remember their names.

"Hi," I said. "I'm looking for Jason."

"Oh, right," said one of the guys. "You're his girlfriend, right?"

"Right," I said.

"Well, he already left," said the other guy.

"He did?" I said.

I'd missed him? I wondered what he'd think when he got home, and I wasn't there.

"Yeah," said the first guy. "He went to a party out on Cortez."

"Right. At Rachel Kline's house," said the other guy.

A party? Jason had gone to a party? After everything that had happened, he'd just ditched me to go off and drink?

"Really?" I said.

"He's been hanging out pretty close with that redhead chick," said one of the guys. "I'm pretty sure going to the party was her idea."

"Oh my God." I shook my head, angry and hurt at the same time.

"Sorry," said the other guy. "Tough break. For what it's worth, I think you're way hotter than that Lilith girl."

Nice. Wonderful.

Fuming, I went back to Jude's car. I filled him in. "They're at Rachel Kline's," I said.

"Oh right," he said. "I totally forgot about that."

"So did I," I said. "You asked me if I wanted to go on Sunday."

"Seems like five years ago," said Jude. "It's been quite a week."

"Yeah," I said. It had been.

"So I guess we're going to Rachel's?" Jude asked.

"I guess so," I said. I couldn't believe Jason was going to a party. Was this some way of getting back at me for going to parties without him all the time? I hadn't realized it bothered him so much.

"Could be fun," said Jude. "It's a party, after all."

Fun? Doubt it. And maybe I'd just been fooling myself all this time, thinking that I went out to so many parties and drank so much because I wanted to cut loose and be free. Truthfully, I thought I might just be running from everything that had happened. I didn't want to face what had happened to me. I didn't want to face who I'd become. But I wasn't a crazy party girl. I was a girl who'd fought off a serial rapist. I was a girl who'd faced down the Sons of the Rising Sun. I was girl who could load a gun and flick off the safety. I was a girl who loved a boy more than life itself. I was me. There wasn't any running from it. Not anymore. I had to be myself. Own up to it.

But I smiled weakly. "Party time," I said.

Jude laughed. He started the car. "You sound so enthused."

As he pulled out of the parking lot, Jude got his phone out of his pocket. "I'm going to give a couple of the guys from work a call and tell them I'm going out to the party, okay?"

I listened while he relayed our destination over the phone and gave directions to Rachel's house. It didn't take long to drive out to Rachel's house. It was close to town. Once there, we had trouble finding a parking space since the entire street was glutted with cars, and they were taking up every possible place to park. Finally, we parked maybe three blocks away and had to walk all the way back to the party.

Rachel's house was one of those McMansions that populate the Sarasota-Bradenton area. Easily worth a half-million dollars, it sprawled amongst houses of the same size in a crowded, planned neighborhood. Inside, there was a lot of space, but not a lot of rooms. The foyer had high ceilings and a large chandelier. Overall, however, the house was a regular three bedroom house. Just a fancy one, with big windows and walk-in closets.

Rachel's parents were out of town for the weekend, and it seemed that everyone in Bayshore High School knew that. The party was packed. Bodies writhed in the living room, dancing to a pulsing stereo. In the foyer, kids chatted in groups, clutching bottles of beer or plastic cups filled with sugary mixed drinks. The kitchen was similarly crowded. There were puddles of alcohol on the floor. There were stains on the carpet. I didn't see Rachel Kline anywhere. I wondered if she were worried about the fact that her house was being destroyed by the entire student body.

Because the party was so packed, I couldn't find Jason or

Lilith. Jude and I made a search of each of the rooms in the lower level of the house. The living room. The foyer. The kitchen. The den. The line to the downstairs bathroom. They were nowhere to be found. Had they actually come to the party? What if they were somewhere else? Together?

Alone?

The thought made me feel nauseated.

"Where are they?" I wondered aloud.

"Should we check upstairs?" Jude asked.

Upstairs? Like . . . in a bedroom? I gulped. If that's where they were, did I want to know?

I chewed on my lip, trying to work up the courage to mount the steps and look. But I didn't have to, because I saw Jason coming out of the kitchen, the plastic cup he held sloshing liquid all over the floor.

Jude touched my shoulder. "You want me to stick around while you talk to him? For moral support?"

I shook my head. "It's probably better if you don't. He doesn't much like you, if you hadn't noticed."

Jude nodded. "I'll be around," he said. "Find me if you need a ride or anything." And then he disappeared into the throng of bodies surrounding us.

I pushed my way through them to Jason.

Jason looked surprised when he recognized me. "What are you doing here, Azazel?" he asked.

"I'm looking for you," I said. "I have something I need to tell you."

He took a long swig of his drink.

"Can we go somewhere and talk? Somewhere quiet?" I asked him.

Jason raised his eyebrows. "What do you want to talk about Azazel? Can't you see I'm drinking here? I'm having fun. I thought you'd be glad. Isn't that what you want me to do? Stop being so serious? Live it up?"

"No," I said. "No, I need to tell you something very important."

"So tell me."

"It's so loud and crowded here. Can't we just – "

"Tell me," he said. "I've got shit to do."

I looked at the floor. "You're drunk."

"Hell yeah, I am," said Jason. "No drunker than you always get, though."

"It's about the bell, Jason."

"Oh, the bell. Come on, Azazel, can't you let that go? I thought Sutherland stuck it in your purse, anyway. Sutherland's not a problem. I told you that, didn't I?"

"Sutherland didn't do it," I said.

"Then who did?"

"The Satanists," I said.

Jason's expression froze thoughtfully. "The Satanists?"

"I found a ritual on the internet telling me that the Invocation to Azazel could be completed with a bell and other stuff. I think the bell was planted to scare me. Or to tip me off. I don't know. Maybe they thought once the ritual was completed, I'd be on their side completely or something."

191

"Wait," said Jason. "The Satanists? Who? Michaela Weem?"

"No," I said. "I mean, I think she's behind it, but I don't think she's here."

"Then who?"

"There's only one person who's close to me, who has ties to the Satanists, and who showed up right before the bell appeared in my purse."

"There is?"

"Lilith, Jason. It's Lilith. And she's obviously trying to seduce you so that I'll get angry with you."

Jason glared at me witheringly before chugging his drink again. "Lilith? Jesus, Azazel, this is ridiculous."

"You don't believe me?" I said. God, what was wrong with Jason? Why didn't he see that what I was saying was the truth?

"Look, I'm drunk, and you're grasping at straws."

"Mr. Sutherland said that someone close to me was trying to complete the ritual," I said.

"And you believed him? He's not exactly a reliable source, is he?"

"He wanted to trade information. He only got violent with me when I wouldn't tell him that you were Edgar Weem's son."

"What?" Jason looked confused. "I can't think about this right now, okay?"

"We have to. Lilith is staying in our house. We have to do something before she — "

"Before she what? Why do you hate Lilith so much, Azazel?"

"This isn't about the way I feel about her. This is about the fact that you and I are both in danger and that the Satanists are – "

"Spare me," said Jason. "I'm sick of your conspiracy theories. If it's up to you, we'll never be safe. We'll never be normal. You see danger everywhere. You're paranoid, and you need to get over it."

Jason drained his glass, turned his back on me, and started back for the kitchen.

"Jason!" I called after him, struggling to push through the bodies and keep up.

He turned on me. "I need some space, okay, Azazel? Just give me one night where I don't have to be the Rising Sun. Just give me one night where I don't have to think about this crap. Just give me one night to be normal. Okay? Is that too much to ask?"

His eyes blazed. Wounded, I hung back. But then Lilith slid between the crowded bodies and moved close to Jason. She was holding two plastic cups. She gave one to Jason. He took it from her and took a large gulp. The two surveyed me.

"Zaza," said Lilith. "You look like you might start crying. Are you okay?"

God. I hated her. How could she pretend to be concerned when she was plotting against me?

Jason laughed. "You should hear her latest paranoid

193

delusion, Lil. She thinks you're working for the Satanists. She thinks you put that bell in her purse after you performed an invocation over her body to invoke the demon Azazel."

Lilith's brow furrowed sympathetically. "Jesus, Zaza." She turned to Jason. "She's been under a lot of stress lately. She was nearly captured and then nearly raped. You shouldn't be too hard on her."

I gaped at Lilith. "Don't play dumb," I said to her. "I know it's true."

Lilith looked into her drink, pressing her lips together as if she were trying very hard to keep from saying something.

"What's your plan?" I said to her. "You think if you seduce Jason that I'll feel betrayed and kill him?"

"Jesus Christ!" Jason exclaimed. "You know I'd never do that."

"I used to think you'd never say I was paranoid and delusional too," I spat out. "I used to think you'd never run off without telling me where you're going and come home covered in blood, too stunned to speak. I used to think all kinds of things about you, Jason Wodden. Now I'm not sure if I even know you."

Jason rolled his eyes. "Screw this," he said. "I can't take this right now." He turned away from me and made his way into the crowd. Lilith started to follow him, but I darted forward and caught her by the arm.

"No," I said. "You don't go with him. There's no way I'm letting you go off with him now."

"You can't control Jason, you know," she said. "He's a big boy. He can do what he wants."

"Yeah?" I said. "Well, he's not doing you. Not on my watch." I started for the door to the house, pulling Lilith with me. "You're coming with me," I said. "We're going to go talk to Hallam. We'll see what he thinks about this."

Lilith struggled, but she walked with me. "I'm not going anywhere with you," she said. "You're going nuts. You're losing it Azazel. None of this is real. You realize that don't you? You're paranoid. Can't you see that you're paranoid?"

"Maybe if I'd been a little more paranoid in Bramford, none of that shit would have happened," I retorted.

I pulled her out the door and onto the porch. Once in the muggy night air, she wrenched her arm out of my grip.

"Don't fool yourself, Azazel," said Lilith. "You didn't have any control over what happened to you in Bramford, just like you don't have any control over what's happening to you now. You're Azazel. The Vessel. The girlfriend of Jason. You're never going to get to choose what you want. Don't you realize that?"

"What are you talking about?" I said. Because it almost sounded to me like she was admitting that I was right. She was a Satanist. She was controlling my destiny. "I know everything that's going on here. I can stop what's going on."

"Well," said another voice, "not everything."

I whirled, looking for the person who owned the voice.

And I couldn't believe my eyes. Walking across the lawn to Rachel Kline's house were my two older brothers, Noah

195

and Gordon. I hadn't seen the two of them since the ritual in Bramford, back in October.

"Noah?" I gasped. "Gordon?" I looked at Lilith. "Why are they here?"

But she looked just as surprised as I did. "I don't . . ." She shook her head.

Noah and Gordon stopped in front of us, both grinning. Noah jammed his hands into his pockets. Gordon rubbed his chin. When I'd spoken to Chance earlier in the week, he'd said that they'd been planning to visit me. Was this that visit?

"Hey Zaza," said Noah.

"Lil' sis," said Gordon.

Suddenly, everything clicked into place. "Oh," I murmured, covering my mouth with my hand. "It was you two. You two stole the bell and performed the ritual."

Noah shrugged. "Well, yeah. After what happened to Mom and Dad, you didn't expect us to just give up, did you?"

"Gotta say, though, we're kind of disappointed in you, Zaza," said Gordon. "You really haven't been living up to your potential. Why couldn't you have just cooperated in October and saved us all this trouble?"

I shook my head. "So, you've been working with Michaela Weem or something?"

"She was really shaken up when she saw the two of you in Shiloh," said Noah. "The things she said she saw . . . Seriously, Zaza. Don't you know that you should get your

196

big brothers' approval before you start dating someone?"

"We don't like this Jason guy at all. He's bad, bad news," said Gordon.

"I'm never going to kill him," I said. "You two must understand that."

They shrugged. "There's some stuff we want to show you," said Gordon.

"You might change your mind," said Noah.

"Never," I said.

"Still," said Gordon, "we'd like you to come with us."

"No way," I said. "You two helped. You two tried to set me up to get raped by Toby. I don't trust you. I don't care if you are my brothers."

"You're talking like you have a choice," said Noah.

Damn it. What did that mean? "So you're going to take me by force?" I asked. Where was a gun when I needed it?

"If we have to," said Noah.

"It would be easier if we didn't have to do that," said Gordon. "You could just come voluntarily."

"What about me?" asked Lilith.

"She'll probably just run off and tell Jason about us if we let her go," said Noah to Gordon.

"Wait," I said. "Lilith isn't working with you?"

"Lilith?" said Noah. "Come on, Zaza. I know she's your friend and all, but she's way too stupid to pull anything like that off."

"Screw you," Lilith said darkly.

I didn't think. I just moved. My hand darted out and

grasped Lilith's. I broke out into a sprint, dragging her along.

We ran across the lawn of Rachel Kline's house. Behind us, I heard both Noah and Gordon cry out in surprise.

Lilith and I might have made it, even though she was slowing me down, her breath coming in gasps.

But before we could get off the lawn and onto the sidewalk (where there were cars to hide in, maybe one with unlocked doors and keys inside) a familiar figure appeared in our path.

"Jude!" I cried out in recognition and relief. "We have to get out of here. I'll explain later." I slowed as I approached him, glancing over my shoulder to see if Noah and Gordon were in pursuit.

I didn't see them anywhere.

Confused, I stopped, pulling Lilith to a stop next to me.

Jude ambled over to us, his arms clasped behind his back. "What's going on?" he asked.

"There are these two guys who were chasing us," I said, struggling to catch my breath. "I don't know where they went."

"I don't see anyone," said Jude.

I just shook my head. "We have to get out of here, anyway," I said. "They'll – "

Jude took his arms out from behind his back. He was holding a baseball bat.

"Jude?" I whispered.

He raised the bat over his head. "Sorry, Azazel," he said.

The bat came crashing down.

And everything winked out, like birthday candles that had just been blown out.

PART TWO

Is it like this
In death's other kingdom
Waking alone
At the hour when we are
Trembling with tenderness

-T.S. Eliot, "The Hollow Men"

CHAPTER TEN

To: Edgar Weem <eweem@risingsun.org>

From: Renegade Son <settingsun007@yahoo.com>

Subject: Big problems

Edgar,

Azazel's disappeared. Jason's gone after her. I don't know where either of them are, and if I find out you've got anything to do with this, so help me.

I still have an email that I could send out, you know. To everyone in the Sons. With all of your secrets, emblazoned for all of them to see.

Get me a secure, untraceable number, so that I can talk to you.

You've got twenty-four hours.

Hallam

"She's not answering her phone!"

The voice was tight with panic. I recognized the voice. I thought.

"Chill out. Maybe she's away from the phone or has it turned off or something."

That was Noah. Noah, my brother. If I could hear Noah talking, everything must be fine.

"She wouldn't be away from her phone right now. There's no way. Something's not right," said the panicky voice. The familiar voice. Who did that voice belong to?

It was dark. It was dark, and my head hurt.

"Noah's right. You've got to calm down. I'm sure she's okay. She's been taking care of herself for quite some time. And she's not a weak woman. She's got spunk, you know?"

Gordon. Both Gordon and Noah? Was it Christmas or something? Had they come home? Was I in my bed, early in the morning, listening to them talk to Mom and Da –

No. Mom and Dad were dead.

And it was dark because my eyes were closed.

My eyes snapped open as it all came back to me. The party. Jude advancing on me with a baseball bat over his head. The pain. The pain in my head had to be because of that.

I wanted to thrash about and scream, but I forced myself not to move so that I could assess my situation.

I was lying on my side in the back of a speeding vehicle. It looked like the interior of a mini-van of some kind. The carpet was gray and mussed. The back seat had been removed. My hands were tied behind my back. My feet were similarly bound. Lilith was lying next to me, also tied up. Her eyes were closed. Maybe she was still out.

I forced my breathing to stay steady and closed my eyes again. I didn't want them to know that I was awake. Maybe if I just listened, I could find out something useful.

"Spunk?" the familiar voice was repeating. It was Jude, of course. "She could still be vulnerable. I'm worried."

"We'll be at her house in fifteen minutes," said Gordon. "Sit tight. We'll check on her."

Her house? Who was this woman they were talking about? Where were we going? I wished I had an idea of how long we'd been travelling. I'd been knocked out. How long did someone stay knocked out, usually? I didn't know. And for all I knew they'd drugged me in some way too. Had I had anything to drink at the party? I couldn't remember, but I did feel very groggy and disoriented.

Similar to the way I'd felt the morning after the party on the beach actually.

"She should have answered the phone a long time ago," Jude insisted.

"Look, what is it you're worried has happened to her anyway?" Noah asked.

"You said that Azazel was accusing Lilith of setting her up when you found her, didn't you?" Jude asked.

"So?" said Noah.

"On behalf of our coven, right?" said Jude.

Coven. So Jude was a Satanist, was he? And I'd never suspected him. How stupid could I get really? Of all the people I could pick to trust, I had to pick the one working for the Satanists, didn't I? God.

"Yeah, but big deal. Why does that matter?" asked Noah.

"What if she told that theory to Jason?" asked Jude.

"What if she did?" asked Gordon.

"If she did, it would take Jason two seconds to connect the dots once Azazel disappeared," said Jude. "He'd know exactly where we were headed."

He would? Then I should be able to figure it out, too,

shouldn't I? Where would the Satanists take me?

Bramford?

Had I really slept through a fourteen-hour car drive? No, I didn't think we were headed to Bramford. That wasn't the center of Satanist activity, anyway. There was one person who'd be at the center of that.

Michaela Weem.

We were going to Shiloh. And Michaela Weem was the woman that they were trying to reach on the phone. I just knew it.

"So what if Jason did figure it out?" asked Gordon. "We've got a head start on him. And what could he have possibly done, anyway?"

"You really don't know anything about Jason, do you?" said Jude. "I'll never forget the night I saw him beat up this guy for saying something suggestive about Azazel. The look on his face. And the way he took that guy down. It was so precise. So deadly."

Jude was right. Jason would be trying to protect me. He might already be with Michaela Weem. He was looking for me, even as I listened to them speak in the front of the van. I could count on Jason. He wouldn't let anyone hurt me. Just the thought of someone trying to molest me would throw him into a rage.

Wait. I groped for thoughts, putting pieces together. I felt groggy. Jude was a Satanist.

Oh, God. Jason had been right all along. Jude had put the damned bell in my purse. Jude had completed the ritual,

206

along with Gordon and Noah. He must have drugged me the night of the party on the beach. Maybe he'd drugged me now.

"I'm calling her again," said Jude.

"You've called her like fifteen times," said Noah.

"You need to calm down," said Gordon.

If Michaela wasn't answering her phone, then maybe it did mean that Jason had found her. Jason would make Michaela tell him where Jude, Noah, and Gordon were holding me. Jason would swoop in and save me. Everything would be okay.

"It's ringing," said Jude. "It's not just going to voicemail. I think that's a good sign."

Jason would come after me, wouldn't he? I remembered the last time I'd seen Jason. His last words to me had been, "You're paranoid, and you need to get over it." He'd been really, really angry with me. What if he didn't come after me? What if he thought that I ran off with Jude? What if he simply didn't care anymore? All of this stuff with the Satanists was my fault, anyway. If Jason had never met me, he'd never have had to deal with them. The Sons were out of the picture, but the Satanists weren't. What if Jason just figured he was better off now?

"Dammit," said Jude from the front of the van. "No answer."

"I'm telling you, we're almost there," said Gordon. "Give it a few minutes. We'll see her."

"I'd just feel better if I could talk to her first," said Jude.

"I'm really starting to get worried."

"Starting to?" Noah muttered.

I opened my eyes again. What if Jason wasn't coming to save me? What was I going to do then? What did Jude, Noah, and Gordon want with me anyway? The last time I'd seen a group of Satanists, they'd wanted me to have sex with Toby and kill Jason. The last time I'd seen Michaela Weem, she wanted me to kill Jason. All things considered, they probably wanted me to kill Jason. But if that were the case, why were they taking me away from Jason? And please God, tell me that they weren't planning some kind of ritual sex with me. Please, God.

They couldn't be, could they? Jude was gay. And Gordon and Noah were my brothers. Okay, we weren't actually blood related, but we'd grown up together. So, they wouldn't. I knew my brothers. I remembered all kinds of things that we'd done together as children, like the time that Noah had gotten a flat tire on Gordon's bike and enlisted my help to try to hide the bike from Gordon. When Gordon had found out, we'd played innocent, like we didn't know how the bike had gotten a flat tire, Gordon had –

My thoughts were interrupted by the shrill ring of a cell phone.

The ringtone cut off abruptly. "Mom?" said Jude's voice.

Mom? Jude was getting calls from his mom? That was weird, wasn't it? I realized that in Florida, I'd never met Jude's parents. Was his mom calling him from Bradenton? Did his mom know he was a Satanist?

"You," Jude's voice said, but it was angry and menacing now. Was he still talking to his mom? "What have you done with her? Let me talk to her."

Wait. Did someone have Jude's mom?

"Sure," said Jude. "I know where she is. I have her, in fact."

He had her? He had his mom? I was really, really confused.

"No," said Jude. "No, absolutely not. No deal."

"Who are you talking to?" asked Noah.

My sentiments exactly. Who *was* Jude talking to?

Jude ignored Noah. "If you hurt her . . ." He paused. "Well, of course I'm not going to hurt Azazel."

Me? He was talking about me? Who was he talking to? What was going on?

"Who is it, Jude?" Gordon demanded.

Jude ignored him. "Listen, there's no way I'm going to trade her for Azazel, you idiot. If you don't let my mother go, I'm going to hunt you down and – " Jude stopped talking, as if he'd been interrupted. He paused for a long time. Finally, he just breathed, "Fuck you," in a gravelly voice.

"Who was that?" Gordon asked.

Jude didn't answer.

"Who was that?" Gordon asked again.

"Turn around," said Jude.

"Turn around?" asked Noah.

"Yeah," said Jude. "We can't go there. He's there."

They couldn't go there? Had Jude gotten a call from their destination? But I thought they were going to Michaela Weem's house.

"Who's there?" asked Noah. "Who were you talking to on the phone?"

"He's got my mother. He's threatening to hurt her if we don't give him Azazel," said Jude.

Who had Jude's mother? And who would want me? And what was Jude's mother doing in Shiloh? Weren't we in Shiloh? Were they taking me to Michaela Weem or not?

"Who's got your mother?" asked Gordon.

"Jason," said Jude. "Jason's got my mother."

Jason had Jude's mother? So Jason was trying to save me! He'd picked a kind of screwed-up way to do it, but he didn't hate me. That was good. Suddenly, I remembered that just hours before I'd argued with drunk Jason, he'd told Lilith that he couldn't exist without me. I couldn't believe that I'd doubted him.

"Big deal," said Noah. "Don't we want Jason dead anyway? We'll just go in, grab him, tie him up and wait until Azazel's ready to do him in."

"You don't understand," said Jude. "Jason was trained by the Sons of the Rising Sun. We'd be no match for him. Not like this."

"He's a kid," said Gordon. "How tough could he really be?"

"He's killed before," said Jude. "A guy named Sutherland owed Mom a favor, and was keeping an eye on Azazel for us. He got fresh, and no one's heard from him since."

Sutherland? Jesus, he was in on it too? He was working with the Satanists? Well, I guess it made sense that he knew about the invocation, then, didn't it? And why did Sutherland owe Jude's mom a favor? Who was Jude's mom, anyway?

"Yeah," said Noah, "but Jason wouldn't hurt Michaela. She's his mother too, isn't she?"

What?!

Oh God.

* * *

Now that I was looking at Jude, I didn't understand why I didn't see it before. Sure, Jude had bright purple hair and multiple piercings. Sure, he was wearing heavy eyeliner. All of that made him look different. Exotic. But his skin was the same shade as Jason's – dusky light brown. His face was the same shape as Jason's – heart-shaped. His eyes were like Jason's too. Big and dark. They looked alike. A lot alike. They were brothers. But before, I'd never made the connection, not even when Jude told me he was a quarter Native American. Like Jason. I was such an idiot. How had I trusted him?

Lilith and I were sitting in the back of the minivan. We were still tied up. We were parked on the side of a country road. The back hatch of the minivan was open, and Jude, Noah, and Gordon were peering in at us. Well, Noah and Gordon were looking at us. Jude was pacing back and forth behind the open hatch, swearing and running his hands through his hair. Noah and Gordon had long since given up trying to calm him down.

"Maybe we could go to a hotel," said Noah thoughtfully, gazing at Lilith and me.

"How are we going to get the two tied-up girls inside without attracting attention?" Gordon asked.

"Good point," said Noah.

"You should just let us go," I said. "You know that Jason isn't going to give up trying to find me. And it's a lost cause to try to get me to kill him. I never will."

"If we wanted your input, Zaza, we'd ask for it," said Noah.

"Well, at least let Lilith go," I said. "She doesn't have anything to do with this."

"Are you kidding?" asked Gordon. "She knows who Noah and I are. She'd run to the police right away."

"I wouldn't," said Lilith.

I glared at Lilith. For some reason, it pissed me off that she was so eager to say she wouldn't try to save us if they let her go. "When Jason finds you, the police are going to be the least of your problems," I said.

Noah rolled his eyes. "The way I figure it, this Jason guy cannot be as big of a deal as you say he is."

"I don't know, Noah," said Gordon. "He did bust Azazel out of Bramford in front of the entire coven. He shot two of the members in the leg, including a police officer."

Jude abruptly stopped pacing. He turned to us, his dark eyes intense. "I've got to go there," he said.

"Go where?" asked Noah.

"To my house," said Jude. "Jason might still be there, waiting with Mom. Maybe I could stop him, somehow. Save my mother."

"You just said that Jason was a total badass and that we'd never stand a chance against him," said Noah.

"I'd have the element of surprise," said Jude.

"Wouldn't matter," I said. "Jason doesn't get surprised easily."

"Shut up, Azazel," said Jude.

I looked from Jude to Lilith. "I sure have some taste in best friends, don't I?" I muttered.

"Shut up, Azazel," said Gordon.

"I'm game," said Noah. "It beats sitting around here. Let's go."

"Not all of us," said Jude. "Just me. If Jason sees Azazel, he'd probably just shoot us all and take her. No, we can't risk getting Azazel captured by Jason."

"Let's get this straight," I said. "If Jason does get me, he'll be rescuing me, not capturing me."

Gordon looked at Jude. "Can't you drug her again?" he asked.

I knew I'd been drugged! "Did you drug me that night on the beach, too, Jude?" I demanded.

Jude ignored me. "I have to go," he said. "She's my mother."

"What could Jason possibly do to her?" Gordon said.

"I told you, she hates him, and he hates her," said Jude.

"She's his mother," said Noah. "He's got to feel something for her, doesn't he?"

"She didn't raise him," said Jude.

"But she's his blood," said Gordon. "That's an important tie. If I ever met my biological parents, I would – "

"God, Gordon, not that again," said Noah. "Listen, Jude, why don't you and I both go? Gordon can stay here with the girls."

"If something happens to me, you two can go on without me," said Jude. "But we can't risk you too, Noah. I have to go alone."

"So how old are you, really, Jude?" I asked. "You can't be my age, like you said, can you? Are you and Jason twins?"

"Of course not!" Jude roared. "Don't ever even suggest that again."

"I don't see why you have to go alone," said Noah. "Wouldn't you be safer with me along?"

"So, then, you've got to be at least a year younger than us," I said. "Is Edgar Weem your dad too?"

"I'm going alone," said Jude. He turned to me. "Azazel, I don't have time for your questions right now. Let's just hope your boyfriend hasn't done anything to my mother that he's going to regret."

"How are you going to get there?" Noah asked.

"I'm taking the van," said Jude.

"So where are we going to be?" said Gordon.

"Here," said Jude.

"What if someone sees the girls?" said Gordon.

"Hide them," said Jude.

"Jude, I don't think this is a good plan," said Gordon.

"Me either," I said.

Gordon, Jude, and Noah all glared at me.

* * *

Jude was gone for a long time. When he returned, it was dark outside. Lilith and I were cold, huddled against a tree, still tied up. Gordon and Noah had led us away from the road, so that we were out of sight in case a car came by. Not many cars had come by, though. It had been an uneventful hour or two. Gordon and Noah didn't say much. Lilith was quiet too, but she had a look of wild terror in her eyes. I felt very, very calm. I wasn't worried at all.

I thought that was strange. I examined my lack of fear the way a scientist might examine a specimen. I felt detached from myself. I didn't know whether or not I should feel afraid. I just knew that feeling afraid wouldn't really do much of anything for me right now. Feeling afraid would keep me from thinking rationally. It would make me more likely to make a mistake, should an opportunity arise to escape. Hell, it would make it more likely that I didn't notice the opportunity arising. Overall, it made more sense to remain calm. Not to be afraid. So, I wasn't.

But I remembered the way I'd felt, just months ago, when Jason and I had been on the run from the Sons. I'd been in constant fear. Terror had gripped me and hadn't let go the entire time. I wasn't afraid anymore, however. Maybe I was desensitized to it. I realized that I hadn't felt that kind of crippling fear in a long time. I hadn't felt it when I'd been grabbed in the parking lot outside of the gun range. I'd been frightened when Mr. Sutherland was trying to rape and kill me, but I hadn't been immobilized. I'd been able to act. To save myself. What had changed?

I remembered that Mr. Sutherland had said, "Maybe you are imbued with the spirit of a demon," as I'd been running away from him. And I supposed that Jude or Noah or Gordon had completed the ritual. Was I . . .

But that was stupid.

I didn't believe in Azazel. I didn't believe that I'd been filled with his essence. No. I was just more sure of myself now. Back then, I hadn't been able to take care of myself. Now, I was stronger. I was capable.

And I couldn't imagine Noah and Gordon really hurting me. Not really.

Of course, I'd trusted my parents implicitly, and they'd set me up to be raped by Toby. Clearly, I didn't pick the best people to trust. I was constantly being betrayed by those I cared about the most and was closest to. I had to admit that I couldn't be sure exactly what Gordon and Noah were planning to do to me. And I couldn't be sure what they'd carry out, given the chance.

Now, they stood over Lilith and me, glaring down at us in the darkness, keeping watch to make sure that we wouldn't leave. Compared to the temperatures I was used to in Bradenton, the early spring Georgia air felt downright frigid. I shivered in my short-sleeved shirt.

I was glad when Jude reappeared with the van. He looked dejected and angry, however. He told Gordon and Noah that neither Jason nor Michaela had been there when he arrived. Instead, there had been a note from Jason, telling Jude that he'd meet him at the house the following afternoon. Jude was to bring me. They would trade. If Jude didn't show up, or didn't bring me, the note said, then Jason would hurt Michaela.

I shivered again when I heard that, not from the cold, but because I didn't like the idea of Jason using his mother's well-being as a bargaining chip for my safety. I didn't think he'd really hurt Michaela. Jason often relied on other people's impression of him as a dangerous guy. He used it as leverage to get what he wanted. When we were escaping from Bradenton, for instance, he'd put a gun to my head. He had no intention of shooting me, but he knew that my father wouldn't stand by and watch me get shot. So, he used that knowledge to get what he wanted. Jason was threatening Jude in the same way.

But it was different, because Jude was Jason's brother. Somehow, it just rubbed me the wrong way. I was relieved, however, because I thought that it meant Lilith and I would be released tomorrow. Jude wouldn't let anything happen to his mother.

But Jude didn't want to trade. He said that he wouldn't give in to Jason's demands, ever. It was too important that Jason be destroyed. Gordon and Noah seemed to agree. I was disappointed.

They decided they couldn't go back to Michaela's house if Jason had it under surveillance. They didn't want to take the chance that he'd sneak in and get me out.

They led Lilith and I back to the van, stuffed us in the back, and we drove for about twenty minutes. When they took us out of the van, we were parked outside an old house. It was dark and difficult to see, but the house looked like a rundown, white farmhouse. The wood siding was losing its paint. The windows were shattered, or missing completely. Vines grew up the sides of the walls. A sapling was breaking through the creaking wood of its porch. There was nothing around, except woods. We were all alone out here.

I had to hand it to Jude. This was the perfect place to hide us. Jason would never know to look for us here. And there was nowhere for me to escape to. It seemed hopeless. If Jude continued to be stubborn and called Jason's bluff, then Jason wouldn't have anything to bargain with.

What was I going to do? I had to get away from these guys. And I wasn't alone. I had Lilith to worry about.

CHAPTER ELEVEN

To: Renegade Son <settingsun007@yahoo.com>
From: Edgar Weem <eweem@risingsun.org>
Subject: Calm down
Hallam,
We both know that it's too dangerous for me to speak to you on the phone. I thought we'd also agreed that it was in everyone's best interests to keep Jason's secrets and my secrets.
Please don't threaten me, Hallam. You shouldn't labor under the delusion that you have power over me. You don't.
I have people on the Jason and Azazel situation. I'm sure we'll be able to locate them soon.
Edgar

Lilith and I slept on the floor in a room in the abandoned house. We were still tied up. It was hard to get comfortable. Jude and my brothers only gave us one blanket, so we huddled against each other for warmth. They told us that one of them would be watching the door at all times. There didn't seem much hope of escape.

I didn't feel much like snuggling against Lilith. Even though it had turned out that she wasn't working for the Satanists, I still couldn't bring myself to actually like her. I knew that I should feel bad for getting her into this situation. But mostly I just felt annoyed. It would be much easier for me to try to escape if I didn't have to worry about Lilith.

It was cold though, so I got close to her for body warmth. We lay in the dark, listening to the sounds of insects in the woods surrounding the abandoned house.

"Azazel," whispered Lilith.

"What?" I said.

"Do you think that they're going to make me go back to Bramford?"

Of course she was only worried about herself. What about Jason? What about me? "I'm going to get us out of this," I said.

"How?" she said.

"I don't know yet," I told her. "But I will. I promise you. And after that . . ." After that, I wanted her to go away, and I never wanted to see her again.

"It's okay," she said. "I know I haven't been the greatest best friend to you."

That was an understatement. I kept my mouth shut.

"I'm sorry," she said. "It's just that girls like you get everything. You're all sweet and naïve, and guys just eat that shit up. They fall in love with girls like you. And just because I'm not like that. Well, no one's ever going to fall in love with me, Zaza. I know it was wrong, but I—I couldn't handle it. I wanted to . . . ruin it, somehow. Like if I couldn't have it, I didn't want you to have it, either."

That was the most twisted thing I'd ever heard. "Lilith," I said, "you're the kind of girl that guys want. They want someone experienced, with big boobs and curves."

"No," she said. "They don't. They might want to have sex with me, but they don't really want someone like me. They want someone like you. No one wants me."

Poor Lilith. I rolled my eyes in the darkness. "I'm sure that someday you'll find someone," I said. "We're only seventeen. We've got time."

Lilith shivered under the covers. "I don't think so," she said. "In Bramford, I met Michaela Weem once. She came to visit after your parents died. She looked into my eyes, and she said that I would never be loved. Not even once before I died."

"Forget Michaela Weem," I said. "Seriously, Lilith. You can't believe that."

When the sun came up, it poured in through the windows, waking me up. Lilith was still asleep next to me. I lay on my back for a few minutes, surveying my surroundings. The room we were in was devoid of decoration or furniture, except for some peeling wallpaper on the walls. The floor was hardwood, splintering and warped in places. Two unadorned large windows blazed sunlight into the space.

Windows!

Why hadn't I thought of this last night?

Probably because it had been too dark to even see that the windows existed. Carefully, I wriggled out from under the blanket. Next to me, Lilith made a noise in her sleep but didn't wake up. It wasn't easy getting to my feet while my hands were tied behind my back, but I finally managed it, scooting to the wall and using it for support. Once standing, I walked over to one of the windows. The glass in it rippled a little. It was clearly old glass, which was probably a bad sign. It looked strong.

But I could probably just unlock the window and open it, provided the windows weren't nailed shut. Then Lilith and I could climb out of the window. We were on the second story, but it looked like we'd drop onto several springy bushes that surrounded the house. That should help to cushion our fall. Plus, as near as I could tell, we weren't up so high that a drop would cause us to break a limb or anything. I didn't think.

Of course, I realized that my hands were tied behind my back. I couldn't unlock or open the window without my hands. Breaking the window was pretty much out of the question too. We didn't have any furniture. Besides, that would be loud, and someone might hear me doing that, come rushing in, and put an end to my escape attempt.

As if reading my thoughts, Jude opened the door and strode into the room. I turned my back to the window, hoping he wouldn't realize I'd been contemplating an escape route.

"You're awake," he said.

I nodded. "I hope you've come in here to tell me that you've come to your senses and you're going to trade me for your mother this afternoon."

Jude sneered. "No way," he said. "Jason doesn't tell me what to do."

Something about the edge to his voice let me know he was serious. He hated Jason. I could see that now. And to think, all that time in Bramford, Jason had known that there was something off about Jude, and I'd never noticed. I should have trusted Jason, but hindsight was twenty-twenty.

"I don't know how he found us, anyway," Jude said. "How could he have had any idea who took you?"

I shrugged. "Well, Jason's pretty amazing." But Jude was right, now that I thought about it. How had Jason figured it out so quickly? He'd beaten us to Shiloh. Was there something odd about that?

Jude glowered at me. "So I hear. Been spending my whole life hearing about Jason."

I didn't say anything.

"My mother never shut up about him. About her visions. About the abomination. But I used to wonder why, if he was such an abomination, she spent so much time talking about him." Jude walked around me and stood at the window himself. He stared through the glass. "If it weren't for the fact that everyone else is convinced that you have to kill him, I'd kill him myself.

"He's so self-righteous," Jude continued. "Thinking he can protect you. That night on the beach, he never knew that I had performed the ritual and placed the bell in your bag. Dingle's bell. There was a certain poetry to the way that it represented Azazel and also fit the ritual. It was just like Azazel to steal something from an authority figure for his own purposes. Like weapons. Like fire. I thought of that. *Me.* And I carried it out. And Jason never knew. He was clueless."

"I'll never kill him," I said. "You have to know that. You know how much I love him."

Jude snorted, still not looking at me. "You two have been arguing a hell of a lot, though, haven't you? And for all you know, he was screwing Lilith."

"He was not. There's no way he . . ." Jude was wrong.

Jude turned back from the window. He took my arm and began to lead me out of the room. "We've got some things to show you, Azazel," he said. He smiled. "But, just between us, I kind of hope you're right. I hope that when it comes down to it, you aren't able to kill him after all, because I'd love to step in and finish the job."

I jerked my arm out of his grasp. "You're no match for Jason," I said.

He snatched my arm back. "We'll just see about that, won't we?"

* * *

Noah had a laptop, which was running off battery power. There wasn't any electricity in the abandoned house. Gordon had the laptop open and was crouched over it on the floor. We were all in a large room on the first floor. Probably a parlor or a sitting room of some kind. There wasn't any furniture in this room, either, but the walls were decorated in graffiti. Someone had spray painted a large message proclaiming that Randy loved Sara, "4-ever +

always." There was also a distorted mural of a naked woman on one of the walls, also rendered in spray paint.

"Gordon, you're going to run the battery down," Noah was saying.

Jude was still clutching my arm. We stood together in the doorway.

"This battery will last hours," said Gordon.

"Not if it's running video," said Noah.

"It's not running video right now," said Gordon.

"No, but – "

Jude cleared his throat. Both of my brothers turned to look at us.

"Where's Lilith?" asked Gordon.

"Still asleep in the room," said Jude.

"Should someone be watching her?" asked Gordon.

Jude glared at him, but he dropped my arm and left the room. Noah got up and came to me. He untied my hands, and I stretched them, rubbing my fingers against each other. I hadn't realized how uncomfortable I'd been tied up until I wasn't. Noah led me further into the room.

"Sit down," he told me.

"What's going on?" I asked.

"We have some things to show you," said Gordon.

"Show me?" I asked. How? What were they going to show me?

Gordon set the laptop down in front of me, so that the screen was facing me. He had a video file open. It was paused, but I could see a woman's face, frozen in the middle of speech.

"What is this?" I asked.

"We're just not sure that you know everything about Jason that there is to know," said Noah. "We want to make sure you're informed, little sis."

"I know Jason better than I know anyone on earth," I countered, folding my arms over my chest.

"So you know about the sorority girls," said Gordon.

"Yes," I said. "I do." But I remembered something that Hallam had said to me, in the kitchen in our apartment. Something about what Jason had done that night. And the way I remembered it, Jason had told me that he hadn't done anything but watch.

Gordon raised his eyebrows. "You do?"

I stared him down.

Gordon reached around the laptop and hit play on the video. The woman's face unfroze. She was young – maybe in her mid-twenties. She had a large scar on her face. It twisted over her features, purple and contorted. Her voice was halting and hesitant.

"They left me for dead," she was saying.

An off-screen voice asked, "So, they didn't leave any intentional survivors?"

"No. They were there to kill us all," she said.

"And do you know why they came to kill you?"

"I don't know. I really don't know. They said something about us running a brothel or something, but that was just stupid. We were a sorority. We had boyfriends. Maybe sometimes, girls even had flings. But we weren't doing anything wrong or anything illegal."

"And they've never caught the men who did this?"

"Caught them? They've hardly even looked for them. At the beginning, there was a lot of media attention and the police made a lot of promises. But they only talked to me once. And they've never made any arrests. They say they don't have any evidence."

I looked at Noah and Gordon. "I don't really think there's any reason for me to watch this," I said. "Jason told me all about it."

"Just keep watching," said Gordon.

I rolled my eyes. Sure, this was a horrible, terrible thing that Hallam had done. But both Hallam and Jason had been acting under the direction of the Sons. None of it had been their idea. And the Sons demanded that their members blindly obey.

"Can you tell us what happened that night?" asked the unseen voice on the video.

The girl looked away from the camera. "I can try," she said, but her voice sounded unsteady.

"Take your time."

The girl took a deep breath. She didn't look back at the camera, but instead down at the ground. "There were two of them," she said. "They were both young. One was maybe twenty or so. The other one was a kid. He couldn't have been more than fifteen or sixteen. That was what disturbed me the most. The fact that he was just a kid. He looked so

227

innocent. He didn't seem the least bit bothered by what was going on. It seemed so normal for him."

I bit my lip. I knew it wasn't normal for Jason. It had really disturbed him. I remembered the way he'd talked to me about it. The haunted, empty look in his eyes. This woman didn't know what she was talking about.

"I didn't know what was going on in the beginning," she continued, "because I was asleep in my bedroom. It was late. Maybe two in the morning or something. I don't know. Anyway, I woke up and there was this figure standing over my bed with a gun. It was the kid. He told me to get up and come with him. He had three of the other girls with him. Apparently, he was rounding everyone up out of their beds. I didn't know why. If they were just going to kill us all, wouldn't it have been more merciful just to put bullets in our heads while we slept? Why did he have to wake me up? Why did he have to make me watch?"

The girl put her head in her hands and started to cry softly.

I looked away. I didn't want to know this. I really didn't think I wanted to know this. "It doesn't matter what you show me," I said to Noah and Gordon. "You can't change how I feel about Jason."

"Just watch," said Noah.

The unseen voice was speaking, gently. "Isn't it true that they did discover some of the girls shot in their beds?"

The girl raised her tearstained face. "Yes, the police said that they did. But there were at least ten of us that the kid rounded up. He took us downstairs, into our kitchen and he made us stand in the middle of the room. He sat on the counter and talked to us."

"Talked to you? What did he say?"

"The stuff about the brothel, like I said. He said that he had to do it, because we were doing illegal and immoral things. He didn't seem upset about it at all. He didn't even seem sorry. He was very matter-of-fact about it. While he was talking, Tami – she was the president of the sorority – she managed to get hold of a butcher knife. I could see that she had it, but I didn't let on. I didn't know what she thought she was going to do with it, but she had it.

"Then," continued the girl, "the other guy came in. The older guy. He and the kid started to argue. The older guy was saying that the kid was making it harder than it needed to be. They should just shoot them and be done with it. There wasn't any reason to drag it out. And the kid was saying that we deserved to know why we were dying. And they were yelling at each other. They were distracted, and Tami snuck up behind the older guy. She had the knife, and she started to raise it to . . . I don't know . . . stab him, maybe, I . . . But the kid saw her. And then . . ."

The girl looked away again, shaking her head.

"What happened then?" prompted the voice.

"I don't really know," said the girl. "It was dark and it was so fast. There was all this gunfire and scuffling. And everyone started to try to run then. But I couldn't move. I just stood there. I was frozen and I couldn't move! The older guy ran out of the kitchen, chasing down the other girls. He was yelling and screaming then. This crazy screaming. Like he was insane or something. There was blood everywhere. And Tami was on the floor. She was bleeding, but she was still alive. The kid was standing over her. He was holding the knife. I was crying.

"I lurched forward all at once. Like I finally had control of my muscles again. I fell on my knees next to Tami and the kid swung the knife at me. He cut open my face, and I crumpled onto the floor and waited for him to kill me. I was bleeding so much. It was getting all over the tile floor in the kitchen. It was everywhere. I could hardly see through the blood. And I couldn't move. Not really. I just lay there. And waited.

"The older guy came back into the room. He shot Tami in the forehead, and she stopped moving. He looked at the kid and he said, 'Thanks. She was going to kill me.'

"The kid didn't say anything. He just stared down at Tami, still holding the knife that was covered in my blood. He dropped the knife. It clattered to the floor.

"'I'll always have your back like that,' said the older guy to the kid.

"But the kid didn't even look at him. 'Is she dead?' he said, pointing his gun at Tami.

"'Yes,' said the older guy.

"And the kid just opened fire on her. He shot her and shot her and shot her. Pumping bullets into her dead body, over and over and over again. And I remember that I could see his face, while he was doing that. And . . . he was smiling." The girl broke down into fresh sobs.

The video ended.

"Is that what Jason told you?" said Gordon pointedly.

I didn't say anything.

"Well is it?" asked Noah.

"He didn't give me a blow-by-blow," I muttered. "It's hard for him to talk about."

"How could you love someone who was capable of something like that?" asked Gordon. He sounded genuinely puzzled.

"How do I know this video is even real?" I asked. "Jason didn't tell me that anyone survived. Maybe you guys just made it up. Maybe you got some chick to tell some bogus story."

"So he didn't tell you much about it at all," said Noah.

"Maybe he even lied to you," said Gordon.

No. I didn't think he'd lied. Why tell me anything about it at all if he were going to lie about it? If he were going to lie, wouldn't he just have lied and said it never happened? That didn't make sense. And what I'd said was true. Jason hadn't talked to me about the evening in detail.

I shook my head. "Or maybe you're lying to me," I said to them. "After all, you've lied to me before. You lied to me about who our family was. You've tricked me and betrayed me and captured me and tied me up. Why in the hell would I trust you?"

"We're your family, Azazel," said Gordon. "We're bound

231

together. You may not understand everything we do, but we do it because we want the best for you."

I snorted. "Right," I said. "You keep trying to turn me into a vessel for an ancient demon so I can commit murder. That's totally the best thing for me."

"That's the best thing for the world, Azazel," said Noah. "Jason is evil. I don't know why you can't see that. He's a being who lives only for destruction and pain. He delights in harming others. He has no regard for human life. The idea of my little sister being under the influence of someone like that is driving me crazy. Yeah, maybe tying you up has been a little extreme. But this is an extreme situation. We're talking about the fate of the human race here."

I gazed at Noah in disbelief. "You really believe that junk? You really believe Michaela Weem?" I looked at Gordon. "You really believe it too?"

"Tradition, Azazel," said Gordon. "This is the way of our family. We can't abandon our roots. It binds us together. It makes us who we are."

"Michaela Weem is a prophet," said Noah.

"Jason's not evil," I said.

"You've seen him kill people," said Noah.

"Only to protect me," I said. "Only to protect himself."

"And the girls in the sorority house?"

"He didn't kill any of them," I said. "That girl didn't see him kill any of them either."

"So you do believe the video is genuine?" asked Gordon.

"No," I said. "I don't. I don't know what I believe. But I

know that I trust Jason more than I trust the two of you."

"You trust Jason?" said a voice. It was Jude. He was standing in the doorway with Lilith, whose hands were still tied behind her back. "That's why you and I went to that party in Bradenton, then, right? Because you trusted him so much."

I looked at Jude. "It's not the same," I said.

"If he was lying to you about Lilith, then he might have been lying about anything," said Jude.

"Nothing was going on between me and Jason," said Lilith.

Jude laughed. "Oh, tell the truth, Lilith. Or are you afraid your friend Azazel won't like you anymore?" He paused. "Oh, wait. I forgot. She already hates your guts. What have you got to lose really?"

"That is the truth," said Lilith. "Nothing was going on."

I swallowed. "What about that conversation I heard you two having? What were you going to show Jason? What did you show Jason?"

Lilith rolled her eyes. "Jesus, Zaza. We're being held against our will by crazy people in the middle of nowhere, and you're worried about whether or not I flashed Jason?"

"You flashed Jason?" I repeated.

Lilith pressed her lips together.

"Ready to see some more?" asked Gordon.

"More?" I said.

It went on for hours. Gordon and Noah had more videos. Testimonies from people in two other incidents. One Jason had told me about. A gang war that the Sons had ordered him to be a part of. One that Jason hadn't. It involved vigilante-style justice carried out on a gang of bank robbers who'd slaughtered all their hostages. The robbers had escaped a jail sentence because of a technicality. In the videos, faces stared bleakly into the camera. They described Jason. He was always wielding a gun. He was always calm. He was never sorry. According to the testimonies on the videos, Jason was a cold and efficient killer. However, I did have to note that none of the testimonies featured a person who had actually witnessed Jason killing anyone. And none of the testimonies were about Jason working alone. Still, there were chilling similarities. According to several people, Jason had surveyed the dead bodies with a smile on his face. Jason also seemed fond of herding people in one place and explaining to them why they were being killed. Whether he actually did the killing or Hallam did wasn't clear. I told myself it didn't matter.

But as the day wore on, I began to wonder if it did.

After a barrage of video, Noah and Gordon dug through the rest of their evidence. Police reports. Transcripts of interviews. Photographs of dead bodies. They showed me the pictures of the kitchen in the sorority house. There was blood spattered on the ceiling. They showed me a picture of Tami's body. Her face was mottled with bullet holes – her features barely recognizable. With everything they showed me, they pressed me. How could someone do these kinds of things and not be evil? How could I claim to love someone like this? Why couldn't I see that Jason was a monster?

I refused to talk to them after a while. I refused to answer their questions. I didn't know what to say. I felt like I knew Jason well, but I was realizing that I knew very little about Jason's past. I had never really tried to get him tell me about it, because I had assumed that it was too painful for him to talk about it. It didn't matter. I loved Jason for who he was. I loved Jason because he was everything to me. So I didn't ask. I didn't demand he spell out everything for me. Besides, after we'd gotten to Florida, Jason had wanted to leave all of that behind him. He'd just wanted us to be normal kids. I wouldn't have ruined that by forcing him to dredge up old memories.

I told myself that the Jason that I knew was a kind and good person. But I couldn't help but remember the way that Jason had ripped at my clothes in a hotel in Pennsylvania, the insistent way his hands had twisted my skin. I couldn't help but remember watching Jason quickly and systematically shoot the members of the Sons in my aunt's dining room. I couldn't help but remember Jason, just a few days ago, covered in blood, staring blankly as I tried to clean him up.

Worst of all, I remembered things that Michaela Weem had said to me when we'd met her in November. Things like Jason was going to burn thousands of people and that he was going to eat me alive. Things like our combined power would drive men mad. And –

It had!

I didn't like to think about that. Jason and I had never talked about it. Maybe it was because it scared us too much to acknowledge that it had actually happened. But a group of ten or fifteen members of the Sons had all gone crazy. Right after Jason and I kissed. They'd been trying to shoot us and then they'd all just come completely mentally unglued, wandering around like frightened children.

It had been easy for me to dismiss the event. I'd told myself I didn't believe what Michaela Weem had said. I'd told myself that she was crazy. I'd told myself that I didn't believe in fate or destiny. I'd told myself that as long as I believed in Jason, in us, then none of that mattered.

But it did matter.

It was time I was honest with myself, even if I wouldn't be honest with Jude and my brothers. I was terrified of Jason. I was terrified of Jason and me together.

It had been easy, all of those months, to blame my uneasiness and fear on external sources like the Sons. If I were afraid of the Sons, I could fight them. I had control. I could learn to shoot guns. I could spin conspiracy theories about Mr. Sutherland and bells being put in my purse. As long as it was something outside of myself, then I could fight it. But the truth was, I was completely out of control.

I didn't know who Jason was. I didn't know who I was. I didn't know who we were together. The Sons thought Jason was the Rising Sun – a messiah who would unite the world under one government. The Satanists thought Jason was evil incarnate – a monster who would destroy free will and enslave the world. The Satanists thought I was the messiah – the one sent to kill Jason and end his reign of terror. As for what the Sons thought of me, I had no idea. I'd thought that I was nothing more than a blip on their radar until Sutherland had showed me those email messages and hinted that the Sons thought that I was the Kali to Jason's Shiva. His dark half. Finally, there were Michaela Weem's prophecies. She said that her visions had changed when Jason had showed up in my life. She said that now she saw visions in which Jason and I did horrible things together.

Whoever you asked, they thought that Jason and I were powerful. And they all thought that there was some sort of capacity for badness in the cards for the two of us.

I was away from Jason now. Maybe I was getting a little bit of distance on the situation. I'd been raised to believe that I made my own destiny. I didn't want to believe that there was anything to what anyone else said about Jason and I. Especially when these people were trying to predict the future, something I regarded as impossible. But the Sons and the Satanists came from completely different backgrounds. They had nothing in common with each other. Except for the fact that they'd both picked Jason and me as either a messianic or destructive force. They disagreed about which was which, but that wasn't really important.

Could it really just be a coincidence?

Or could it be true somehow? Were Jason and I powerful? Did one of us or both of us together have the capacity to destroy the world?

I didn't know what I thought about the stories that Gordon and Noah were telling me. I didn't know if I believed them. And I didn't know if it mattered to me if Jason were actually a killer or not. I was really more concerned, I realized, not with the fact that Jason might have killed people, but with the idea that Jason might have lied to me about it. I'd always thought that the first people he'd killed had been the members of the Sons who'd killed my parents. I did know that I had to face up to the evidence about Jason and me.

As more and more of it piled up, I had to realize that Jason and I weren't normal. That we were vastly different than most teenagers. And that there might be something about us, something special, something powerful, something destructive. Even though the thought seemed insane, I was going to drive myself insane if I didn't accept it.

I was sinking in my thoughts, drifting away. I didn't see the documents that floated in front of me. I didn't hear Noah's or Gordon's voice anymore. I lost track of all the things they showed me. None of it mattered anymore.

There was only one thing that mattered, and I told them when they were finally finished. The floor of the abandoned room was littered with papers and manila folders. I was sprawled Indian style on the floor, surveying my brothers, Jude, Lilith, and the evidence. The afternoon sun streamed through the windows, giving everything a lazy, tired glow. I looked them in the eye, one after another, and I said, "It doesn't matter. I won't kill him. I'll never kill him. I don't care what he's done."

I knew that was true, too. Even if I became convinced that Michaela Weem was absolutely right, and that lurking somewhere inside Jason was the monster she said was there – dangerous, destructive, violent – even then, I couldn't kill Jason. I loved him too much.

Everyone stared at me as if there were something completely wrong with me.

Jude's phone rang. We all turned to look at him as he answered it. He didn't say much, just listened. I watched his face contort in a mix of rage and pain. He ripped the phone away from his ear and dashed it against the floor.

No one said anything.

Jude seethed, pacing in a frenzy.

Finally, Noah said, "What? What is it?"

Jude stopped. "It was him," he said.

"Jason?" asked Noah.

"I have to go," said Jude. He crossed the room to a suitcase that sat in the corner. Knelt by it. Twisted the combination. Opened it. He took out the keys to the van. So that was where they kept them, was it? Now, if only I could figure out some way to get down here to that suitcase. Maybe tonight. But how was I going to get past the combination?

"Wait, you can't just go," said Noah. He was on his feet, moving to intercept Jude.

"I'm going," Jude said, weaving around him.

Gordon had stood up too. "You can't hurt Jason!" he

called after Jude. "Azazel has to – "

"Fuck Azazel," retorted Jude, and he was out the door.

We heard the van start and drive off.

"Dammit," said Gordon, staring after him.

* * *

Less than twenty minutes later, the door to the house burst open and Jude came barreling back in. He was carrying a bundle of cloth. It had red stains on it. Was there something inside it?

Gordon got to his feet and stalked over to Jude. "You can't just run off like that," he said. "You can't just take the van. What if there was an emergency?"

"Emergency?" repeated Jude. "This *was* an emergency."

"What happened?" asked Noah.

Jude clutched the bundle tighter. "If he'd only been there when I'd gotten there, I would have – "

"You wouldn't have done anything," said Gordon sharply. "Because this isn't just about you."

"But it's about my mother!" Jude said, his face twisting like he was about to cry. "He's got my *mother*. Do you understand that?"

"What happened?" said Noah.

"What happened?" repeated Jude. "What happened! That bastard!" And Jude choked up.

"Jude?" prompted Noah.

Jude flung the bundle of cloth at Noah. Noah caught it awkwardly. He knelt and set it on the floor. Then he stared at it. It was close to where I sat. I could see it better now. It looked like a ripped piece of dress or skirt. And the red stains had a brown tint to the edges. They were some kind of liquid. The liquid was still wet.

I refused to let my brain make the logical connection. Jason wouldn't have . . . Jason had been bluffing, like I'd thought. When Jude called his bluff, he hadn't . . . He couldn't . . .

"Unwrap it," Jude ordered, his voice harsh.

Noah hesitated.

"Do it!" Jude said.

Gingerly, Noah began to pull away at the edges of the cloth, peeling it back so that he could see what was inside.

Abruptly, he jumped back and cried out a little, tossing the bundle away from him.

It landed right in front of me. I swallowed hard, but I couldn't help myself. I leaned forward. Looked inside.

It was a finger.

CHAPTER TWELVE

Text message transcript between Jason Wodden and Hallam Wakefield, 03/15/09, 05:15 PM

Jason Wodden: any tips for cauterizing a wound?

Hallam Wakefield: are you hurt? where are you?

Jason Wodden: am fine. not my wound. have u done it before or not?

Hallam Wakefield: tell me where you are!!!

Jason Wodden: can't. i tried to do it and botched it. wound still bleeding heavily.

Hallam Wakefield: give me your location.

Hallam Wakefield: jason?

I let out a little gasp. Muffled it immediately with my hand. I wanted to look away, but I couldn't. The severed finger sat inside the stained cloth, blood still seeping from it. It was a woman's index finger. She had a long, manicured nail. "Oh," I whispered, shaking my head. "Oh, oh, oh."

Gordon pushed past Jude to see what was in the bundle. He turned on his heel and went back to Jude, grabbing Jude by the shoulders. "How did you get this? What happened?"

Jude was sobbing. Huge tears were spilling out of eyes. He didn't talk. He didn't look at Gordon. He just cried.

Gordon shook Jude hard. "Stop it," Gordon ordered. "Talk to me, Jude."

"He called me," Jude said through his tears.

"We were all here when that happened," said Gordon. "What did he say?"

"He said . . ." Jude's sobs cut him off.

Gordon shook Jude again. "What did he say?"

"He said, 'Your mother has something she'd like to tell you.' And then I heard her screaming and screaming and screaming. And then he hung up." Jude sniffled. "When I got there, I found this. It was still warm."

"Oh," I whispered. "Oh. Oh."

"Jesus," said Noah.

He did it. He did it. He actually hurt Michaela because I didn't show up. Oh God. Oh God. Jason.

"There was another note," said Jude. "It said that if I didn't bring Azazel tomorrow, I'd find more pieces." He shuddered.

"She's his own mother," said Gordon, dropping Jude's shoulders and coming to look at the finger again. "How could do that to his mother?"

"He's evil," whispered Noah. "He's just pure evil." He looked at me. "And you won't kill him."

I stood up then. "It's a trick!" I screamed.

"What?" said Jude.

I advanced on Jude. "It's a trick," I repeated. "It's not a real finger. It's not a real finger. You're just trying to get me to kill Jason. You're all lying to me!" I shoved Jude then, hard.

He stumbled back from me, surprised. There were still tears in his eyes and his nose was running. He recovered, rubbing his nose with the back of his hand, a movement that made him look so much like Jason, it hurt. "You think I'm faking this?" he demanded.

"You faked everything else," I shrieked, shoving him again.

Jude shoved me back.

"Hey," said Gordon, grabbing me and pulling me away from Jude. "Don't shove my sister."

Jude flipped him off. "Her fucking boyfriend is cutting up my mother!" he yelled. "I'll shove her if I feel like it."

Gordon put me behind him. "Jude," he said. "Give me the keys to the van."

"No," said Jude. Jude reached behind Gordon and grasped my wrist. He yanked me over to him. "No," he said. "No, I'm taking Azazel, and I'm taking the van, and she's going to tell me where the hell Jason is."

I tried to pull away from Jude. "I don't know where he is," I said.

"Jude," said Gordon, "let go of Azazel." He moved forward, reaching for me.

"No," said Jude, and he reached into his jacket and pulled out a gun.

Gordon stopped moving.

"Shit," said Noah.

"Put down the gun, Jude," said Gordon, but his voice was shaking.

Jude aimed the gun at Gordon, then at Noah. Then he put the gun to my temple. In a sick sense of déjà vu, I remembered Jason holding me this way, tight against his body, a gun to my head. But I'd trusted Jason. I didn't trust Jude.

"We're going," said Jude. "Don't try and stop me."

Jude backed up, dragging me with him.

"Jude," said Noah, "let's talk about this."

"One more word," said Jude, "and I blow her head off."

I didn't think he was serious. After all, his big plan was to get me to tell him where Jason was, which he couldn't do if I was dead. But I didn't know. Jude was pretty upset. I willed Noah and Gordon to shut up.

They stared after us as Jude led me to the car, their eyes wide and luminous.

Once outside, Jude threw open the door to the van and forced me inside. He slammed the door after me and hurried around to the other side. I watched him as he started the car, backed up the van, and pulled away from the house. I turned away from him once, to see that Noah and Gordon had both come out on the ruined porch of the abandoned house and that they were gazing after the van as it left. Then I turned back to Jude.

Jude was steering with one hand. The other hand was gripping the gun so tight that his knuckles were white. I thought about saying something to him. I decided not to. He was the one with the gun, after all. He was in charge.

We drove in silence for some time. The road ahead of us wound through the backwoods of Georgia. Eventually, we emerged in Shiloh, the small town where I'd met Michaela

Weem just a few months before. Jude drove up and down the streets, looking around. Did he think he was just going to see Jason, walking around?

"He's got to be here somewhere," Jude said more to himself than to me. "He's close. Close enough to cut off her finger and leave it there still bleeding. Where is he?"

I didn't say anything.

"Where is he, Azazel?" he said, rage filling his voice.

"I don't know," I said softly.

"And if you did, you wouldn't tell me, would you?" he said.

It didn't really seem wise to answer that question. "I don't know where he is," I repeated.

Jude swallowed. "You understand why I'm so upset, don't you?" he asked.

What was this? Was he looking to me for reassurance? He was the one with the gun.

"She's my mother," he continued. "She's all I've ever had. Maybe sometimes I got angry with her. Maybe sometimes I even hated her, but I can't let anything happen to her."

"Trade me tomorrow, then," I said. "What do you care? Your mother will be safe."

"No," said Jude. "No, I can't do that. Then Jason wins. I can't let Jason win."

"Even if it means your mother gets hurt?" Maybe it wasn't a good idea to push him like this, but he seemed vulnerable. Besides, if I could focus on how Jude was feeling, then I didn't have to think about the fact that Jason had cut off his own mother's finger. My Jason. Had tortured someone. What did that mean?

"You don't understand," said Jude. "She'd never forgive me if I gave in like that." He shook his head. "If I gave you up, she'd hate me. Us finding you and getting you and convincing you to kill Jason is the most important thing in the world to her. If I ruined that for her, she'd . . ."

"She'd what?" I asked. "She wouldn't be grateful that you saved her life?"

"Of course not. Her life isn't important. Not unless she gets you to destroy Jason."

We'd reached the end of Shiloh. It wasn't a big town. Jude took a turn, taking us down another windy country road. I realized that he must know his way around here pretty well.

"Did you grow up in Shiloh?" I asked, wanting to change the subject. Maybe if I could get Jude to talk about happy memories, he'd calm down enough to think rationally. Maybe then I could . . .

I could what? Did I think Jude was still my best friend or something? He had just threatened to kill me.

"Yes," said Jude. "I've lived here my whole life. Until I went to Bradenton to find you."

Jude took another turn, this time onto a dirt road. The van bumped along the rocky road.

"I hate it here," he said. "I was so happy to get away."

He hated it here? "But your mother is here," I said.

"I hate my mother," said Jude.

What? "But you just said that – "

"I know what I said." Jude pulled the car over onto the shoulder. He put his gun inside his jacket. He turned the keys in the ignition and pocketed them.

"We're stopping?" I said.

"I can't talk to you while I'm driving," said Jude. "I can't concentrate."

"Okay," I said. What did he want to talk about?

Jude shook his head. "Oh, Azazel," he said, looking close to tears again. "I don't know how everything got so screwed up."

For that matter, I didn't either.

He looked away from me. Up, at the interior of the van. "You don't know what it was like growing up here. Everyone knew my mother was Crazy Lady Weem. Everyone hated me. I defended her, but they used to beat me up anyway. And when I got home, it wasn't much better. All she talked about was Jason. All the time. The abomination. How to destroy him. How to end the madness she'd created.

"My mother got pregnant with me almost as soon as she'd had Jason," Jude said. "And she never told me who my father was. She always said that I was her second chance. That I was the great light. What she had brought into being to correct her mistake. But she never really seemed to love me. She never seemed to see me as anything other than a tool she could use to stop Jason. So, I was always lonely. But I didn't know that I was. I didn't know what it was that I wanted. I'd never had anyone. I'd never had any friends. Not until you."

"Jude – " I started, then stopped. What was I supposed to say to that?

"I know," he said. "We're not friends. Not really. But that time that I spent in Bradenton, with you. Hanging out. That was the happiest time of my life. And I wasn't faking everything."

"You faked a lot," I said. "You faked who you were. You're not even gay, are you?"

"No," he said. "But I thought I'd be less threatening to Jason if you thought I was."

"That worked well," I muttered.

Jude laughed. "Yeah, I guess he was still pretty threatened."

"He knew," I said. "He saw through you." And I hadn't. And what was I doing now? Was I comforting Jude? Jude, who'd betrayed me? I sighed. "You drugged me, performed Satanic rituals on my sleeping body, hit me with a baseball bat, and most recently threatened to blow off my head."

"I know," said Jude. "And I'm kind of sorry about that. I don't know. I wish that . . . that it could be real. The way things were. The way we talked. All of that stuff."

He looked at me with sad eyes, and he was my old Jude again. Was this an act? Was he trying to get something out of me by acting like this?

"I don't know where Jason is," I said. "Saying this stuff isn't going to make me tell you where he is."

"I know that," said Jude. "I know you don't know where

he is."

"So, then, why'd you take me away?"

Jude looked at his fingers. "I don't know," he said finally. "I didn't really think about that. I was really angry and upset. I didn't know what to do."

This wasn't the way that Jude should be acting after he'd captured me. He wasn't supposed to get all vulnerable and honest. How was I supposed to react to that? If he'd been cruel, if he'd been angry, if he'd waved the gun in my face, then I would have known how to act. After all, I'd been in that situation before. But now, with Jude so unsure of himself, I suddenly felt unsure of myself.

"You liked me, didn't you?" Jude asked. "You trusted me?"

I looked at him. I half-smiled. "Of course I liked you, Jude. You were my best friend. I told you everything."

"Not everything," said Jude. "You kept your secrets. Yours and Jason's. You were very loyal to that."

"I wanted to keep you safe," I said. "Back then, I thought that you didn't know anything about all of this. I thought if you knew, you'd be in danger."

"You were worried about me?"

"Of course."

"No one's ever been worried about me before," Jude said.

"That can't be true," I said. "I'm sure your mother – "

"No," said Jude. "She doesn't worry about me. She expects me to worry about her, but she doesn't care if I live or die."

250

"Jude – "

"No one cares if I live or die," he said.

We were quiet for several long minutes. Then finally, I said it, because it was true. "I care."

"No, you don't."

"I do," I said. "God knows why. You've done nothing but betray me."

Outside, twilight was stealing over the Georgia landscape. The sun was sinking slowly into the trees. I gazed out over the fields. "I guess everyone I ever cared about has betrayed me. My parents. Lilith. My brothers. You." I paused. "Even Jason. Jason went after Sutherland. He cut off your mother's finger. For all I know, he's actually a cold-blooded killer. Everyone's betrayed me." I turned back to him. "But it doesn't mean that I don't still care about those people. Maybe I shouldn't care about them. But it's like if I stopped, I wouldn't know who I was anymore. I'd lose my connection to the world. I'd stop being me. Maybe I'd stop being human. I care about you, Jude. I think I always will."

He smiled at me through the darkening interior of the van. "Thank you," he whispered.

We didn't speak again for quite some time. Outside, it got darker. The stars began to peek through the blackening blanket of the sky.

"I'm sorry about your mother," I finally said. "I don't . . . I don't know why he did that."

Jude didn't respond at first. Then he said, "I do."

"You do?" I was confused.

"He did it because of you," said Jude. "He did it because he'd do anything to get you back. Don't you remember what you said to me back in Bradenton? You said that if Jason knew someone had hurt you, he'd kill that person. Do you remember that?

I did. "Yes," I said. "But—"

"You said it scared you."

I turned away.

"Does it still scare you?"

I hesitated. "Yes," I said.

"It scares me when you're scared," said Jude. "You're so brave, Azazel. I saw you take down Sutherland when he tried to carry you off outside the shooting range. I couldn't believe you actually went after him the next day. You're brave."

"I was scared," I said. "You saw me after I ran away from Sutherland."

"Yeah," he said. "You were crying. I held you."

I remembered. I remembered the feeling of Jude's arms around me and how similar they'd felt to Jason's arms. How obvious it should have been to me then. They were so similar. Why couldn't I have seen that they were brothers?

"I liked that," Jude said.

"You were very comforting," I said.

Jude's hand snaked across the van to snatch mine. "But I'm not him," he said.

"Jude?" I asked.

"I'm not as comforting as he is," he said. "I can't protect

252

you the way he does."

I squeezed Jude's hand. "I'm not sure if I particularly like the way Jason is protecting me these days."

"Because he scares you?"

"Yeah."

"Do I scare you?"

I cocked my head, trying to look at him in the scant light, considering. "No," I said finally. "You don't scare me."

"Good," he said. "I don't want to scare you."

"Really?" I said. "Is that why you dragged me off at gunpoint earlier?"

"I just wanted to get you away," Jude said. "I don't know. I wanted to talk to you." He sighed. "It's weird. But I was upset, and the only person I could think of that I wanted to be around was you."

He was still holding my hand. It was dark inside the van, and I could barely make out his outline as he leaned closer to me, his face inching nearer and nearer to mine.

Was he going to kiss me?

Jude kept leaning in towards me.

He couldn't be trying to kiss me, could he?

His nose brushed mine.

He *was* trying to kiss me.

I hesitated for a second, and then I let him. I held my breath as his lips touched mine. They were warm and soft. I slid my hands inside Jude's jacket, tracing the outline of his ribcage.

And grasped his gun, drawing it out of his pocket.

Jude pulled back, surprised, but I already had the safety off and my finger on the trigger. I whipped the gun up, resting the barrel under Jude's chin.

"That was very, very stupid, Jude," I said softly.

His eyes were wide. "Azazel?"

"You couldn't have really thought that I wanted to kiss you, could you?" He'd bought it. He'd actually thought that I was feeling sorry for him. He'd thought that I had romantic feelings for him. I didn't. Jude disgusted me. I might sort of half-pity him, like a wounded dog or something. But he wasn't my friend.

I smiled, feeling pretty damned proud of myself. "Here's what's going to happen, Jude. Very slowly, you're going to give me the keys to the van. I'm going to take them. Then you're going to open the door and get out of the van. You're going to start walking away from the van. While you're walking, you're going to count. You'll keep walking until you've counted to, I don't know, a hundred. And you're going to keep walking and counting, even if you hear the van start and you hear me drive away, because if you do turn around, I'm going to shoot you. And you were with me when we went to the shooting range, Jude, so you know that I could very probably hit you, even if I'd driven the van away. You might think that maybe I'd be paying attention to driving and that I wouldn't see you turn around, but you aren't going to want to take that chance, so you're going to keep walking and keep counting. Do you understand?"

"Yeah," Jude said hoarsely, still looking astounded at this

turn of events.

"Good," I said. "Give me the keys."

Jude reached into his pocket and handed them to me.

"Now open the door and get out of the van," I said, moving the gun away from his chin and aiming it at his forehead. "Slowly."

Jude tried to move slowly, but he lost his balance and tumbled out of the van. As he got up and brushed himself off, I moved into the driver's seat. I rolled down the window and pulled the door shut, aiming the gun at Jude through the open window. "Now turn around," I said. "And walk."

Jude started walking, his back to me.

"Count to a hundred!" I yelled after him as I started the van.

And I peeled out of the dirt road as fast as I could, without one look back at Jude. Back on the main road, I turned back towards Shiloh.

It was harder to drive the van than I'd imagined. I'd never driven a car that was this high above the ground before. Also, it was disconcerting not to be able to see the nose of the van. I didn't feel bad at all for leaving Jude out in the middle of nowhere. It was only a few miles out of town, after all. Plus, he'd taken me away at gun point.

Mostly, I guessed I was grateful. An emotional Jude had been much easier to get away from than both of my brothers and Jude. I also now had wheels. Things were definitely looking up for the first time since I'd been captured in Bradenton.

It was odd that Jude had bared his soul to me in so much detail, but I really didn't care. There were much more important things to worry about, like where Jason was. If I could get to him, then I could get him to stop hurting Michaela Weem. The both of us could get out of here.

Would we go back to Bradenton? Would we be safe there? What if Gordon and Noah tried again? Was I going to spend the rest of my life on the run from my brothers?

It didn't matter right now. I needed to find Jason first. We'd figure out the other details later. Right now, the only thing I should be focusing on was where Jason might be. And that was the problem, because I had no idea. We didn't have anywhere to stay in Shiloh. When we'd been here before, we'd stayed in a hotel outside Shiloh. I couldn't picture Jason checking into a hotel with a hostage. So, where was he? Was he in another abandoned house like we were? Wherever it was, Jude was right, it had to be relatively close. By the time Jude had returned, the blood on the cloth binding her finger had still been wet.

I blanched inwardly at the thought of Jason cutting off someone's finger. How could he have done that? What was happening to him? But I shook it off. I didn't have the luxury of worrying about that either. I had to find Jason.

I just had no idea where to look. If only I had my cell phone. I could just call him. But I didn't have a cell phone. Sutherland had taken it. And even if he hadn't, I was sure my brothers would have taken it when they captured me. I'd look for a payphone, but I still didn't know Jason's number.

Was there any real point in trying to find a payphone, then? And where did they even have payphones these days? Convenience stores?

So what was I going to do? Drive up and down the streets looking for Jason? Go looking for other abandoned houses? Go door to door asking, "Have you seen a teenage boy and a fingerless woman?"

That was ridiculous.

I drummed my fingers against the steering wheel, willing myself to think. Think. I didn't have anywhere to go, except back to Florida. Could I do that? Was Hallam there, or had he gone out looking for us? If I could call Hallam, he would have Jason's phone number. Of course, I didn't know Hallam's phone number either. God. This was so stupid. When I'd been back in Bramford, I'd had everyone's phone numbers memorized. Back before I'd had a cell phone. They were nice and all, but there were definite drawbacks.

Suddenly, I was beginning to feel as if things were not exactly looking up now that I was away from Jude. Sure, I wasn't being held captive anymore, but I didn't know what I was going to do. And what about Lilith? Sure, I hated her, but could I really leave her at the hands of my brothers?

As if to add insult to injury, a car abruptly pulled out in front of me, a few hundred feet up the road. It halted in the middle of the road, blocking my lane and just stayed there, like it was a police roadblock or something. I swore and slammed on my brakes, screeching to a halt just a few feet shy of colliding with the car. It was dark, but I could see that the car was a shiny, new expensive one.

I leaned out my still open window, hurriedly stowing the gun inside the waist to my jeans. "Everything okay?" I called.

The door to the car opened, and Noah stepped out. "Azazel?" he said. "Where's Jude?"

Jesus! How had he gotten that car?

I threw the van into reverse and backed up at full speed, putting as much distance as I could between their car and the van. When I saw that Noah was getting back in the car and they were starting to pursue me, I immediately put the car in drive and turned around in the middle of the road, my tires squealing.

I took off at top speed, frantically checking my rear view mirror. They were in hot pursuit. And their car could go much faster than the ratty old van.

Damn. Damn. Damn.

Where had that car come from? I'd thought they were stranded back at that abandoned house. They'd gotten a really, really nice car lightning fast. How had that happened? How?

I had to slow down for the turns in the road, because I wasn't used to driving it. With every passing second, Noah was gaining on me. I tried to go faster, but I was losing control of the van as I rounded the curves. I pushed myself to take them faster and faster, not to worry about being able to navigate the road.

But then it happened. I hit a turn way too fast and when I

turned the steering wheel and braked a bit, I skidded. Panicking, I pressed harder on the brake, realizing belatedly that was exactly the wrong thing to do. The skid deepened and the van wobbled. It tumbled off the road, falling on its side.

I wasn't wearing my seatbelt, so I was thrown to the other side of the van – *hard*. I thudded against the passenger side door. The crank for the window jabbed my thigh. My head cracked against the window. Pain shot through my body, bright like carnival lights. I bounced, collided again, and was still.

I groaned.

I knew that I needed to get up and run, but everything hurt so, so bad.

"Azazel?" Noah's voice.

"Zaza, are you okay?" Gordon's voice, getting closer.

I felt in my pants for the gun. It was still there.

Oh God. That had really, really hurt. I'd never wrecked a car before. I knew it was supposed to be a normal teenage experience. Trust me to make sure I had it in the most abnormal way possible, running from my crazy Satanist brothers who were trying to get me to murder my boyfriend. Could this possibly get any worse?

Oh yeah. They'd found me. I'd escaped, and now I was getting recaptured.

The driver's side door to the van opened. It was funny, watching it open above me like that. Open onto the night sky.

Noah and Gordon peered in at me.

"Are you hurt?" Gordon asked.

"I'm fine," I managed.

"We've got to get you out of there," said Noah.

"So you can tie me up again? No, thanks," I said. This really, really sucked.

"Zaza, you must realize we're just trying to help you," said Gordon.

"You're not helping me," I said. "You're ruining my life."

"How can you say that?" asked Noah. "We're saving the world."

"By sacrificing your baby sister?" I demanded. "You two stood by while Toby almost raped me. Brothers who cared would have stopped that."

"Well, it wasn't exactly rape, now was it?" said Noah. "Honestly, Azazel, you're overreacting."

"Really, Zaza," said Gordon. "Do you have any idea how much time I've had to take off of work to be here?"

That was the last straw. His work?! Really?

I ripped the gun out of the waist of my pants. I didn't think. I didn't speak. I didn't threaten. It was quick. It was easy. It was very, very simple. And it felt natural too. Like the most obvious, most normal thing in the world to do.

I shot them both very neatly in the forehead. Their bodies toppled over into the van. They hadn't even had time to cry out.

For a few very strange seconds, I felt calm and relieved. I felt proud of myself. I'd just fixed everything.

Then I looked into their faces, dangling over mine, blood dripping over their eyebrows and down their noses.

And I convulsed.

What had I just done?

CHAPTER THIRTEEN

To: Renegade Son <settingsun007@yahoo.com>
From: Edgar Weem <eweem@risingsun.org>
Subject: (none)
Fine, Hallam. We'll play it your way.
011-44-020-5555-7032

Lilith was in the back of the car, tied up and gagged. I opened the door and looked at her. "You okay?" I asked.

She made a muffled noise. I reached in and pulled the gag out of her mouth.

"Fine," she gasped. "Are you?"

"I'm great," I said. "Come over here so that I can untie you."

"Zaza, what – ?"

"If I've told you once, I've told you a thousand fucking times. Don't. Call. Me. Zaza." I waved the gun in her face for emphasis.

She shrank from me. "Sorry," she mumbled.

"Now, come over here," I said, exasperated. She scooted over, and I untied her hands and feet.

"Azazel, you're head is – "

"It's fine," I said. "You wanna sit up front?"

"Uh . . ."

"Stay in the back, then," I said. I closed the door, and got in the driver's seat. I sat down. Buckled my seat belt. Felt the ignition.

And burst into laughter. I turned back to Lilith. "Keys!" I said to her. "I forgot the keys."

Still laughing, I got out of the car and ambled over to the bodies of Noah and Gordon. Noah had been driving, so he probably had them. I felt in his pockets. Sure enough. Keys.

Before I could think much about the fact that I'd just shot and killed both of my brothers, I went back to the car.

I jammed the keys in the ignition and started the car. I pulled the car back on the road and headed towards Shiloh.

"Now," I said to Lilith, "before I was interrupted, I was thinking about where the fuck I was going to go. Now that I've just committed murder, I'm even more confused." I looked back at her. "Where do people go after they kill people?"

"Watch the road," she said, her voice shaky.

I turned back to the road. "Sorry," said breezily. "I think sometimes people go hide out. They need . . ." I paused, feeling exactly like a cartoon light bulb had lit up above my head. "Sanctuary," I breathed.

I grinned at Lilith, but in the rearview mirror, not by turning around. "We're going to see Father Gerald."

"Father who?" asked Lilith.

"Gerald," I said. "At Christ is King Catholic Church. Hallam stayed with him for months before we found him in November. I know he'll know how to contact Hallam. They're friends. And if I can get in touch with Hallam, I can get in touch with Jason."

"Okay," said Lilith. "Great. I guess."

"Hey," I said. "How about a little gratitude? I just rescued you."

"You shot them," she whispered.

Right. Well, there was that. But I wasn't thinking about that right now. I couldn't think about that right now.

* * *

Christ is King Catholic Church was boarded up. There was a big sign on the front of the church which said, "Reopening in April." Hmm. I guessed that the big shootout between us and the Sons really had destroyed the sanctuary. I felt kind of guilty for a minute. I hoped that Father Gerald didn't blame us for the destruction of his church.

The lights were on in the rectory, where he lived, so I supposed I would find out in a few minutes anyway. I dragged Lilith with me, and together we knocked on his door.

There was no answer at first, so I knocked again.

After the second knock, the door opened. Father Gerald peered out at us.

"Hi Father Gerald," I said meekly.

"Azazel Jones?" he said in recognition. "What happened to you?"

"Happened to me?"

"Your head is bleeding."

"Is it?" I gingerly touched my head and looked at my fingers. Yep. Red. I shrugged. "I was in a car wreck. I was wondering if we could use your phone?"

"Come in," said Father Gerald. "Come in, come in."

Lilith and I stepped inside the rectory. It was sparse and functional. White walls. No decoration except for a crucifix on one wall.

"Your friend?" he asked.

"This is Lilith," I said.

He raised an eyebrow. "Lilith and Azazel?" He shook his head and crossed himself, mumbling something about never thinking he'd see the day he was opening his door to those two. He started out of the room we were in, which was the kitchen, heading back the hall. "I'll get something for your head," he said.

"It's okay, really," I said. "I just need to call Hallam. You have a number for him, don't you?"

Father Gerald stopped. "Well, yes. I was just about to call him myself, actually. Some strange events have recently unfolded. I thought he'd want to know."

"Strange events?" I said.

"With the Sons of the Rising Sun," he explained. "It's a little convoluted."

I waved it away. "The Sons aren't actually a problem for me this time. Can I just call Hallam, please?"

"Certainly," he said, pointing at the phone. He gave me the number. As I dialed, he said, "I'm going to go get some bandages. If my guest wanders out here, don't be alarmed."

Guest? Priests had guests?

Whatever. The phone was ringing on Hallam's end. Lilith

stood behind me, looking frightened. If I still liked her, I would have grabbed her hand or done something reassuring. But I didn't like her. Not at all. She felt scared? Good.

For a few terrible seconds, I was convinced that Hallam's phone was going to go to voicemail, but at the last second, he picked up.

"Father Gerald, what is going on?" he said. "Did you release the email without telling me? Why does Edgar Weem think that I'm playing games with him?"

"Edgar Weem?" I said. "You're in communication with Edgar Weem?"

"Who is this?"

"It's Azazel. And why the hell are you talking to Weem?"

"Azazel, Jesus, where are you?"

"I'm in Shiloh," I said. "I got captured by Satanists. Now you answer my question."

"Oh, Christ, Azazel, it's complicated. Look, I'm actually on my way to Shiloh. I should be there in an hour or so. Hang tight where you are, and I'll fill you in when I arrive. I don't want to talk about it on the phone."

"Hallam, are you still working for the Sons?" I was floored. Shocked. Appalled. After all this time, after I'd trusted Hallam as much as I did, was he betraying us?

"No, of course not. Please, just stay with Father Gerald. When I get there, I'll explain everything."

Behind me, Lilith screamed.

I whirled.

A man had just walked into the kitchen. He was bruised and beaten, his face swelling in odd places. Bandages decorated every part of his exposed skin. "Azazel," he said, his damaged mouth curving into a sly smile.

I dropped the phone. "Sutherland," I breathed.

He took a step toward me.

I grabbed Lilith's hand. "Let's get out of here," I said to her.

We tore out of the kitchen, out of the rectory, back into the car. As I drove away, I glanced in the rearview mirror to see that Sutherland had followed us outside. He was standing outside the church, in front of the re-opening sign, grinning like a jackal.

* * *

"How did he get there?" Lilith was asking.

She was sitting next to me in the passenger seat. We were driving aimlessly in the dark. Through the streets of Shiloh. Out into the surrounding country roads. Back into Shiloh. I didn't know where we were going. I didn't know what we were doing.

"I don't know," I said. "I thought he was dead."

Sutherland was alive. Jason hadn't killed him. Hallam had been wrong when he'd asked Jason where Sutherland's body was. It looked like Jason had beat him up very, very badly, but he hadn't killed him. As frightening as it had been to see Sutherland, the news made a part of me sing. Jason hadn't done that. He wasn't the killer that Noah and Gordon had claimed he was.

Of course, I'd killed . . . I shuddered again.

"He's not dead," Lilith said.

"Maybe . . ." I said, turning it over in my head, " . . . maybe he was following us. Following me. Maybe he followed us into the rectory."

"No," said Lilith. "I saw him come into the room. He didn't come through the front door. He came from the hallway."

"He was waiting for us? He knew we'd go there?"

"He sounded surprised to see you. Pleasantly surprised, but surprised."

She was right. He did.

I didn't like this one bit. First there was this car we were driving. This car that had come out of nowhere. Then there was Sutherland appearing also out of nowhere. So many unanswered questions. "There are too many things I just don't understand," I said. "How did Noah and Gordon get this car?"

"Gordon called your grandmother," said Lilith.

"Grandma Hoyt?" I said. "Why?" I couldn't even finish the thought, it was too preposterous. But I guessed it made sense. Grandma Hoyt had money. She could get them a car fast. "Why was she helping them?"

"I don't know," said Lilith.

More unanswered questions. More things that didn't add up. My mind was reeling. Chance had said that Gordon and Noah had gone to see Grandma Hoyt, and then she'd consented to pack Chance off to Italy. Could they have told her what they were planning to do? Had she decided to send Chance away so that it would be safe for him? But why was she helping the Satanists out? My grandmother hated the Satanists. She'd disowned my parents because of their Satanist ties.

But none of this was important right now, because . . . Because . . .

"We have to find Jason," I said.

We were driving through the streets of Shiloh. Impulsively, I turned onto Spring Street. Drove the car past Michaela Weem's house. I stared at it. And suddenly, it came to me. Last week.

Jude was driving Jason and me home. We were talking about the kidnapping of the Lindbergh baby. And Jason had said . . .

"I always thought," said Jason, "that would be a good way to pull off a kidnapping."

"What do you mean?" I asked.

"I mean, kidnap someone in their own house," said Jason. "Tie them up and knock them out, and keep them in their own attic."

I yanked the wheel to the right and turned into Michaela Weem's driveway. Of course, of course, of course. This was the place close enough to cut of Michaela's finger and leave it downstairs, still warm and wet with her blood. This was the place that Jason could leave notes. It was a safe place. Not a hotel. Not an abandoned house. And it was the last place anyone would think to look for him, because it was too obvious. Jesus.

"What are you doing?" asked Lilith.

"I know where Jason is," I said.

"You do?"

Quickly, I explained to her what I thought, as I parked the car and turned off the ignition.

"He's been keeping her here in her own house?" Lilith was incredulous.

"Brilliant, isn't it?" I said.

She shook her head. "Yeah," she admitted.

Lilith sighed. Then – she moved. She pulled me close against her body, her forearm going around my neck, making it tough for me to breathe.

"Lilith!" I protested.

Then I felt it. The cold, sharp point of a small knife at my neck. "Lilith?" I said.

"You really are way too trusting, *Zaza*," said Lilith, her voice ugly.

CHAPTER FOURTEEN

Text message to Hallam Wakefield, 11:12 P.M.:

We've got a trace on the car, thanks to Hoyt. We should know where they are in a matter of minutes. Coordinates to follow.

"But-but – " I sputtered. "They tied you up. And you kept trying to make Jason suspect Jude."

"Well, I did want to bang Jason. I'm not gonna lie about that. I figured any path in a storm, right?"

"You're mixing your metaphors," I said.

"AP English rears its ugly head," she mocked me. "As for the tying up part, I was supposed to keep an eye on you that way. Monitor what you were feeling. They thought you'd trust me."

"I didn't trust you," I said.

"Which is why you untied me."

"Fuck you," I growled.

"Tisk, tisk. It's not a good idea to be rude to the girl who has a knife to your throat."

Ugh. She was right. I *was* stupid. I was way too trusting.

"Noah and Gordon had no vision," Lilith said. "They thought they could convince you to kill Jason. I know better. You're never going to think it's the right thing to do."

"It's not the right thing to do," I said.

"Like I said, you're never going to think that," said Lilith. "When Jason is dead, Michaela is going to see just how special I am. I'll make her eat those words. Someone will love me."

"I don't get it," I said. "You want Jason dead too? You just said you wanted to bang him."

Lilith chuckled. "Boys aren't good for much other than sex, Zaza. They're all expendable, really."

"But you think Jason is evil incarnate, like they do?"

Lilith didn't answer for a few seconds. "Stop talking," she said. "I'm calling the shots here. I've got a knife at your throat. I could kill you at any second. You shut up, okay?"

I didn't say anything, but I could tell I'd gotten to her.

"Look," she said, "I figure it doesn't really matter how it goes down, as long as you kill Jason. So, we'll go inside. We'll find Jason. He'll do whatever I say as long as I've got a knife to your throat, right? Even take a gun, put it in your hand, hold it to his own head, and make you pull the damned trigger. He'll do that. Won't he?"

She was right. He would. He'd die for me. I didn't like Lilith's plan at all. For someone who didn't do very smart things very often, she'd put together a pretty good plan. I had to keep pushing. She could threaten to shut me up all she wanted, but if she killed me now, then I couldn't kill Jason. And if things were really about to go down the way she'd just explained, I far preferred to die for Jason than for him to die for me. Not when there was some way I could stop it.

272

"You sure you want Jason dead?" I asked. "I was listening when you flashed Jason, you know. It got quiet for a long time." This was killing me, but it was more important that Jason lived than anything. Than anything. "And when I walked into the room, I could swear he looked guilty. How do you know that he doesn't want to be with you anyway? Maybe that's how you could show Michaela she was wrong."

Lilith pushed the point of the knife a little deeper into my neck. "You think you're so smart, don't you?" she hissed at me. "You think you can play mind games with me, but I'm not as dumb as you think I am."

"I'm not saying your dumb," I said. "I'm just not sure what you're motivation here is. Why are you still working for the Satanists? I mean, what have they ever done for you?"

The knife stabbed at my neck. It broke the skin. I let out at little yelp.

"I said shut up, Zaza," said Lilith, "and I meant it."

Suddenly, this little exercise in trying to manipulate Lilith seemed really, really difficult. I wanted to see Jason. I wanted this nightmare over.

But I didn't want to hurt Lilith. I'd done enough damage for one evening. I knew that. I also knew that there were things I'd done in the past hour that would haunt me for the rest of my life. I didn't want to add to that. I remembered the way Jason had sobbed in my arms after killing the members of the Sons. I knew the way Jason's eyes always looked.

There were depths in them. Depths of pain and guilt and confusion. I didn't want to go there myself. But I was frustrated, and I couldn't help but want to do things the easy way.

As I hesitated in those few moments, I saw it all so very clearly. This way was seductive. It was simple. It was quick. It made the immediate problems go away. There were obstacles in the way of my goal. I needed to eliminate them. I saw that. I saw that I was starting down a path of simplicity. A path of casual violence. And I also knew that if I took that path, it would be harder to resist it in the future. I saw all of that.

And I made my choice. Because, in the end, no matter what anyone said about fate or Shiva or the power of Azazel, it was all about my choices. In the end, I wouldn't be able to blame ancient religions for my life. I'd have to take responsibility for it.

I moved as quick as Lilith had, and it meant that her knife took a pretty nice-sized chunk out of my neck. The pain was sharp, and I felt blood begin to trickle from the wound. But in one movement, I got the gun out of my pants with one hand, slapped the barrel against Lilith's temple, wrenched the knife away from her with my other hand, and twisted so that I could see her face.

I smiled at her. "Lilith, if you're so smart, why didn't you take my gun?"

"I-I – " Lilith was startled.

I didn't let her finish. I just pulled the trigger.

Her blood got on my face.

I looked at her for a while after it was done. The bullet didn't cause too much destruction going in. Sure there was a big bloody hole. But it was the exit wound that was so bad. Blood spattered all over the interior of the car, an exploded firework of red fluid and brain matter. The other side of Lilith's head caved in. It didn't really look like a skull anymore. Instead it was a broken Easter egg. A shattered Christmas ornament.

I don't know why I looked as long as I did. I think I just needed to see what I'd done. To understand that I'd killed her. I needed to look at it, look at the utter horror of it, the gore of it, the incomprehensible, repulsive reality of it, and make sure that I understood that I was responsible for it. Because I'd decided that my life and that Jason's life were more important than hers, I'd taken her life. I needed to recognize that, force myself to face it and acknowledge it.

I wasn't telling myself that it was the right thing to do. I wasn't trying to excuse it. I was just facing it. Taking responsibility for it.

As I got out of the car, my heart clanged against my rib cage. My legs trembled. I stood outside the car and closed the door behind me, shutting away the dreadfulness of the remains of Lilith.

Gripping the gun tightly, I started forward. Halting steps carried me over the threshold of Michaela Weem's house and inside.

* * *

Inside the house it was dusty and dark. I stumbled over shadowed shapes of furniture, looking for the staircase. I remembered that it was in the foyer, just as you entered the house. I wanted to go upstairs because I figured Jason was in the attic.

I felt blindly ahead of me and connected with the railing to the stairwell. As my eyes gradually adjusted to the darkness, I eased up the steps. I wanted to go faster, but I felt sluggish. Gingerly, I reached up to touch my head. How much blood had I lost? Could I have a concussion? If I had a concussion, I wasn't supposed to go to sleep, right?

I labored up the steps, gazing around me in the scant light. The steps opened onto narrow hallway. Moonlight came in a window at end, illuminating an antique wooden table overflowing with burnt candles and several framed photos on the wall. My feet creaked as I moved forward. Could Jason hear me? If he could, would he come down to investigate?

I had a horrible thought. Maybe Jason wasn't here at all. Maybe the comment he'd made in Jude's car had been nothing more than an offhand remark, and he wasn't even in the house. I didn't move, biting my fingernails nervously. If that were true, then the only thing I'd be able to do would be to get back in the car . . . But I couldn't sit next to Lilith's body. No. *No.*

I looked up. How did I get to the attic? Was there a pull-down set of stairs in the ceiling somewhere? Or was there an actual built-in staircase?

Then I heard a woman moan.

Above me.

They were here.

She moaned again. She sounded so close. Where were they? How did I get to them?

"There's someone here," said the woman's voice.

"Shh," hushed a voice. Jason?

"I won't be quiet," said the woman. "Help m—" she yelled, but her voice was muffled before she could finish.

"Shut up," said Jason's voice. It was his, unmistakably, even though it had a threatening tinge to it that I'd never heard before. "If you make one more noise, I'll kill you. I can cut parts off your dead body just as easy as your live one."

I shuddered. Jason sounded ugly. Hard. Cruel. And I couldn't believe he was talking about cutting off body parts.

Michaela Weem was his mother, no matter how awful she was. Jason shouldn't—

But did I have any right to judge him? After my evening?

Noah's and Gordon's empty eyes danced in front of my face, dangling inside the van's open door, staring at me.

"Go on, kill me," said the woman. "Do it. It's what I've always known you'd do. Evil spawn. Abomination."

"Shut up!" Jason insisted. "I'm not going to warn you again."

"*Kill me!*" shouted Michaela Weem.

"Jason!" I yelled. "Jason, it's me!"

Michaela Weem shrieked.

"No!" I yelled. "I'm here. Stop!"

From above me, the shrieking died off. There was a gurgling noise, like there was blood in her throat.

"Jason!" I called, my voice hoarse.

Behind me, a square of light appeared in the ceiling. A set of steps folded down and settled against the floor.

"Azazel?" said a voice. Jason's voice.

I flew to the stairs, scrambling up them as fast as I could. "Jason?" I said. "Jason?"

He caught me in his arms at the top of the steps. I dropped the gun I was holding to wrap myself around him. He smelled like sweat and blood, but I didn't care. He smelled like Jason. My Jason. I kissed his lips. His cheeks. His forehead. His chin. His neck. I couldn't stop kissing him.

"Jason, Jason, Jason," I murmured between kisses, feeling his arms tight around my waist.

But Jason was pulling away from me.

He held my face in his palms and forced my face away from his. "You're hurt," he said. "You're bleeding."

"I'm fine," I said, tears starting to stream down my face. He was here. I'd found him. Nothing else mattered right then. I'd found Jason. We were together. Everything else was just periphery. I didn't care about anything except the fact I'd found him.

"What happened to you?" he said.

There was so much. "I got away," I said. "I had to shoot people. They're dead."

"Jesus," he breathed. "But your head . . ."

"I was in a car accident."

"We've got to get you to a hospital."

I shook my head. "No. I'm a murderer. I can't go – " I broke off. Speaking of being a murderer. "Where's Michaela?"

"Who cares about her?" said Jason. "Let's just go. Both of us. Let's just go. Now."

I peered around Jason, actually looking at our surroundings for the first time. The attic was low-ceilinged. It had exposed rafters. It was lit entirely by candlelight. At least twenty candles squatted on the floor, between boxes and broken pieces of furniture. There was an old sewing machine, the kind with a pedal. In the corner, lying on several bloodstained rags was Michaela Weem.

She lay on her back. Her hand was bandaged, but the bandage was crusted with dry blood. Her head twisted towards me at an unnatural angle. Her eyes were wide and staring.

"Oh, Jason," I whispered. "What did you do?"

He touched my face again, turned my chin to face him. "I didn't know where you were," he said softly.

Slowly, I disentangled myself from Jason. I went to Michaela. Kneeled next to her. She looked so old, lying there. Old and broken.

I looked at Jason. "She's your mother," I said.

Jason shook his head. "I don't have a mother," he said.

Suddenly, Michaela moved.

I leaped back, but not in time. She reached over, with her good hand and grasped my wrist. She sat up, gasping for breath.

I struggled against her grip, but she held me fast.

Jason rushed towards us.

Michaela pulled me top of her. I was lying with my back on top of her body. She snaked her arm around my neck. She tightened it.

"Stop, Fiend," she said to Jason.

Jason stopped, his eyes murderous.

I could breathe, but it wasn't comfortable. And to think I'd been feeling sorry for this woman. I really *was* an idiot.

"That's your Vessel you're strangling," he rasped.

Michaela's mouth was close. I could feel her breath on my neck. I heard her voice in my ear. "Azazel," she said. "Oh Azazel. It's all gone wrong. My visions . . . they're swimming in confusion. Muddied. Swirled up. What have you done?"

I swallowed.

"I remember," Michaela continued, "what I saw when I first put my hands on your mother's belly and knew you were growing inside her. How delighted I was. You stood, strong and proud, clutching a spear of fire. You would vanquish the abomination. And your mother a Hoyt. It was too perfect."

"Hoyt?" I managed. "What's my mother's family got to do with this?"

Michaela Weem laughed, a high-pitched maniacal sound.

"You don't know, do you?"

Jason shook his head. "Not *those* Hoyts," he said.

"Yes," said Michaela Weem. "Yes."

"You're twisted," said Jason. "You and my father both. You claim it's got something to do with ancient power or fate or destiny or anything like that, but it's all about you — your revenge — your ability to do what you want."

"I don't understand," I said.

"Your great uncle is Weem's successor," said Michaela. "Where did you think all that Hoyt money came from? It comes from the Sons of the Rising Sun. To use their own blood against them. To use you . . ." She laughed again. "It was too perfect."

Wait. My mother's side of the family had ties to Sons? That would make sense, considering my grandmother hadn't wanted anything to do with the Satanists. But . . . "But the Sons killed my Aunt Stephanie," I protested.

"The Sons are very rarely concerned with women's lives," said Michaela. "Very rarely concerned. And you, my dear sweet Azazel, you were going to be a thorn in their side. You were going to strike a blow to their foundations. Such a blow . . . But now . . . now I can't see. It's all a haze." Michaela's grip on my throat loosened a little bit. "It was so clear before. Two figures. One an agent of Chaos. One an agent of Order. One light. One dark. But now I can't see which is which."

What was she talking about? And she had to be wrong anyway. The Hoyts had nothing to do with the Sons. They couldn't. "Why was my grandmother helping Noah and Gordon, then?" I asked. "Why did she send them that car?"

Michaela cackled. "Oh, there are many, many things you don't know about Arabella Hoyt, Azazel. Many things." She smiled, humming to herself for a second. Then she stopped. "The Sons never would have noticed you, you know," she continued. "If you'd just struck. Smote him down. But now they know who you are. And they must control their precious Rising Sun. Oh, they must, mustn't they? But I can't see anymore, Azazel. I can't tell who you serve. Or who he serves. Do you use the power of Rabbit for evil, girl? Which of you, which of you, which of you should die? Which one?"

If my grandmother had ties to the Sons, then that would mean that the car that I drove to the house was a car that belonged to the Sons.

I looked up at Jason. "Jason," I said. "The Sons, they – "

And I was cut off by the sounds of several cars outside the house, all pulling to a stop.

"They know where we are," I finished.

"Oh, I know, I know that only you can kill the abomination. But if you won't kill him, and both of you live, what worse things could happen? One of you must die!" And she pulled her arm tight around my neck.

I gagged, my eyes going wide. Frantic, I scrabbled at her arm with my nails, raking her skin, drawing blood.

Jason raced to us, fishing out a gun. He put the barrel against Michaela Weem's head. "Let her go," he said.

Michaela only laughed. "Must die, must die, must die!"

she squealed.

Jason shot her.

Immediately, her arm fell away from me lifelessly. Her body thudded back against the floor behind me.

I crawled away from her, into Jason's waiting arms.

I didn't look back, but Jason was staring at her. He didn't look away.

And the Sons were entering the house. We could hear their footsteps as they mounted the stairs, their voices as they opened doors.

"Jason?" I said.

He didn't look away from Michaela.

I only looked for a second. I only peeled my eyes away from the entrance for one moment, to look at what he was looking at. Michaela's body, frail and twisted, a sick smiled still on her lips.

A second was all it took.

I heard the gun shot, and I turned, but it was too late.

Jason didn't even make a noise. He just collapsed against me, blood seeping out of his forehead.

"Jude?" I said.

He was standing at the opening to the attic, holding the gun I'd dropped.

He smiled at me. "Hi Azazel," he said.

"Jude," I repeated. I'd left him alive. Of all of them, I'd left *him* alive. And it was funny. He'd seemed like such a bad shot at the target range. But he hadn't had any trouble this time. Right on the mark.

I looked back at Jason, his head slumped against my chest. His blood was flowing onto my shirt. He was – But no. No, that –

"Mother's gone," said Jude. "But so is he now. And now, Azazel, there's no reason we can't be together."

I started to tremble, then to shake. Spastic jerks. No. *No.* *NO.*

CHAPTER FIFTEEN

From: Arabella Hoyt <arabella.hoyt@gmail.com>
To: Michaela Weem <mweem@thegreatgodazazel.com>
Subject: Is it done?
Michaela, you've been out of touch with me for days now. I just received communication from my grandsons. You promised me that this would be quick. I need word and soon. I'll only keep my end of the bargain if you keep yours.
Arabella

I could still hear the Sons scrambling through the house. Someone was coming up the steps behind Jude.

It was Hallam. He tackled Jude, knocking Jude flat on his face on the floor of the attic.

Behind him came a swarm of men dressed in black. Men toting guns.

But it was like it was all moving in slow motion. Like reality had just snapped whatever hold it had on me. I couldn't grasp the thread of events that had transpired. I couldn't make my brain put them together.

"Jesus, Azazel," said Hallam, "why couldn't you have waited for me?"

I looked at him. I looked through him. What was going on? I shook Jason. "Jason," I said. "Wake up."

Jason's body jerked lifelessly with the force of my shaking. His head lopped forward. His chin bounced against his chest. I shook harder. "Jason!" I said insistently.

Hallam came to me. Behind him, the Sons were restraining Jude. Tying his hands behind his back. Hallam knelt. "Azazel," he said. "Stand up."

I glared at him. "No," I said.

I turned back to Jason. I guided his head back. I placed it in my lap. I cradled him, and I rocked. "This didn't happen, did it?" I asked Hallam. "He isn't . . ." I couldn't make myself say it.

Hallam reached across me, taking Jason's wrist. He was feeling for a pulse.

"Azazel," he whispered. "He's gone. Come away from the body."

"NO!" I shouted. I clutched Jason to me tighter. "No."

I gazed down at Jason's face. Unlike Lilith's, it still looked so perfect. There was only one small hole marring the beauty of his face, high on his forehead, just below his hairline. It wasn't even bleeding that much. There was no exit wound. I traced his nose and chin with my forefinger.

He couldn't be dead. I'd just found him. It had been so hard to find him, and I'd had to go through so much. I'd shot three people in the head to find him. I'd faced the darkest part of myself. Resigned myself to future nightmares. Done things I'd never believed myself capable of. So, he couldn't be dead. After all of that, it just wouldn't be fair. It wouldn't be right.

"No," I whispered, caressing his cheek with the back of my fingers.

286

Hallam stood up and crossed the attic to the other members of the Sons. I heard him giving them orders, telling them what to do with Jude. Telling them to leave us alone for awhile. But I couldn't really focus on the words. Everything still seemed fuzzy. There was a gauzy curtain between the world and me. I couldn't see straight. This couldn't be reality. Because Jason couldn't die. That wasn't the way things were supposed to go!

I loved Jason. He and I were supposed to ride off into the sunset together. He and I were supposed to live happily ever after. He wasn't supposed to die! And how, how, how, how could I possibly face the idea of being alive if he wasn't? It just wasn't true. It couldn't be true. It couldn't be true!

I looked down at his face. It was true. Jason was dead.

The realization settled over me with icy certainty. Its truth seemed to crystallize the air in front of me. Things began to move at the proper speed. Things began to look clear again. That almost made it worse. Because everything was still going on, moving on, and Jason was dead. I felt like the world should stop. Like everything should stop functioning the way it usually did. How could everyone just keep going when Jason was dead?

Hallam sat down next to me again. We watched as the Sons left the attic. Then it was just me and Hallam. And the bodies.

"I'm sorry, Azazel," said Hallam.

"Yes," I said.

"But I'm glad I didn't have to do it," he said.

The statement should have made me angry. It didn't. I didn't really think I had the capacity for emotions right now. "You thought you'd have to kill Jason?"

"I hoped I wouldn't," said Hallam.

I held Jason close to me, still rocking his quiet body. My brain was still putting pieces together, even in the face of this. Would nothing stop me? Wasn't the death of Jason enough to stop me, even if it was enough to stop Jason?

"You've been working for the Sons this whole time, haven't you?" I said.

"No," said Hallam. "I don't work for the Sons."

"You brought them here," I said.

"It's complicated," he said.

"Were they coming to capture Jason?" I asked.

"I don't know why they were coming," said Hallam. "I just know that Weem put me in touch with them."

Right. He'd been talking to Weem. "Why were you in touch with Edgar Weem?"

Hallam didn't speak for a moment. His eyes darted from Jason's head in my lap to my eyes. "Are you sure you want to talk about this now?" he asked.

"No," I said. "Not sure about much of anything right now. But you might as well tell me."

"It's a long story," said Hallam.

"Guess I'm not going anywhere," I said. All my captors were dead or captured. The threat to me had been neutralized. Overall, I guessed I was safe. But the price . . . the price had been Jason's life, and the victory felt empty.

Shouldn't I be crying now? Shouldn't I be a mess? Why was I so calm? Dry-eyed? Was this the price I'd paid for killing my brothers and Lilith? Had I lost my ability to grieve? I remembered just minutes ago, when I'd been crying in joy at the sight of him. Now, when I'd never get to do that again, I was a stone. I didn't understand.

"Tell me," I said to Hallam, not looking away from Jason's face.

"Okay," said Hallam. "In November, you remember, I went to talk to Edgar Weem, to work the deal for you and Jason."

"Yes," I said.

"I arrived in Weem's office that evening after flying to England. Weem was waiting for me. He already knew that I had documents about Michaela, so I figured that he was sure of the scale of what I'd discovered about him. During our phone conversation, he'd seemed worried and confused. By the time I arrived, he seemed even more so. I chalked this up to my impeccable detective skills. But once I got settled and we began talking, he started to tell me things.

"He seemed very contrite and very sad. He seemed very old. He told me that the whole business with Jason had happened when he was a younger man. He said that he'd been stupid then, thinking he could create the Rising Sun. He should have known that he couldn't mess with forces like the ones he'd been intending to mess with.

"I didn't understand what he meant. I told him frankly that I didn't believe in any forces anymore. I had evidence that the entire Rising Sun debacle had been engineered by him, and I wasn't inclined to listen to anymore mumbo-jumbo about ancient powers and magics and whatever other ridiculous nonsense he wanted to spew at me. I told him that I'd had enough of that while I was working for the Sons thank you very much, and I didn't want anymore of it now. I was here to work a deal, plain and simple.

"He said that I was mistaken. He said that yes, it was true that he had manufactured Jason, that he had fathered him. But, he said, I mustn't think that because he'd engineered the entire thing that there weren't very powerful things that had transpired in Jason's creation. He told me that I didn't know what depths he'd plummeted to in the search for that kind of knowledge. Then he went on some kind of extended comparison between him and Faust, about making deals with the devil for knowledge.

"I was starting to tune him out. Look, I said to him, it didn't matter whether or not he thought Jason was actually the Rising Sun or not. The fact was that once everyone else in the Sons found out what he'd done, they wouldn't think that Jason was the Rising Sun. I had the power to destroy the organization and to destroy him if he didn't cooperate with me.

"He laughed then. He said that I shouldn't assume that he was trying to tell me that Jason was the Rising Sun. Quite the opposite, he said. He'd done awful, terrible things when creating Jason. He and Michaela had participated in rituals that were illegal and immoral and repulsive. He told me about some of them. I don't want to repeat much. He invoked powers dark and mysterious, powers that slumber in ancient texts, too horrible to be named, let alone be awakened. He said that he didn't think Jason was the Rising Sun at all.

"He said, 'No, Hallam, I think I've created a monstrosity.'

"I told him he was insane. I'd spent years with Jason. He wasn't monstrous in any way.

"Weem began to give me examples of things. He pointed out the work Jason and I had done for the Sons. Violent work. He said that Jason had taken pleasure in it. I denied that. Jason hadn't. I said that I'd never even witnessed Jason taking another human life.

"Weem said that Jason had killed members of the Sons in New Jersey. He told me how efficient it was. He said Jason's work was the work of a trained assassin, one who has killed many times. He hinted that I might not know how many people Jason had killed or when.

"I still didn't believe him, and I said so.

"He said that finally, there was the fact that Jason had killed his mentor, Anton.

"I was appalled. 'You people killed Anton,' I said. After all, it was that action which had been the impetus for my leaving the Sons. I couldn't believe he would pin the event on Jason. It was low, I thought. Low and ridiculous. And I couldn't figure what it was Weem wanted to accomplish by lying to me in this way.

"Weem shook his head. He insisted that Jason had

actually killed Anton. And he could prove it."

I interrupted Hallam. "He could prove it?" I said. "But Jason didn't do that. There's no way. He loved Anton."

Hallam sighed. "This isn't a good time for me to be explaining this to you," he said. "We should wait. Later, when you're calmer – "

I silenced him with a look. "I'll never be calmer than I am now."

He nodded once. "He had a video, Azazel."

"He faked it!" I said.

Hallam shook his head. "I don't think so. Faking a video is a pretty tricky business. No, I'm sure it was Jason in the video. It was a security video. Grainy and black and white, but very convincing. If you could have seen it . . . Jason and Anton were clearly arguing. They were shouting at each other. There wasn't any sound, but I could tell they were both upset. Then Jason pulled out a gun and shot Anton. Over and over. And the expression on his face . . . Azazel, I've seen that expression. The first time I saw it was at that sorority house. He was just unloading his gun into Anton and he was . . . Azazel, he was smiling. Smiling.

"After, Jason stood over Anton for a long time. He crouched over the body. He started crying. But, there's no doubt in my mind that he killed Anton.

"After I saw the video, I was completely stunned. Weem told me that he was frightened about what he'd unleashed on the world. He said he was more than happy to sever the ties the Sons had with Jason. He wanted to wash his hands of the entire business. But he asked me to watch Jason. To see if this kind of behavior continued. To see if Jason was dangerous. And that's what I've been doing.

"I know you're hurting right now, but I think this was for the best," Hallam said to me. "I think that there was a side to Jason that maybe neither of us knew about. There was a part of him – a violent, dark part. It was starting to surface within him. All the fighting he was doing in Bradenton. It was just a matter of time before it got worse. After he killed Sutherland, I was worried that I was going to have to do something. Stop Jason somehow."

"Sutherland's alive," I said to Hallam.

"What?" Hallam said, looking genuinely confused.

"I saw him," I said. "At Father Gerald's rectory."

Hallam's look of confusion switched to a look of alarm. "Sutherland was with Father Gerald?"

"Yes," I said.

Hallam furrowed his brow. "It doesn't make sense. Why would Jason leave Sutherland alive?"

"He wasn't what you said he was," I said. "That's why. He wasn't violent or evil or dark. Sutherland knew that. He showed me emails he intercepted from the Sons. I'm Kali. Jason was Shiva. He was the good one. I was the dark one." I stroked Jason's face. "You were all wrong. All of you."

I leaned close to Jason. "I'm sorry," I said to him. "I'm so sorry. I love you. I love you forever."

Things had to be dealt with. I couldn't sit here forever, cradling Jason's dead body, listening to Hallam's stories.

Instead, I had to get moving. My captors might be out of the way, but the Sons were here, Weem was still alive, and Sutherland was still out there. From the look on Hallam's face, that wasn't a good thing.

Tenderly, I pressed my lips against Jason's, for what I knew would be the last time. I had to leave him, let him go. If nothing else, I had to make sure that everyone understood that he wasn't what they thought he was. Not a monster. Not the man who would enslave the world. Just Jason. My Jason.

I lingered on his lips for too long. I didn't want to let go. This was the final step in accepting the horror that had just occurred. Once I stopped kissing him, stopped holding him, his death would be real. I didn't want to face that.

But I had to. I broke away from Jason. I turned to Hallam. "What do we need to do?" I asked.

And Jason coughed in my lap.

Coughed.

We both jerked our heads to look at him. His eyes were fluttering. He was coughing, as if air had just filled his lungs after a long break.

"Jason?" I whispered.

Was I dreaming?

"Hey," he said, looking around.

"No," said Hallam. "He was dead. I felt his pulse."

Jason struggled into a sitting position, putting his hand to the wound on his forehead. "I'm not dead," he said. He smiled at me lopsidedly. "Didn't Michaela Weem say that only you could kill 'the abomination?' It's not the first time she's been right."

"He was dead," Hallam said.

I touched my lips. "I thought you were dead," I said.

"Who could be dead through a kiss like that?" said Jason. He pulled me close and kissed me again. My heart stopped in my chest.

Hallam scrambled to his feet. "Isis and Osiris," he muttered. "You *are* the Rising Sun. Your consort breathed life into you. It's one of the signs."

Jason stood up too and helped me to my feet. He shrugged at me, taking my hand. "Well," he said, "gotta say it's good to be a dying god. But I really think this bullet didn't do much damage. It doesn't even hurt."

"You were dead!" Hallam said. "You didn't have a pulse!"

Jason laughed. "Right, Hallam. It's a miracle." He grinned at me. "Of course, I guess we did drive a bunch of men mad a few months ago. Maybe we really are, like, magic or something." He laughed again. "Come on, Azazel, we've got to get out of here."

"You can't leave," said Hallam.

"Got to," said Jason. "Don't you know that I must be about screwing up my father's business?" He took his phone out of his pocket and hit a few numbers. Holding it to his ear, he said, "I've got her. Meet me out front. When can you get here? . . . Good." Jason hung up his phone. He turned to Hallam. "You double-crossed me. You've been in touch with

295

Weem all this time."

"Did you overhear while you were . . . dead?" Hallam said.

"No," said Jason. "No, I've got a source. Listen, Hallam, you and I have a history. Just let me and Azazel walk out of here, okay? I'm willing to just let you go. You were my friend."

Hallam looked confused. "Where are you going?"

"I never want to see you again," said Jason. "If I do, I'll have to kill you."

Jason took my hand and led me through the house. When the Sons saw us, they dropped their guns. They fell to their knees. They whispered amongst themselves things like, "He's alive" and "He *is* the one." On the front porch, two of the Sons were wrestling with Jude. When Jude saw us, he went nuts.

He yelled after us, "This isn't over, Jason! You killed Mother! I won't ever forget that, and I'll make sure you don't either!"

But in the tired darkness of the wee hours of the morning, with the moon sagging in the sky above us, a car pulled up in front of Michaela Weem's house. Jason led me towards it.

"Jason," I said, "who . . .?"

"You'll see," he said, opening the door for me.

We slid into the back seat together, and Jason slid his arm around me, holding me tight against him. It felt so good to be close to him.

The driver in the car turned around. "Where to, kids?" he

said.

I looked at Jason in alarm.

The driver was Sutherland.

EPILOGUE

Twenty hours later, Jason and I were standing at the Trevi Fountain in Rome, Italy. It was midmorning in the eternal city. Bright sunlight filtered through the ancient buildings and a crowd of tourist had already gathered around the fountain. The water cascaded over the statues, which were so life-like, I thought the stone horses were going to leap out at us over the frothy water and gallop across the square. Of course, that might have been just because I was ridiculously sleep deprived.

I hadn't slept – really slept anyway – since the night that I huddled with Lilith in the abandoned house. Instead, Sutherland had taken both Jason and I to the airport, where we'd caught a flight to Rome, prepaid by the Catholic Church. I was confused. I tried to ask Jason questions as we waited for the plane, but it wasn't until we boarded and got settled that we really got to talk.

During the long flight to Rome, Jason had explained as best as he could what had happened. "First of all," he said. "I owe you an apology. I kept saying you were paranoid, and that there wasn't any danger, and you were right all along."

"No," I said. "I thought it was the Sons. I was wrong. And I was totally clueless about Jude. I should have listened to you."

"I should have listened to *you*," Jason said. "I can't keep running away from this stuff. It follows me everywhere. It's part of who I am. I won't forget that again. Okay?"

I kissed him. "I'm just glad you're alive."

He grinned. "Well, so am I."

Jason began to explain. After beating Sutherland to an inch of his life, Sutherland had begged Jason to let him live, promising to tell Jason information that he knew about the Satanists and Jude. Disgusted, Jason had left him, coming back to me that night, dazed from his violence. After I'd disappeared, Jason remembered what I'd said to him about the Satanists. He'd hunted Sutherland down and beaten the information out of him.

"Sutherland and I made a deal," Jason said. "In return for his cooperation and any information he knew about me or you, I told him who my father was."

Sutherland, in return, had told him that Michaela Weem had engineered the capturing of me. He'd been doing Michaela a favor by watching me. That was why he'd been in Bradenton. Sutherland also told Jason that Jude was actually Michaela's son. Further, he told Jason that Hallam was in contact with Edgar Weem.

Armed with this knowledge, Jason had gone to Michaela's house, tied her up, and left the note for Jude to find. Sutherland had used his knowledge to contact the biggest enemy of the Sons that existed – the Catholic Church.

I was surprised. Jason said that he was too. Since Jason knew that Hallam was working for Weem, he got

Sutherland to work a deal with the Church. In exchange for sheltering us, we'd help them fight against the Sons. That was why we were in Italy now. We were guests of the order of Reddimus, here in Rome. It seemed that it was our lot in life to stay with people who wouldn't let us have sex.

Because of Sutherland's actions, big changes were going down in the Sons. Weem had purportedly stepped down and had been succeeded by Ian Hoyt, my great uncle, who I'd never heard of. There were things I didn't understand about the connection between the Hoyts and the Sons. Was Grandma Hoyt working with the Sons? Was she working with the Satanists? Now that we were in Italy, I also fully intended to visit my younger brother Chance at his boarding school. I thought it was strange that my grandmother had sent him away right before everything had gone down with Gordon and Noah. I didn't know what was going on with my grandmother.

Then I'd spent some time catching Jason up on everything that had happened to me. I was breezing past some of the things at first, like how Noah and Gordon had showed me hours of videotape and documents proving that Jason was actually a cold-blooded killer. Jason stopped me and asked me about it though.

"They showed you what?" he asked.

I explained again, but slower. He wanted to know about the video of the girl from the sorority house. He made me explain it in excruciating detail. I felt embarrassed, frightened that Jason would think that just because I was telling him the story, I also believed it. I didn't. But I was confused. I wasn't sure what to think.

"She said I was smiling?" Jason repeated.

I toyed with the tray table – the remains of the snack that the flight attendant had yet to collect from us. "A lot of people said that about you. That you were smiling."

"Really?" said Jason. He looked disturbed. He settled back into his chair and looked into the aisle of the plane.

"And Hallam said it too. He said that he saw you kill Anton on a video tape and that you were smiling when you did it."

"Really," Jason repeated, still not looking at me.

"I don't believe it," I said. "Or . . . even if it is true, it doesn't matter."

He turned to me then. "You mean that?" he said.

"Of course I mean it," I said.

"No matter what I've done."

"No matter what you've done, I'll always love you," I said. "I overheard you saying something like that about me to Lilith."

He nodded. "I did. It's true."

"Did you . . . did you kill people before you met me?"

Jason stared down at his fingers. He shook his head. "No," he said. "No, of course not."

I nodded. Of course, he hadn't. How could I have believed . . .? I hadn't, though. I hadn't believed. We were quiet for a little bit, then Jason prompted me to go on.

I finished explaining what had happened to me,

everything, including shooting Noah and Gordon and killing Lilith. Jason squeezed my hand tight when I thought I might cry. And I didn't.

"It's good that we're talking about all of this," Jason said. "I don't think we've been communicating enough lately. We've been avoiding things that are true. We never talked about what happened in Shiloh. About the Sons going nuts."

I was glad he said that. I'd been thinking about that too. In the house with Noah and Gordon. "I know," I said. "We've been running from who we are. From what we are."

"We tell each other everything from now on," he said.

"Yes," I said. "And it doesn't matter what it is. Because I trust you, and I want to know you. And I want to know everything you've ever felt or done been."

"Then we tell each other everything."

"Everything."

* * *

Once in Rome, our wounds bandaged, we'd gone sightseeing. The monks of the order assured us that the Sons wouldn't bother us in Rome. The entire city was a sanctuary of sorts, considering its history and ties to the Church. We wandered freely through the streets, feeling a kind of liberty we hadn't felt in months.

Next to us, a tour guide was telling her tour that throwing one coin over your shoulder into the fountain would ensure you returned to Rome, two would mean that you'd find new love, and three would mean your current lover would break up with you. Jason and I didn't have any coins, so we didn't throw any.

But it wouldn't have mattered anyway. We were going to be in Rome for quite some time. Returning wasn't an issue. As for love, we had exactly what we wanted. True love. Honest love. Forever.

* * *

Later, as twilight was falling on Rome, we wandered through the stone streets, hand in hand. We paused and sat down on the Spanish steps. I lay my head on Jason's shoulder. And he took my hand. Then he whispered in my ear, "I lied to you."

I started, moving to look at him.

"One thing," he said. "And I guess I've been lying to myself about it for a long time too, because I didn't want to face it. But when I'm with you, I don't feel like I'm who I used to be. And when I'm with you, I feel like . . ."

"You can tell me anything, Jason. You know that."

"He called me an abomination," said Jason. "The same words Michaela Weem used. When she said them, I thought of it. That night, he came to me, and he said that I was a thing of great evil. He was all I ever had. And he wanted me dead."

I took Jason's hands in mine. "You killed Anton, didn't you?"

He nodded.

Trembling for more?

<u>Tortured, Jason and Azazel, Book Three</u>

Keep reading for a sneak peak at the first chapter.

Want freebies, information on new releases, discounts, and more?

Visit my website to join my email list.

vjchambers.com

TORTURED, CHAPTER ONE

April 17, 1990

Professor Weem commented on my paper to the entire class today. He said it was the best discussion of ancient religions he'd seen in all his years as a teacher. All of the girls in class hate me even more than they did before. Everyone has a crush on Professor Weem. Even though I'm learning more here than I ever imagined, sometimes I just want to go home.

Above me, stained glass windows loomed in the darkness, fractured pictures, casting multi-colored bits of light over the wooden pews. Back when the Sol Solis School was first built, it was a monastery, and this building was the church. Now we used it for assemblies and performances. I was lying back on one of the pews. My boyfriend Jason was kissing me.

I tried to pay attention to the softness of his lips, to the hard curves of his muscular chest against my body. But I couldn't help but stare up at the stained glass.

It was late at night. Jason and I had snuck out of our dormitories to meet each other here. Jason could pick locks and get us into pretty much any building on campus. Except the library, of course. Jason could have picked the lock without any problem. But the library was always guarded. It was frustrating, because the whole reason we'd come to the Sol Solis School was to get into that library.

Jason brushed a stray hair out of my face. He looked deep into my eyes. "Azazel?" he whispered.

"What?" I said, shifting uncomfortably on the wooden pew.

"Are you okay?" he asked.

I nodded. "Fine," I said, attempting to smile.

He kissed me again, closing his eyes. I tried to close mine, but they fluttered open again. I looked back up at the stained glass above me. We were making out in a church. A church. And we'd planned to come here to do more than make out. I eyed the stained glass suspiciously, feeling ill at ease.

As if in response to my thought, Jason eased his hand under my shirt, his fingers cold against my skin. I jumped.

Jason pulled away. He sat up. "You aren't into this, are you?" he asked.

I sat up too. "I'm into it," I said. And I was. Hadn't I been wanting to be with Jason for months?

"So, then how come you're so tense?" he asked.

"I'm not tense," I said.

Jason sighed. "Hey," he said, "I thought we promised to be honest with each other."

Jason had been brutally honest with me. He'd shared with me his darkest secret, something he'd never admitted to anyone. Something he'd barely admitted to himself. His mentor, Anton, had come to him one night, telling him that he'd found out things about Jason. That Jason wasn't the Rising Sun, or the messiah of the world, but actually a thing of evil. Anton had tried to kill Jason but Jason had killed him

306

first. Jason had told himself over and over that it wasn't really his fault. That it was the fault of the Sons themselves, who'd made Anton believe in things like the Rising Sun or things of great evil power. But Jason had finally told me about it. He'd been honest. I owed it to him to be honest too. Still, this hardly compared. This wasn't some dark secret that I had. This was just something I was too uncomfortable to talk about.

Jason folded his arms over his chest.

I shot one more look up at the stained glass windows. "Well," I said, "we ARE in a church."

"It's not a church anymore," said Jason. "Besides, what are you afraid of? The wrath of God raining down on us or something?"

"No. Not exactly. But, you know, weird things do happen to us, Jason. Especially when we kiss."

Like driving a group of men absolutely insane. Or Jason coming back from the dead.

Jason laughed. "Yeah, okay, point," he said. "But I think we're okay here. No one comes in here at night. And it's been so long." He reached for me again.

I ducked out of his grasp, chewing on my lip.

"What?" he said. "What is it?"

I shook my head. "Nothing," I said.

Jason sighed. "Don't do that, Azazel. It's something. It's something or you wouldn't be trying to get away from me when I want to touch you."

"I'm not trying to get away from you!" I said. Honestly, I didn't know what was wrong with me. I wanted Jason. I did. I loved him more than life itself. And we hadn't been able to do more than hold hands since escaping from Shiloh two months ago. We'd been living with a group of monks in Rome most recently. Now we were attending the Sol Solis School, the same boarding school my younger brother Chance attended.

It was just that in the past couple months, everything had gotten so serious between Jason and me. Everything had been so focused on what we were trying to figure out. I'd almost forgotten about this part of our relationship. "Shouldn't we be focusing on how to get into that library?" I asked Jason.

"The library?" he said. "We are. We're trying to figure something out. But we've only been at school here for two weeks."

"I know that," I said. "But it's why we're here, isn't it?" Jason and I were trying to find some ancient documents on the history of the Rising Sun. We wanted to know why we'd been able to do the weird things we'd done when we were kissing. We wanted to know if we had supernatural powers.

Jason had been brought up to believe he was the Rising Sun, a savior of sorts for the human race. It was prophesied that he would unite the world under a global government and usher in an era of peace and prosperity. My Satanist family had groomed me as the Vessel of Azazel (a Jewish demon). My purpose had been to destroy Jason and stop him from uniting the world. Jason and I had fallen in love. I hadn't killed him. Ever since then, all kinds of very strange things had happened to us. We'd been chased by one organization or another across the United States. Finally, we'd taken refuge here in Italy. But we had questions, and it seemed that no one had any answers. We were hoping that the answers were here.

"It's not why we're here tonight," Jason said, gesturing at the walls of the old church. "We're here tonight to—"

"I know," I said, cutting him off. I took a deep breath and leaned in to kiss him.

His arms went around me, pulling me tight against him. His lips parted mine with his tongue. His fingers lightly stroked my back, the nape of my neck.

I pulled away again. "What if we tried to distract the guys who are guarding the library?" I said.

"You're really fixated on this library thing," said Jason.

"I'm not fixated," I said. "I'm determined. We're here for a reason, and I think we should do our best to try and make sure we follow it through."

"How do you propose we distract them?" Jason asked. "Treat them like dogs and throw them a big juicy steak?"

"No," I said. "One of us could pretend to be hurt. Or we could say that someone had been hurt."

"They'd just radio someone else to take care of it," said Jason. "You know all of the guards carry around walkie-talkies."

The Sol Solis School had pretty heavy security, and not just because children of the most wealthy and influential people in the world attended it. The Sol Solis School was an institution sponsored by the Sons of the Rising Sun, a secret society. They housed their secrets in that library. They didn't want to let anyone in. Especially not Jason or me, if they knew who we were.

"I could flash them," I said.

"Great," said Jason. "You're offering to show your breasts to complete strangers, but you won't even let me hold you."

I looked away.

Jason touched my arm. "What's going on?" He sounded concerned. "Is everything okay? Are you mad at me?"

"No," I said. What was going on? Why was I being like this? "We haven't been together like that since Bradenton."

"That's true," said Jason.

"Since before Lilith," I said. Immediately, I felt as if a weight had been lifted from my chest. That was it! That was why I was upset.

"Lilith?" Jason reached for my chin and turned my face so that I was facing him. "Is this about Lilith?"

I nodded.

"You don't still think that something happened between me and Lilith, do you?"

I shook my head.

"Are you sure? Because I told you nothing happened. She tried to get me to do something, but I didn't. You know that, right?"

310

"It's not about that."

"So then what is it about?"

I looked down at the wooden pew between us. At the whirls in the wood grain. "She said things," I said.

"Like what?" Jason wanted to know.

Now that I'd started to talk about it, I really didn't want to. "Never mind."

"Not never mind. Tell me what you're talking about."

How could I even put this? "She said things about being ... pleased."

Jason looked confused. "Pleased? When?"

"I overheard that conversation you were having. You remember. When she tried to seduce you."

Jason furrowed his brow in confusion. "I don't remember anything about ..." He paused for a second, a different expression taking over his face. "Oh," he said.

I inspected my fingernails, feeling my face heat up. I was glad it was dark, and Jason couldn't see that I was blushing.

"I didn't believe anything she had to say," said Jason. "I know that we're ... that you're ... she was just trying to make me think that you were cheating on me with Jude."

"Right," I said. "That's all she was doing. So it doesn't matter what she said."

"Well, it wasn't true anyway," said Jason. He looked at me. "Was it?"

I hesitated. I didn't know how to talk about this. I'd never known how to talk about this. "Look, let's just forget it," I said. "I don't want to talk about it anymore."

"Oh," said Jason. "So it is true?"

Flustered, I stood up, folding my arms and shrugging. "What's true?"

Jason floundered. "Well, she said that you weren't ... satisfied."

I shook my head quickly. "No," I said. "I am. I'm totally satisfied. I love you, and everything we do is amazing. I'm very, very satisfied."

"Yeah," said Jason, "but I don't think that's what she meant."

"Let's just drop it," I said.

"You brought it up."

"I don't know why I did."

Jason stood up too. He touched my shoulder. "I told you before," he said softly, "I don't know what I'm doing."

"Yes you do," I said. "You're wonderful. Besides, it's not your fault, anyway. It's like she said, she had to show ..." I couldn't continue. My face was on fire. "This is just too embarrassing."

"Hey," Jason said, "you don't have to be embarrassed. It's me. Besides, we said no more secrets. If you're thinking about this, I want to know."

"I just worry that what she said is true. That if I can't do that, then you'll think that I don't appreciate you. And I don't want you to think—"

"No," he said, "this isn't about me. This is about you."

"I know," I said. "There's got to be something wrong with me, right? I mean, shouldn't it have happened already?"

"Well," said Jason, "and keep in mind that I haven't spent a large part of my life listening to locker room talk or having many friends that were my own age. From what I understand, though, it's, like, harder for girls to ..." He laughed. "Okay, well, I'm embarrassed too."

I giggled nervously.

"There's nothing wrong with you," said Jason, "but I think I must be doing something wrong."

"No," I said, "no, I don't think so. I mean, everything's working okay for you."

"But it's not working for you."

"It's fine."

"So, then why are we talking about this?"

"I just wanted to make sure that you knew I appreciated you, that's all. And I wanted to tell you that I was ... I don't know ... that something was wrong with me, and I didn't know if you—"

"Stop it, Azazel. There's nothing wrong with you."

I plopped back down on the pew.

Jason sat down next to me. "Look," he said, "if you told me what to do, you know I would do anything you wanted. I want you to be happy. I want—"

"I don't know what you should do!" I interrupted him. "I don't know how to do it. And that's what Lilith said. She

313

said she had to show guys what to do. And I DON'T KNOW what to do."

Jason absorbed this for a few seconds. "Okay," he said finally. "So, we'll figure it out then. We'll just try stuff."

I bit my lip. "You think that will work?"

He grinned. "It's sex, Azazel. Cavemen could do it. It can't be that hard to figure out."

I tried to smile.

Jason kissed me again. I tried to just let myself melt into him, to concentrate on nothing but his lips. Eventually, however, I pulled away. "I'm just not really in the mood," I muttered.

Jason didn't say anything for a while. Finally, he said, "Okay."

"You're mad."

"I'm not mad," said Jason. He kissed my forehead. "We've got time," he whispered. "We've got our whole lives."

* * *

My roommate Palomino was crying in the bathroom when I got back to my dorm. Palomino was the daughter of an American senator. She was also my brother Chance's girlfriend. As was the plight of the children of the incredibly rich, she'd been stuck with a totally weird first name. She was cool, though, despite the fact that she was actually dating my dork of a baby brother. Chance was fifteen and so was Palomino. They'd met when Chance lived with my grandmother in New Jersey. Chance and Palomino had claimed they were "just friends" for months before finally admitting they were girlfriend and boyfriend.

When Jason and I had first realized that the information we were looking for about the Sons and the Rising Sun prophecies were all housed in the Sol Solis School, we didn't have any idea how we were going to get in. The monks we were staying with—the Order of Reddimus—didn't have any connection with the Sons. The Sons themselves had broken off from the Order of Reddimus back in the Renaissance, but that was hundreds of years ago. The organizations no longer had any ties.

Chance and Palomino had really helped us out. Since they both attended the school, they knew the ins and outs of it. They told us which of the people who worked in admissions were total space cadets and would let two seniors into the school two months before graduation. They told us how to make sure we got assigned to room with them. Chance and Jason shared a dorm across campus. I roomed with Palomino.

The only thing the Order of Reddimus really had been helpful with was money. The Catholic Church was willing to throw tons of money at us, considering we were working to overthrow the Sons. The Church hated the Sons. They were their biggest enemy on earth.

Our tuition was paid for, and we didn't have to live with strangers. Plus, this was a good school. I was ridiculously behind on my studies, considering this was the third high school I'd attended during my senior year. Jason was a freaking genius, so he wasn't having any trouble. Palomino and Jason were both helping me study, so I was glad of the assistance.

I knocked tentatively on the door of the bathroom, which was a heavy, old door, made of dark oak, and engraved with ornate decorations. "Palomino," I called. "Are you okay?"

Only the muffled sound of sobs came through the door. I looked around at our dorm room. For a high school dorm, it was a pretty nice room. Quite big. Unlike most dorm rooms, rooms in our building—Bianchi Hall—didn't have rooms that looked like cookie cutter images of each other. Each room had a little bit of character. Our room had two large windows on the far wall and a small sort of L-shaped alcove where our closet was. Like all dorms in Bianchi, our bathroom was off our dorm room.

Some students' parents paid enough for private rooms, but Palomino's apparently wanted her to learn what it was like to live with another person. They said it was a social skill. As for me—the Catholic Church was being generous, but not that generous.

I tried the door handle. It was unlocked. "Can I come in?" I asked.

Palomino didn't answer.

When I entered the bathroom, I saw her sitting on the green tile floor, her head between her knees. Her shoulders were shaking from the force of her sobs.

I knelt down next to her, concerned. "What's wrong?" I asked.

She still didn't answer. I put my hand on her back and patted it gently. "Mina," I said softly, using her nickname. "Talk to me. Is it Chance? Was my brother a total dickhead to you?"

"I broke up with Chance," she said, hiccupping and raising her face to look at me. Her eyes were puffy and red, but she was still a really pretty girl. Her long white-blonde hair cascaded over her shoulders. My brother was a lucky guy. Well. He had been, anyway.

"What?" I said. "Why'd you break up?"

"I just don't want to see him anymore," she said, rubbing her eyes with the heels of hands.

"What did he do?" I asked.

"Nothing," said Palomino.

Really? "Okay," I said. "So why'd you break up with him?"

"It's not him, it's me," she said, standing up and going to the sink.

"Um," I said, getting up behind her, "that line might work when you're dumping your boyfriend, but it doesn't work when you're explaining it to your friends."

Palomino surveyed herself in the mirror, making a face at her reflection. "I'm fine," she said. "I don't want to talk about it."

"Come on," I said. "You're upset. Anyone can see that."

She shrugged and splashed water on her face.

I came closer, leaning on one side of the sink. "Look," I said, "I know my brother is not always the politest or even nicest guy ever. I grew up with him, remember? But I know he likes you. He really, really likes you —"

"He won't, though," said Palomino. "He won't when he finds out. This way, it's a clean break. I did it first." She swept out of the bathroom, collapsing on her bed in the bedroom.

I followed her. "Finds out what?" I asked, sitting down on my bed, which was opposite hers.

Palomino pulled a pillow over her head.

I sat back. "I can't imagine that anything you did would make him like you less," I said. "You're a really awesome girlfriend."

She pulled her head out from underneath the pillow. "I'm an idiot."

"No," I said, "you're not."

"It was my idea," she said. "I told him it would be okay. In health class at my old high school, they said it would be okay. You're not supposed to be able to when you're on your period."

I furrowed my brow, a niggling suspicion running through me. "Palomino," I said, "did you and Chance have sex?"

She looked at me like I was an idiot. "We've been having sex," she told me. "Since before I came to this school."

Really? "But Chance said you weren't his girlfriend," I said. "Back when you were hanging out in New Jersey. He said you guys weren't dating. You were doing it then?" This was kind of blowing my mind. Chance was my younger brother after all.

"I knew I was coming here for spring semester," she said. "I didn't want to get attached."

"So you were just randomly hooking up with my brother?" I demanded.

Palomino rolled her eyes. "Azazel, you're such a prude. You wouldn't understand. Never mind." She buried her face in her pillow.

The furrow in my brow deepened. I lay back on my bed, staring at the ceiling. "I'm not a prude," I said. Of course, I had just skipped out on my chance to have sex with my boyfriend. My first chance in months. Was I a prude?

"You've only done it with Jason, right?" said Palomino.

"How many people have you done it with?" I asked.

"Three," she said.

"Really?" I said. Palomino was fifteen. How did you fit three boyfriends into fifteen years? When had she started having sex? When she was twelve? "It doesn't make me a prude, because I've only been with one guy."

"Whatever," said Palomino, "and I'm sure you guys are always super careful. You probably make him wear two condoms."

"Just one," I said. "And I don't MAKE him do it. We've just always ..." Truthfully, Jason and I never talked about the condoms. He always had them. I sat back up and fixed Palomino with my gaze. "What are you saying? Are you saying you haven't been careful?"

Palomino didn't look up from her pillow. Her voice was muffled. "I'm pregnant, Azazel."

* * *

Jason was scrubbing at the blood on his hands. He stood over the sink, the water rushing over them from the faucet. I stood in the doorway, watching him.

"Where did the blood come from?" I asked him.

He turned off the faucet, flinging his wet hands once, so that water spattered against the sink. It was pink with blood.

He came to me, holding his hands out to touch me.

I backed away. "Where did the blood come from, Jason?" I asked.

Jason advanced on me.

I backed into the closed door behind me. I fumbled for the doorknob behind my back.

Jason was coming for me, blood dripping from his hands and fingers, dripping onto the floor, red like roses. The blood was all over his hands. All over his arms. Smeared on his white t-shirt.

"I don't like it when you come home covered in all this blood," I whispered, still trying to turn the doorknob behind me.

It was locked.

Jason stopped in front of me. He put his hands on my cheeks.

I pushed him away. "I don't want the blood on me," I said.

"But it's your blood," said Jason.

"No, it's not," I said.

"It is," said Jason. "Come here and see our beautiful baby."

"What?" I said. "What are you talking about?"

I looked down at myself. I was naked from the waist down. My thighs were covered in smears of deep red blood. And now, suddenly, I could feel it. It felt like something had clawed its way out of my uterus. There was nothing between my legs but tatters of skin. I collapsed onto the bathroom floor, cold green tile against my skin.

Behind the shower curtain, something screamed.

Jason smiled at me. He pulled aside the curtain of the shower with a presentational flair, like he was a showman at a circus. "Isn't he beautiful?" he said.

Behind the shower curtain, a long black worm-like shape slithered over the lip of the bathtub. Its sharp teeth glinted in the lights. Pieces of my flesh still clung to it. Wherever it slid, it left a trail of blood.

I backed away, backed into the door again, shaking my head, muttering, "No. No."

"He's our baby," said Jason.

"No," I said.

"Yes," said Jason.

"No," I said. I stumbled to my feet. "It has to die," I said, lunging for the worm-shaped thing, ready to strangle it.

"Stop!" cried Jason.

* * *

And I woke up.

It was dark in the dorm room and quiet. Quiet the way it is in the morning before the sun comes up. Still. Peaceful.

But my heart was beating out of my chest.

Goddamn dreams.

I'd been having bad dreams—nightmares—ever since Jason and I escaped my crazy Satanist family in Bramford, WV last fall. Recently, however, they'd started to get much, much worse. I had one nearly every night. Sometimes more than one. They never made much sense. Sometimes they had a basis in things that had happened. For instance, this one was clearly an amalgamation of Palomino's news and the time Jason had come home in Bradenton covered in blood. And maybe it had something to do with the fact that I wasn't quite sure if Jason and I weren't ... evil.

Jason's own mother had tried to get me to kill him. She'd had visions. Visions in which Jason did horrible things.

What if my dreams were like visions? What if ...

I tried to calm down. Monitor my breathing so that my heart would slow down. It wouldn't help anything to think like that. People didn't have visions of the future.

At least I didn't think so.

Sometimes, though, Jason was so violent. I tried not to think about it, because nothing had happened in quite some time. But I'd watched Jason shoot his own mother in the head.

He'd been protecting me.

He'd never talked about it.

The things that I thought about when I woke up from the dreams were sometimes worse than the dreams themselves. I didn't like the dreams, and I didn't like thinking about whether or not Jason was too violent. I didn't like thinking about it at all.

There was only one thing that worked to keep it all at bay, and I'd been so caught up in listening to Palomino tell me about being pregnant that I hadn't bothered with it before bed. Not like I usually did.

It was dark. It was quiet. And my bed was warm. I didn't particularly want to get up.

But I wanted to turn my brain off, and I only knew one way to do that. I climbed out of bed and knelt beside it. Feeling under my mattress, my fingers brushed the cold metal of my gun. It was good to know it was there, but it wasn't what I was looking for.

Instead, I slid out a glass bottle of vodka.

It was easy to buy liquor in Italy, even though I wasn't technically quite old enough to purchase it. The drinking age was lower in Europe. I never had problems. And it wasn't like I was buying it to party. It was like medicine.

I gulped the burning liquid down my throat, feeling the oblivion rush into my temples.

* * *

I had a headache. I always had a headache. Drinking as much liquor as I did every night before bed (or in last night's case, in the middle of the night) tended to make me pretty much constantly hung over. I sat in my morning class, bleary-eyed, barely listening to Professor Moretti's lecture on Post-Colonialism. I'd been through various approaches to education my senior year of high school. The first had been honors classes in the West Virginia public school system. Then general classes in the Florida public school system. Finally, here I was, finishing out my high school career in a posh, English-language private school in Europe. The approaches all had some things in common, but here at the Sol Solis School, the emphasis was on lecture. I came to class. Professors talked at me. I took notes. Later there was a test. It was the most challenging program I'd ever taken part in.

In my pocket, my phone vibrated.

Looking around to make sure Professor Moretti wasn't looking, I eased the phone out of my pocket and eyed the text message Jason had sent me.

"whats up w/c and p?" it said.

Careful not to look down at the phone too much, I quickly texted back: "what did chance say to u?"

I made a show of scribbling down something on my notebook paper, waiting until my phone vibrated again before looking at it.

"p broke up w/ him? she say why?"

I chewed on my lip, considering. Jason and I had made a pact not to keep secrets from each other, but this wasn't my secret. Last night, Palomino had made it clear to me that she didn't want Chance to know. She was convinced that Chance would leave her if he found out. Apparently, she'd been sort of seeing a guy before Chance had transferred in

324

the early spring. She hadn't had sex with the guy, but Chance didn't believe that. Palomino was sure that Chance would blame the baby on someone else. I told her my brother wasn't like that.

At any rate, I didn't think Palomino wanted her business blabbed to anyone, not even Jason. I trusted Jason, but since he was living with Chance, it would be really hard for him not to want to tell his own roommate. Still, I didn't think Palomino should keep this to herself for too long.

Conflicted, my fingers hovered over the keys of my phone.

"Ms. Smith," said Professor Moretti.

I didn't look up at first. My name was Jones. But we were undercover at the Sol Solis School and we weren't using our real names. I was going by Amy Smith. My head snapped up.

Professor Moretti was standing right next to my desk. He could see that I was texting.

I blushed and shoved the phone back into my pocket. "Sorry," I mumbled.

Professor Moretti looked concerned. "Ms. Smith," he said kindly, "you really need to heed your studies. Your grades can't afford distractions like this." He was referring to the D I'd gotten on my last test. I couldn't help that I wasn't studying so much. What with nightmares, hangovers, and trying to figure out a way into the library, I was distracted. School didn't seem so important anymore.

I looked down at my desk, ashamed.

Professor Moretti moved on. "The next chapter of THINGS FALL APART for tomorrow, then," he addressed the class.

Around me, students began to gather their belongings. Shove their notebooks into book bags. Stand up. A low buzz of chatter started to fill the classroom. The class was over. I didn't move for a few seconds. The noise was making my head pound.

Slowly, I stood up and began picking up my own stuff.

Jason appeared beside my desk, his book bag already slung over his shoulder. "Sorry," he said.

I shook my head. "I should have kept my eye out for Moretti."

"No," said Jason, "it was my fault. And I shouldn't distract you in class, anyway."

Way to rub it in. Jason had, of course, gotten an A on the test. "Right," I said. "Your stupid girlfriend needs to concentrate, or she'll flunk out of school."

He kissed my forehead. "Don't be silly," he said, taking my hand as we left the classroom and spilled into the hallway with the other students. "I just already know this stuff. When people think you're the messiah, they cram your head full of all kinds of useless knowledge."

I elbowed him. "Shh. Don't say that stuff so loud. Someone might hear."

He tickled my ribs. "Paranoid Azazel," he teased.

"Don't say my name either," I hissed.

"You're in a bad mood," he said. "Did you drink last night again?"

"No," I said. "I forgot. I had a dream that we had a monster for a baby, and it ate its way out of my body."

Jason made a face. "Eew," he said.

I shrugged. "So then I downed half a bottle of vodka at like four in the morning."

We made our way out of Rossi Hall and into the bright, spring day. Outside, other students like us walked in groups of two or three across the sprawling campus. They wound through old brick buildings that had been standing for hundreds of years. Jason and I were heading towards the dining hall for lunch. We usually met up with Palomino and Chance. I wondered how that was going to work out today.

Jason shook his head. "I don't think it's good for you to drink so much."

"And the nightmares? Are they good for me?"

"I just worry about you. You know that."

I did know. I squeezed his hand. "I'm okay."

We walked without speaking for a few moments.

"You don't ever have bad dreams?" I asked him. "After everything you've seen?"

He shrugged. "Used to," he said. "A long time ago. After the sorority house. But not so much anymore."

The Sons had assigned Jason and a man named Hallam, who we used to live with in Florida, to kill a house full of sorority girls. They'd told them the girls were running a brothel, but that had probably been a lie. No one really

327

knew, because they were dead. Jason hadn't done any of the actual killing, but the night had scarred him deeply.

"So, you think it'll get better?" I asked.

"Maybe we should take you to a doctor. Like a psychiatrist or something."

I snorted.

"I didn't mean that you were crazy or anything," he added hastily.

"We both need loads of therapy," I told him. "And we won't be getting it any time soon. Let's just find a way into this library and figure out what we need to know."

Jason stopped walking, looking thoughtful. I stopped too.

"Then what?" he said.

"What do you mean?"

"What if we find out that I actually am the Rising Sun? What if we find out that collectively we're going to bring about the end of the world? What do we do then?"

I didn't say anything. After a few seconds, I started walking again. I didn't look back to see if Jason was catching up.

I spotted Palomino standing in front of the dining hall, hugging herself. Chance was nowhere to be seen. I half-waved at her, and she waved back. As I walked over to her, Jason fell into my stride next to me. Out of habit, I reached for his hand, and he took mine.

"Hey Mina," I said.

"Hey," she said.

"Why'd you break up with Chance?" said Jason.

I elbowed him. Did he have no tact?

Palomino swung around to face Jason, her eyes welling up with tears.

I dropped Jason's hand and touched her shoulder. "You okay?"

She shook her head. "I couldn't make it through my last class. I started crying, and I had to leave. Everyone saw."

"Wait," said Jason. "Are you upset about breaking up with Chance? Because he's out of his mind, okay? He was freaked out when I got back to the dorm last night. What's going on with you two?"

"Jason," I said.

"No," he said. "Look, if you both still like each other, and you're both sad that you aren't together, you should get back together."

"Chance is a jealous dick," said Palomino. She turned on her heel and stalked into the dining hall.

Jason went after her, and I followed Jason. "Is this about that guy you were seeing? What was his name, Skylar or something?"

Skylar. Another rich kid doomed to a weird name.

"Because," Jason continued, "Chance is really sorry he said anything. And he totally trusts you."

Palomino whirled. "I don't want to talk about it, okay?" She thrust the door open to the dining hall.

Jason stopped and looked at me. "You should back me up here," he said. "He's your brother."

"It's complicated," I said.

Jason rolled his eyes. "Whatever," he said. "It's always complicated with girls."

A line to the serving area had already formed. Jason and I got in line behind Palomino. We got through the line quickly and sat down at our regular table. Jason and I looked at Chance's usual seat. It was empty.

"Where's Chance?" I asked Jason. It didn't seem fair that he had to find another seat.

Jason shrugged. "Don't know." He turned to Palomino. "You know," he said, "Azazel and I had some issues with jealousy. She thought I was sleeping with her best friend."

I glared at him. "And you thought I was sleeping with a gay guy."

"He wasn't actually gay," Jason pointed out. To Palomino, "He was actually my brother, and he tried to kill me."

He DID kill Jason. At least, he put a bullet in Jason's skull. Jason stopped breathing His heart stopped beating. Until I kissed him.

My life was too weird.

"Anyway," said Jason, "the point is that we worked through that. We talked about how we felt. And we're still together."

Palomino sighed. "I don't want to talk about this, okay?"

"Why not?" said Jason. "What did Chance do?"

She glared at him. "Did Chance put you up to this?"

"No," said Jason, but he didn't meet her eyes.

"I don't want to talk to him," she said. "It's over. Just tell him it's over."

"Mina," I said, "are you sure you shouldn't just talk to Chance about—"

She shot me a murderous look. I shut my mouth. I'd promised not to say anything. But this was huge. My younger brother had fathered a CHILD. And his girlfriend wouldn't tell him. How was I supposed to keep this to myself?

To distract myself, I looked around the dining hall. It was a big, open room with high ceilings. Long tables lined the room. I spotted the Weem twins, Faruza and Fairie (more hapless victims of rich people's wacky ideas of names), sauntering across the dining hall. I didn't feel sorry for the Weem twins, despite their names, however. They were awful gossips who were always rude to me. They picked on pretty much everyone except people who had the right last names. People who were related to members of the Council of the Sons.

Since their uncle, Edgar Weem, had stepped down from his post at the Council, the Weem twins had gotten even meaner. They seemed to resent the fact that their uncle had been demoted, as if it threatened their social status. They walked by our table, casting withering glances in our direction. I seethed, imagining how satisfying it would be to let them know that Jason was actually their cousin, since Edgar Weem was his father.

Faruza stopped next to our table, holding her tray and looking down at us. "So, Mina," she said. "I heard about the nervous breakdown in class today. I'm so sorry." She sounded about as sorry as Hitler was for killing Jews.

Palomina glowered at her. "Thanks, Faruza," she said. "You're always so concerned and kind."

Faruza smirked. "So is it true that you found out your skuzzy adopted boyfriend gave you herpes? Because I hear that's what you get when you date Jersey trash."

"Chance isn't even from New Jersey," I said. I couldn't help it. The Weem twins just pissed me off so much.

Faruza turned to me as if she'd noticed me for the first time. "Was I talking to you?" she asked.

"I don't know," I said. "I think you were leaving, actually, weren't you?"

"Because God knows where you and your boyfriend came from. You're probably charity cases. At least, he's definitely performing some kind of charity by dating something that looks like you."

Jason's jaw twitched. "Don't talk to her like that," he said.

"Ooh," said Faruza, "I guess I struck a nerve."

Faruza's boyfriend, George Churchill (victim of being named after his super rich grandfather), slid in behind her, one arm snaking around her waist. "Hey babe," he said. "You gonna waste your whole lunch here?"

She smiled up at him. "Just catching up," she said.

"Actually," said Jason, "she was insulting my girlfriend."

332

George shot me a look. "She'd be kind of hard to compliment, wouldn't she?"

Jason stood up, knocking over his chair. "You should really reconsider that statement."

I watched his fist, clenching and unclenching at his side.

www.ingramcontent.com/pod-product-compliance
Lightning Source LLC
Chambersburg PA
CBHW060514180626
46817CB00002B/357